The Porpoise Watcher

The Porpoise Watcher

by Kenneth S. Norris

W · W · NORTON & COMPANY · INC ·

NEW YORK

To my father, Robert DeWitt Norris,
*who showed me how to walk quietly
in the woods,*
and my mother, Jessie Matheson Norris,
*who was patient about horned lizards
in my dresser.*

Contents

Illustrations

Introduction

During the last twenty years, when the stories in this book were happening, even my life at home seems to have been related to the sea and its animals. First, when we lived in Portuguese Bend, California, we looked down on a little cove where, a hundred years previously, California gray whales moved south, often within a few dozen yards of the rocky headlands. Then came Hawaii, and from our living-room window I often saw the last pitiful remnants of a once populous humpback whale population. These awkward-seeming giants are gaining in number, but the whalers nearly did them in, and the Hawaiian population of a few hundred animals may be one of the world's largest. Now, back in California at Santa Cruz, I stand on our oak-shaded hill looking down through the deep canyon V to a wedge of pale sea near Davenport. Like Portuguese Bend, it was the site of hand whaling before the gray whale tribe dwindled and all but disappeared from the earth.

When I began learning about porpoises and whales, many things were different. For one thing, we were just beginning to realize what wonderful creatures these animals are. For another, massive whale killing, the like of which the world had never known, lay ahead in the early 1960s. Public consciousness about these curious giants was low. We really didn't understand, when I started the story told here, that porpoises could navigate by sound. No one had caught a live whale for observation and exhibit; in fact, no one knew how. Enough had been learned about the behavior of captive porpoises to know that they were remarkably flexible and intelligent creatures, but next to nothing was known about their lives at sea. Even today the sum of our ignorance more than equals what we know.

This book is about my experiences and the knowledge I gained. It is not intended to be a scientific book, but it is about the excitement of science as I have known it. For me, science is a deeply human endeavor. It is simply human curiosity channeled toward the truth, with our normal human tendency toward fish tales and exaggeration weeded out. The book is about some of the people who have worked with me. Some were fishermen, like Frank and Boots, about whom I will have much to say, and others were pirates at heart, but collectors or seamen by trade, which bought them the freedom a seaman regards as his birthright. Their ships were their domains as surely as a king owns his castle.

The book is certainly about the animals I have worked with, whose lives became deeply enmeshed with my own. Populating my story are peppery young porpoises; crafty ones that nearly beat us at our own training game; sweet, docile old-lady porpoises; and big bovine whales whose innocent but ponderous moves could injure fragile humans nearby.

As much as anything, the book is about the exhilaration and insight I have experienced in glimpsing nature. Such excitement and wonder at nature's marvels can be shared by all perceptive people. One does not have to be a scientist to wonder at a little jeweled lantern fish lying in the dark folds of a net, its brilliant bluish lights shining like buttons on a waistcoat. I think that's where it all starts with any naturalist, professional or amateur: with wonder at the intricacy and beauty of living things. But science helps one to understand, and that too has its own special excitement.

Like many another naturalist, I came to my profession via the route of the hunter and outdoorsman. Very early in my life, my father taught me how to tell a doe from a buck by footprints, how the Indian places his feet to keep twigs from snapping as he walks, how to build a smokeless campfire. I learned how to leach the tannin from acorns so they become fit to eat, how to make soap or rich food out of the bulb of the amole, and how to stun fish with the juice of the doveweed. This latter practice is universally frowned upon by Fish and Game departments, but I'm glad to know it anyway. To my father, I suppose, must go both thanks and blame. At any rate, his fascinating lore was the steppingstone to the formal natural history that now engages me.

My mother knew that my father's lessons were powerful brew. Although she may have been shaken when my carnivorous collared lizard ran across the hearth on his hind legs during a party, or when the skunk in my "animal tail" collection got too ripe, she encouraged me.

Many of my friends also had parts to play in these adventures. Only a few have been mentioned here. I hope the others will understand.

Working with porpoises and whales is often expensive, as the reader may perceive. During several of the years encompassed in this book my work received support of one sort or another. Some was done with the help of the National Science Foundation, much of the hearing work was performed with National Institutes of Health help, and especially the Office of Naval Research has been willing to lend a hand as my career took its many twists and turns. Such folks as Sidney Galler, Deane Holt, and Chuck Woodhouse were remarkably patient, now that I look backward for a change.

My final wish, before leaving you to the book, which I hope you will enjoy, is to give acknowledgment to several stalwarts who saw me through the trauma of writing. I was blessed with an editor, Mrs. Peach, of such forbearance as can scarcely be countenanced in a commercial organization. She forbore from hounding me unmercifully when I took years to get the book down on paper, and by doing so she allowed me to do most of the things recounted here. Not only that, she knows a lot about sentences, commas, and things like that. Two others, Dick Strout and my daughter Nancy Norris, have helped immeasurably with careful editing and coddling of my spirit when I needed it most.

KENNETH S. NORRIS
Bonny Doon, California
October 1973

The Porpoise Watcher

CHAPTER ONE

Scammon's Lagoon

The surface of the lagoon lay flat, imperfectly reflecting cumulus clouds and distant beach dunes. The three of us lolled sleepily in our skiff listening to the burbling outboard motor. Suddenly a forty-foot gray whale broke the surface near us and rose ponderously, almost straight up into the desert air. The sea cascaded from its body. It rose ten, fifteen, twenty feet, until only its tail remained in the water. One of its huge paddle-shaped flippers reached into the air as it arched and fell back on its side. The water surface slapped together over the twenty-ton bulk, sending a geyser of spray high into the air. A family of concentric waves rocked us crazily as we looked incredulously at where the whale had been.

Two things struck me about this incident. The first was the seeming slowness with which the whale rose from the water; all its movements were in slow motion, like a rocket launching. The second was a sort of inscrutable fixed smile that the animal wore during its aerial sortie. Now I know that even dead gray whales have this smile. It results from fleshy extensions of the lower lips outside the upper jaws. However, at the time I read nebulous meanings into this emotionless grin and felt a strong foreboding at invading such a powerful creature's home grounds.

This encounter happened deep in Scammon's Lagoon, or Laguna Ojo de Liebre, as the Mexicans call it. It is one of several inland bays that flood into the desert along the central and southern Baja California coast of western Mexico. Most of the year these remote sheets of water host only tiny events; coyotes padding along the shore searching for food among the flotsam, or flocks of sea birds probing the sand flats for crabs. An almost overwhelming quiet and sense of timelessness grips the visitor. Then, each year in January, come the whales; hundreds and hundreds of them. The peace is shattered by their leaps, by the birth and nursing of fourteen-foot young, and by the deep, resonant snoring respirations of the whales that drift along immobile, nearly submerged, and, I suppose, asleep. I've seen the lagoons wearing both of these faces and would be hard pressed to choose between these sharply differing moods. Each is gripping in its own way.

My first visit came in midsummer as a young ichthyology student, when I was sent into the lagoon to collect fishes, and then, ten years later, I returned to study the whales.

In 1950 I enrolled at Scripps Institution of Oceanography at La Jolla, California, as a graduate student under the guidance of a world-renowned authority on fishes, Dr. Carl L. Hubbs. Like other graduate students, I expected to enter, at least peripherally, into my professor's world, helping where I could and learning by watching, listening, and asking questions. I soon found myself tagging frantically along behind a human whirlwind. The doctor proved to be bursting with an animal energy that often appalled his students. He was curious about everything. He strode relentlessly across the desert salt flats ahead of his straggling students, searching for the desert pupfish; he climbed sea cliffs looking for Heermann's gulls with special white wing feathers; and he identified and examined in exhaustive detail every fish he could catch. He dug for fossil bones and read the history of Indian peoples from the trash of their campsites, sent nets into the deep sea, and visited every dead whale or porpoise that washed ashore within a hundred miles of Scripps, no matter how rotten it was.

Professor Hubbs had pioneered studies of fish distribution along the Pacific coast. One curious fact he uncovered was that a regular change from cold-water fish species in the north to warm-water types in the south did not exist, except in the broadest sense. Instead one found pockets of warm-water animals and plants in bays and coves far to the north, while cold-water forms occurred in subtropical waters to the south in places where cold water came locally to the surface. Hubbs predicted that Scammon's Lagoon would provide an enclave for warm-water species. but no collections had been made to test the idea. So he asked me if I would lead a small collecting party along the central Baja coast and into the lagoon. Nothing, needless to say, could have suited me better, so we commenced at once to make plans.

Dr. Hubbs arranged for us to use the Scripps Institution vessel *Paolina-T*, a sturdy eighty-foot converted purse seiner. My collecting crew, green but eager, consisted of three young fellows just graduated from high school. Howard Harper, a strapping, amiable young man, was one. Howard had never been to sea before and knew little about field collecting and its rigors. He remained uncomplaining, though, as he was dunked repeatedly in the surf and kept up many nights hauling on a soggy seine rope. Jack Littlepage and Wes Farmer, both of whom have since become professional biologists, completed my crew, and they too proved their mettle before the trip was over.

Finding such good companions was blind luck. There are few endeavors like concentrated field work to bring out the worst in people. Tempers sometimes flare after a few days of exhausting labor. Sand and dirt and salt-water baths don't help either. Food is usually hastily eaten between seine hauls, but not until the final fish has been pickled and tagged under the harsh light of a gasoline lantern can one crawl into the sleeping bag. But the four of us maintained our sense of humor and ultimately made good collections for Professor Hubbs.

After a week's work along the coast to the south we entered Sebastián Vizcaíno Bay and charted a course for Scammon's Lagoon. The *Paolina-T* hove to about five miles off the low desert shore and lay heaving slowly on the glassy early-morning swell. As dawn brightened we could see a distant beach lined with huge sculptured sand dunes. Gear was passed down from the mother vessel and stowed in the sixteen-foot skiff rocking alongside. The *Paolina-T*'s skipper was unfamiliar with the tricky entrance to Scammon's and decided to let us negotiate the channel in the open skiff. He would, we decided, work the coast to the north while we were in the lagoon. Our only chart, dating from the late 1800s, showed the entrance channel starting several miles from the lagoon and running between an offshore sand bar and the beach. In rough weather a boat entering the lagoon must cross this shallow bar and slip in between a surf booming on the beach and a long, threatening line of spume-capped rollers on the sea side.

Fortunately for us, our misty morning scene presented no such frightening aspect. Everything seemed propitious, but I wondered what might lie in store for us, especially if the weather turned while we worked inside. We were laden to within a few inches of the water, and our collections should drop us even lower. And, to be sure, we were a softer breed than the whalers of the 1800s. My companions seemed not to give these possibilities a second thought. They seemed to trust implicitly in the wisdom of their leader. The only look of apprehension I noted occurred when I asked the captain for a handful of flares. With these stowed in the bow and an emergency code worked out—one green, *we will stay in another day;* two red, *we need help,* etc.—I felt a bit easier.

Action usually cures such forebodings. We settled in among the gear. I pulled the outboard motor cable and the engine started with a gurgling roar. Minutes later the mother ship was a gray silhouette on the horizon, but we scarcely looked back for her. Our eyes were ahead, straining to see any signs of the offshore bar and channel.

No rising swell on the gently heaving water marked the bar for us, so we simply turned our prow toward where we supposed the entrance to Scammon's would be. For two hours we skirted along the desolate sand mountains that line the coast, finally turning into the broad lagoon mouth. There an aquatic welcoming party of a dozen Pacific bottlenose porpoises leaped toward us. This was my first close encounter with these mild-mannered and playful animals. They frightened me a little, since some were only about four feet shorter than our bulky skiff and they seemed inclined to take unusual liberties with us, surfacing within a few feet of our bow, puffing their almost explosive breaths, and diving again. I was relieved when they turned and left us, swimming back toward the channel entrance. Now that I know more about porpoises, I wonder if they left to wait for the next boat into the lagoon. Their curiosity being what it is, they probably couldn't bear to miss it, even if it came six months later.

The sky was a cloudless and pale blue. By the time we entered the lagoon and cruised along close to the sand-dune-lined shore, the fierce summer sun became oppressively hot. To the south of us lay the main lagoon, a vast expanse of glassy water extending as far as the eye could see, marked here and there with shimmering sand islands. Through the dancing heat haze to the west a low range of bluffs, seared and sand-colored, could be seen. Our solitude was absolute. The seemingly limitless landscape of flat water and desolate shore had quietly closed around us as the moving water of the open sea was left behind. A loneliness akin to fear pervaded me, because I knew it was more than fifty miles on an almost impassable sandy track to the nearest habitation.

I nosed the good skiff, which had suddenly become very dear to us, into a hard beach, and we stepped out onto an intimate little sand flat set between low dunes. Gear was quickly unloaded and the skiff hauled up above the reach of the tide. With the noisy outboard stilled, we became sharply aware of the pervasive quiet of this uninhabited lagoon. We stood silent, listening. Tiny noises took the stage: the gentle lapping of the water on the sandy beach; the far-distant scream of a flock of terns circling over an island two miles away.

Our trip had begun in the cool air before dawn, but now the relentless noon sun glanced at us from a dozen angles off the

dunes and we grew drowsy. A brief siesta seemed in order.
Each of us built a shelter from the pieces of our gear and dozed
on the warm sand. The silence became so complete that Howard
woke with a start and swore that the culprit was a little shore
bird noisily padding up and down, stamping its feet thoughtlessly on the hard-packed sand.

Later we cooked a sparse lunch over a driftwood fire. From
the quantity of timbers, planking, masts, and other debris half
buried in dune sand, it was obvious that many a ship must have
found a grave in this lagoon. Captain Scammon, who fished this
lagoon for whales ninety-four years earlier, may have used similar
wood to fire his try-pots.

We ate, reloaded the skiff with our possessions—now truly
everything we owned in the world—pushed off, and turned toward a little crescent-moon-shaped sand bar known as Shell Island. Its north shore was fringed by a broad bed of sea grass. I
headed the skiff along its outer edge until we found a sandy
channel running through the grass, leading directly into the shell-
pavemented beach. Eagle stingrays rocketed away from our prow,
stirring up boiling trails of mud with their beating wings.

Nearing the island, we could see that it was home for dozens
of bird families. The skiff first touched the beach near a group of
nesting cormorants. The parents fled, but two young birds apprehensively stood their ground in a volcano-shaped nest. They were
ridiculous black-skinned, downy creatures with fluttering yellow
throat pouches, seemingly not sure whether we presaged danger
or brought food. A short distance down the beach a reddish egret
family nested in an old, bleached crate. Their scraggly fledgling
had no illusions about us. He advanced threateningly, clacking
his bill each time we trudged back and forth by him to set up
camp. Farther down the five-hundred-yard-long island a large
flock of brown pelicans marched and countermarched nervously
at the unaccustomed sight of invaders. Two hundred or more
terns screamed and wheeled over our heads for half an hour
before settling in silence at the very farthest tip of the island.
Other bird species also lived on the island; oyster catchers with
their glistening black plumage and red bills flew low over the

water, while dowitchers, sanderlings, willets, black-bellied plovers, and curlews scurried along the beaches. A lone fish eagle, or osprey, sat grandly unruffled by the chaos around him—atop a tall driftwood plank wedged endwise in the sand.

The four of us laid our sleeping bags on soft beds of dried sea grass piled two or three feet thick by the spring tides. Since the island would be our home for two or three days, I constructed a little driftwood shelter for our gear. Later we dug a pit in the sand for our campfire, eased back against the soft sea grass, and ate our dinner while contemplating a beautiful desert sunset, whose red light tinged the water and the distant sand hills. This island was ours for the moment, in spite of the hundreds of avian eyes looking suspiciously our way. For the first time since entering the lagoon we felt wondrously peaceful. We talked quietly about the changes that must be wrought yearly by the arrival of several hundred gray whales, and of times past when whalers lay at anchor in the deeper channels blotching the sky with black smoke from tryworks aboard. Very different from now, I thought.

The setting sun didn't mean rest to us. The best time to catch fish was at hand. Many fish can detect a seine easily in the daylight, so it is best to fish in the dark. We arose from our sea-grass beds, gathered up collecting gear, and set off in the darkness to see if the doctor's theory was correct. It was midnight before we returned, soaking wet and exhausted. In our collecting cans were dozens of tiny fish, most of them unfamiliar to us. The answer to Dr. Hubbs' question had to wait on patient study in his laboratory at Scripps, where we later learned that he was correct; many fishes in our take were most common along the southern coasts of Baja California, western Mexico, or even Panama. For the moment, however, we were cold and our backs ached from pulling the heavy seines through the mucky sea-grass beds. We boiled coffee in a bean can left from dinner, talked for a few moments around the flickering campfire, and crawled into our sleeping bags with no more than a fleeting glance at snapping bright desert stars overhead.

After two days we moved camp to a sandy flat near the base

of the barrier sand mountains between the lagoon and Sebastián
Vizcaíno Bay outside. Our choice of campsites proved poor, for
after dark we found the tide rising on all sides and were soon
again on an island, this time cut off from shore by a fast-widen-
ing channel. As high ground dwindled, it became apparent that
it would probably disappear entirely in twenty minutes or so.
There was nothing left to do but load the skiff again and pile
back aboard like animals into Noah's ark. In pitch-blackness we
felt our way along the shore and finally, a mile or so away from
our original camp, located a tiny sandy shelf above high-tide line
at the base of a great dark dune rising out of sight into the black-
ness. Once again the boat was beached and the gear was la-
boriously carried above high-tide line. With camp secure, the
night's collecting began.

All the nearby beaches were of Aeolian, or wind-blown, dune
sand. It is far finer than the usual beach sand and, when wet,
forms a watery gruel that will scarcely support a man's weight.
To set our net, we plodded back and forth into the lagoon, sinking to our knees with every step. The net dug deep into the
sand with each tug. Such water-covered, wind-blown sand
seemed to be as inhospitable to fish as to us, since most sets produced "water hauls," i.e., not a fish in sight. The night's collecting would have been a dismal failure and our precious time lost
had we not found a peculiar black-and-white flatfish, almost as
round as a silver dollar, flapping among the folds of the net on
our last haul. It proved to be a perfect specimen of an unusual
flatfish (*Achirus*) that is rare in collections from this region.

Next morning we woke to find ourselves camped directly at
the base of a hundred-foot sand mountain that dropped directly
into the bay. While munching our pancake breakfast, we looked
at that dune. What fun it would be to slide down it! By noon-
time the urge got the better of us. With scarcely a word, Jack
and I left the contents of our pockets in the skiff, jumped ashore,
and scrambled up the slipping dune face. In a few minutes we
lay puffing at the top looking directly down the thirty-seven-de-
gree slope at the tiny figures of Howard and Wes in the skiff

below. It seemed as if we could drop straight down onto them from our vantage point.

After a few slides we all shucked our clothes and slid right down the slope into the clear, tepid water amid cascades of hot sand. Pure animal pleasure! Hot sand, bare skins, and warm water. We crawled out on the sand and sat drying like seals in the sun.

Wes looked up along the coast and suddenly spoke in a hushed voice. "What's that fin up there? It looks like it's coming our way."

In a moment we all spotted it, scarcely a hundred feet away. Not wanting to frighten whatever it was, we sat in silence as a dark-gray hooked fin cut alongshore only a few feet from the edge of the water. Very shortly we recognized a lone Pacific bottlenose porpoise lazing along, minding its own business. It passed within about eight feet of us, swimming in such shallow water that it was rolled partly on its side to keep from stranding. As it went by, it looked up at us with one quizzical eye. Not having been conditioned at that time by either the captive porpoises of oceanariums or those on television, we were still wary and afraid to swim again with it so near.

That night we made camp along the shore of the entrance channel behind the cast-up timber of a long-dead ship. The wind began to rise shortly after we landed, whipping sheets of stinging sand against us. We could stand the sand in our clothes, food, and eyes, but I knew we had to protect our precious outboard somehow. So I commandeered our ground cloth, wrapping it around the engine. A shelter was dug behind a great, splintery old mast that lay half buried in the beach. Driftwood, old crates, and logs were piled up until a fairly windproof shelter was built. Personal comfort, however, was the least of my worries. We were scheduled to leave Scammon's Lagoon the next morning to make the passage in our heavily laden skiff between the offshore bar and the beach and to locate the *Paolina-T*, which was supposed to be lying somewhere ten miles away out to sea. The rising wind filled me with apprehension.

In the evening we packed our seine down to the beach and

fished far into the blustery night. Our catch was a nice heap of
fish. It included several examples of one form well known to us,
the smooth puffer fish (*Sphoeroides annulatus*). This innocuous-
looking little fish carries in its liver and viscera one of the most
violently poisonous biological substances known. Its Mexican
name—*botete*—is an uncomplimentary term used to describe a
man who visits one's wife while one is away from home. I've
never been able to reconcile a connection between fish and phi-
landerer, except possibly that this fish is used as a coyote poison
in some areas. The several *botetes* among our catch showed no
sinister tendencies and only grunted and puffed themselves full
of air when we hauled them ashore. Their white bellies became
round and taut as little baseballs in the net.

Wearily we shouldered our gear in the dark, plodded up the
windy beach, and crawled into our damp, gritty sleeping bags.
In spite of the wind-blown sand sifting about us, all was soon
quiet in our comfortless camp.

I awoke before dawn. Wisps of fog trailed around our shelter,
and to my great relief there was only a slight breeze. As the sun
grayed the sky over the dunes, I prodded my sand-encrusted
crew awake. We loaded quickly and launched the heavily laden
skiff through a low surf. The blessed motor, unswathed of its
protective wrappings, started easily enough as we pushed out
into the channel. Luck was with us. The open bay outside proved
calm. An hour later Jack sighted the mast of the *Paolina-T*,
which lay hull down on the horizon, and soon we were aboard
stowing our fish cans in the hold and plotting our next collection
with the skipper.

We four had been drawn closer together by our brief stay in
that lonely lagoon, and, I suspect, felt a trifle superior to the
boat-bound crew members who hadn't pioneered it with us. Our
experiences had been mostly mild and pleasant ones and the
dangers slight, but we had all been, I suppose, a little afraid at
times. We seemed closer, I noticed, after that. I suppose that is
why secret societies have initiation ceremonies. We had uncon-
sciously had ours. Now, over twenty years later, if we four were
to meet, I suspect some of those feelings would still be there.

Even though my work with Professor Hubbs was primarily concerned with fish, he also gave me my first introduction to the whale tribe. Two pilot whales stranded and died on a beach not far from Scripps Institution. With obvious relish, Professor Hubbs gathered samples and measurements from them. His major prizes were their heads, which he chopped off and packed back to Scripps, where he placed them in two big wire baskets. The baskets and their bloody cargo were lowered off Scripps' pier in about twenty feet of water. There, for two weeks, the severed heads lay washing back and forth in the surge, being chewed upon by crabs and other assorted marine creatures. These tiny beasts were expected to clean off all the blubber and meat, leaving a nice white skull, which could be deposited in the San Diego Museum of Natural History for future study.

Trouble develops if one leaves such mementos too long. The sea creatures disarticulate all the bones, and the teeth fall out, and it becomes a bewildering job to reassemble the parts. Dr. Hubbs, I suspect, was a little impatient with his marine invertebrate helpers anyway, and decided that his vertebrate assistants on shore might finish the job with more dispatch, even if with less enthusiasm. He had the cages hoisted. When the whale heads appeared, they were great mottled globs of whitish jellied blubber, striped here and there with strands of connective tissue. Somewhere deep beneath the fetid air-whale interface were the skulls that we had to unearth.

Howard Harper and I spent several days scraping and picking at those whale heads. A cloud of Eau de Pilot Whale enveloped us, impenetrable to anyone not under the stern direction of his guiding professor. Howard, who thought himself headed for a career in biology, soon abandoned the study of living and recently dead things, took up a clean, odorless slide rule, and became a mathematician. I have a poor sense of smell and stayed on to become a biologist.

Another outlet for the professor's energy was counting California gray whales. He made this seemingly indolent pastime into a test of anyone's stamina. Every year during December, January, and February a procession of these whales passes along California's coast, headed for lagoons in Mexico, of which Scammon's is one. There young whales are born. Gray whales swim close along the shore at La Jolla on their southward passage. It was not uncommon for us to look out of our laboratory windows and see one or two of these ponderous mammals apparently foundering in the surf. We never saw them strand themselves though, and they always returned to deeper water and continued on their way. The majority of the migrating whales cruise farther offshore. They swim at about four knots and can often be located by their "mushy" spouts, which form plumes of white against the sky. With binoculars we could see their knobby, finless backs arch up, and from time to time we could see them throw their broad tail flukes free of the water in preparation for a deep dive.

Professor Hubbs counted them as they passed. He wanted to know if their numbers were increasing or not. In the middle 1800s whalers located their breeding lagoons and learned their migration habits. Relentless killing followed, and the whales seemed gone from the earth, but they miraculously revived their species from a few secretive members, and sometime after their rediscovery they were placed under international protection. Many hundreds made the yearly migration by the time I reached Scripps.

Dr. Hubbs started his observations by climbing out of the upstairs window of his huge old campus house onto the steep shingle roof. Soon he could be seen there, wind, rain, or sunshine, peering through binoculars at the horrizon. Most of the time his wife, Laura, was with him taking down the counts as he made them. The whale count spread like a consuming passion into an Institution-wide operation. Graduate students, secretaries, mailmen, and research associates were pressed into service and stood "whale watch" fifteen minutes out of each hour. If one was an eager graduate student, one stood at least ten minutes longer than the prescribed time and wrote copious notes. A whale-watching shed was built on the roof of Ritter Hall, complete with telescope and azimuth circle, clipboards, and whale-accounting forms. The miscellaneous whale-watching crew had to climb up four floors of stairs, into an attic, and up an iron rung ladder onto the roof. It was a great improvement over Dr. Hubbs' unprotected roof, though, particularly on rainy days, when the intrepid whale watcher at the old station would have been soaked for his pains.

There was, however, one disadvantage that soon became apparent. Like a bird nesting in a mailbox, the good doctor refused to abandon his old post. Each watcher studied the sea with the knowledge that Dr. Hubbs was probably back there, straddling the ridgepole of his house, shouting counts down to his wife, his crew cut bristling in the wind. When a comparison of notes took place later, the doctor often had seen more migrants than the watchers in the cozy Ritter Hall penthouse, and nobody doubted that he saw them, either.

The penthouse had its advantages. Afternoon watches, just as the sun dropped below the horizon, casting its fading amber light over the sea, were often magic times of delicious calm. Even the watches on wild, windy days had their charm. We watched storm waves dash against the cliffs north of the Institution, crashing with such ferocity against the end of Scripps' pier that clouds of spray obscured the instrument shack at its outer end. Whales were hard to see at such a time, with the sea a mass of whitecaps, but we stood our watches anyway on the off chance that a dark-gray back would roll into view. Then, too, I courted my future wife, Phyllis, on watch. In case Dr. Hubbs should worry about his data on this account, I can assure him that our watch was scrupulously kept.

This whale watch continued while I was a student at Scripps Institution but has since been discontinued. It revealed that the California gray whale is in the process of making a solid comeback. The population now numbers over ten thousand animals.

Though these whales once entered San Diego Bay, California, in such numbers that it was risky to cross in a skiff at migration time, today the main place for the birth and nurture of their young is Scammon's Lagoon, named in memory of the remarkable seaman mentioned before, a self-made naturalist and artist,

Captain Charles Scammon. The Captain commanded the whaling ship *Boston* during the 1850s, while gray whales were still abundant.

Captain Scammon first fished the lagoon in the winter of 1857–58. He had located the inland lagoon on an earlier trip and noted that it was the home of the gray whale. This species, which some whalers called the "devil fish," was notorious in Scammon's time for the destruction it sometimes wrought upon whalers and their frail cedar whaleboats. This reputation failed to deter the Captain. The sight of hundreds of whales filing into a single inland lagoon, where the calm waters were optimum for capture and where plentiful driftwood was available to fire the try-pots, overcame such concerns.

On Scammon's first whaling venture into the lagoon, his ship anchored some miles north of the entrance, while his scouts charted the bar and entrance channel. Two days later they returned with news that there was enough water for the mother vessel to enter. The Captain recorded his historic passage and some of the events that took place in his classic volume *The Marine Mammals of the North-western Coast of North America together with an Account of the American Whale-Fishery*. Parts of this graphic record are quoted here to re-create those boisterous days of hand whaling. Scammon writes:

> It was afternoon before we got underway. A brisk breeze was blowing, and would have carried us to a land-locked harbor before evening, had it not failed us when nearly on the shoalest part of the entrance, obliging both vessels to anchor, the tender having previously joined us. Night came on, dark and misty; and as the tedious hours wore away, an increasing heavy swell rolled in, breaking fitfully around both brig and schooner. Nothing could relieve us from our perilous situation but a strong land breeze, to take the vessels back to the first anchorage or to sea. Not a soul on board slept during that night. A light puff of wind, at long intervals, came through the mouth of the lagoon, each time giving us hope for the desired land-breeze; but it only increased the dismal sound of the angry surf as it beat upon the sandy shores. At daylight, a gentle air came in from seaward, when signal was made for both vessels to get underway; but be-

fore the anchors were lifted it fell calm again, and near noon the wind came from the northward, when we were quickly under all sail, and soon passed through the turbulent passage, and cast anchor behind a sheltered point of the lagoon.

The Captain then relates how his boatman accidentally set all the whaleboats adrift, how the ship's carpenter was lost trying to save them as they drifted out in the swift tidal current of the entrance channel, and how they finally swept back into the lagoon on the following tide and were regained. After enduring a gale, the embattled vessels finally began exploring the vast lagoon, and near its head many whales were found.

On the next day the boats were sent in pursuit, and two large cows were captured without difficulty, which gave all hands confidence in our ultimate success. Early next morning, the boats were again in eager pursuit; but before the animal was struck, it gave a dash with its flukes, staving the boat into fragments, and sending the crew in all directions. One man had his leg broken, another had an arm fractured and three others were more or less injured—the officer of the boat being the only one who escaped unharmed. The relief boat, while rescuing the wounded men, was also staved by a passing whale, leaving only one boat afloat. The tender being near at hand, however, a boat from that vessel rendered assistance, and all returned to the brig. When the first boat arrived with her freight of crippled passengers, it could only be compared to a floating ambulance crowded with men—the uninjured supporting the helpless. As soon as they reached the vessel, those who were maimed were placed on mattresses upon the quarter-deck, while others hobbled to their quarters in the forecastle. The next boat brought with it the remains of two others, which were complete wrecks. Every attention was given to the wounded men, their broken limbs set, cuts and bruises were carefully dressed, and all the injured were made as comfortable as our situation would permit; but the vessel, for several days, was a contracted and crowded hospital. During this time no whaling was attempted, as nearly half of the crew were unfit for duty, and a large portion of the rest were demoralized by fright. After several days' rest, however, two boat's crews were selected, and the pursuit was renewed. The men, on leaving the vessel, took to the oars apparently with as much spirit as ever; but on nearing a whale to be harpooned, they all jumped overboard, leaving no one in the boat except the boat-header and the boat-steerer. On one occasion, a bulky deserter from the U.S. Army, who had boasted of his daring exploits in the Florida War, made a headlong plunge, as he supposed, into the water, but he landed on the flukes of the whale, fortunately receiving no injury, as the animal settled gently under the water, thereby ridding itself of the human parasite.

The Captain finally caught many whales by use of the revolutionary new bomb lance. He set his remaining boats alongside a narrow channel through which the whales passed, and had his gunner shoot from the shore. In spite of the skepticism of the old whalers, the method proved spectacularly successful, and the *Boston* was soon loaded. She returned to home port with decks awash and whale oil in every available cask, including those normally used for bread, those used as coolers, and those used for deck try-pots.

The story of Scammon's success inevitably spread throughout the whaling fleet. The following season a large flotilla flocked to the lagoon, though only six of the whaling ships actually made the difficult passage into the lagoon. Many stood outside and sent their crews and longboats in to catch what they could. Scammon described the resultant scene in the upper reaches of Scammon's Lagoon:

> Here the objects of pursuit were found in large numbers, and here the scene of slaughter was exceedingly picturesque and unusually exciting, especially on a calm morning, when the mirage would transform not only the boats and their crews into fantastic imagery, but the whales, as they sent forth their towering spouts of aqueous vapor, frequently tinted with blood, would appear greatly distorted. At one time, the upper sections of the boats, with their crews, would be seen gliding over the molten-looking surface of the water, with a portion of the colossal form of the whale appearing for an instant, like a spectre, in the advance; or both boats and whales would assume ever-changing forms, while the report of the bomb-guns would sound like the sudden discharge of musketry; but one cannot fully realize, unless he be an eye-witness, the intense and boisterous excitement

of the reckless pursuit, by a large fleet of boats from different ships, engaged in a morning's whaling foray. Numbers of them would be fast to whales at the same time, and the stricken animals, in their efforts to escape, can be seen darting in every direction through the water, or breaching headlong clear of its surface, coming down with a splash that sends columns of foam in every direction, and with a rattling report that can be heard beyond the surrounding shores. The men in the boats shout and yell, or converse in vehement strains, using a variety of lingo, from the Portuguese of the Western Islands to the Kanaka of Oceania. In fact, the whole spectacle is beyond description, for it is one continually changing battle-scene.

By the time of my first visit to the lagoon, those boisterous days had, of course, gone, and the desert had taken back its own, a rare enough event in these days of "progress." Before telling of my second trip, as a member of a well-equipped expedition to learn about the sounds of gray whales, I should first chart the path that led me there, since many things happened in the intervening decade. It all began with the chance to assemble the exhibit at an oceanarium, Marineland of the Pacific.

CHAPTER TWO

Marineland of the Pacific

The best way to get to know a porpoise or to understand the personality of a whale is to work with it in one of the big marine exhibits, or "oceanaria." In 1952 only one oceanarium, at St. Augustine, Florida, existed. But it had been such a surprising success that plans were being laid for another in Los Angeles. One of my professors told me that the curator's job was open, and he suggested that I apply. I thought long and hard about the idea, and finally, filled with trepidation about how little I knew, I applied, and was hired. I still wonder why they hired me. The manager who interviewed me later told me he felt I was terribly formal and "academic" and, considering the spotless new suit I was wearing and the way my hair was slicked down, he wondered if I would be any help with the rough outdoor work connected with assembling an exhibit. Actually I'm neither of those things. I love field work and am happiest in old clothes in the midst of the dirty job. I can only conclude that I was available, cheap, and that some of my professors spoke a good word in my behalf.

I also realize that my notions about what went into building a display in a vast oceanarium were rather naïve. We would need, I thought, a three-hundred-foot beach seine, some fishing poles, reels, hooks and lines, a skiff with an outboard motor, a little boat to go to the main collecting grounds at Santa Catalina Island, and perhaps a few lobster traps. This inadequate assemblage was to do the job, along with liberal application of hard work.

Almost nothing developed as I expected. I eventually ordered and received my precious beach seine, but within a month my collectors had cut it to pieces, refashioned it into a totally unfamiliar-looking net, and used it in ways I had never heard of. Then, too, while we often dropped a hand line into the water, I soon learned that the fishing pole was a useless item designed to remove the fishline from your hand, where it belongs. We used skiffs and traps, but not the ones I had in mind. For the most part we fished with gill nets, equipment I had dismissed completely because I supposed they would damage the fish. I guess the only element I envisioned correctly from the start was the work. We had plenty of that.

Marineland of the Pacific was planned as the world's second oceanarium, and, of course, it would be bigger and better than the first one. It would have two huge three-story tanks, holding in aggregate more than a million and a half gallons of sea water, one for fish and one for porpoises, plus many smaller exhibits. I would have a staff of about twenty people to catch, train, and run the show: collectors, laboratory technicians, announcers, divers, aquarists, and artists.

Since those who built the first oceanarium at St. Augustine would be part owners, ours would be a lineal descendant of that first remarkable effort, which began in the late 1930s. A group of innovative film makers were then pondering how they might make moving pictures of life beneath the sea. This was before the advent of the aqualung, before all but the most crude submarine cameras, and before the invention of most other submarine equipment we take for granted nowadays. The film makers had little to go on but their own ingenuity. One of the men had photographed African veldt animals by enclosing them in a huge corral—so large that no fences could be seen on camera. The corral did its work. It restricted the animals so that they appeared on camera with predictable regularity. "Why not do the same thing for the sea?" the film makers reasoned. And so Marine Studios (now Marineland, Florida) was built far off the beaten track on a soggy parcel of inexpensive real estate at the end of a badly kept two-lane road, out in the palmetto swamp. It had big steel, concrete-coated tanks that could "corral" hundreds of fish, and dozens of ports through which photographers could work.

As the world's first oceanarium grew toward completion, so did local curiosity about it. It gradually became obvious that the tanks might be valuable as a tourist attraction as well as for photography, and thus Marine Studios was opened to the public. The first day the doors swung open, nearly fourteen thousand people crowded down that back-country lane to see the marine life. Through a hectic and sometimes desperate learning process, the owners discovered how to capture and keep turtles, sharks, reef fishes, and finally porpoises and small whales. I was to learn what I could from them and to have a display on hand when Marineland of the Pacific opened.

My start as curator was far from auspicious. Directly after hiring me, the manager assigned me two tasks. First, I was to inspect the old beach cave on the property. He had heard that it was teeming with rattlesnakes, of which he was deathly afraid. And, second, I was to care for the two goldfish someone had given him. The cave inspection went well enough. No rattlesnakes. But both goldfish promptly died. Since goldfish are among the world's hardiest fish, this was a matter of considerable embarrassment for one who planned to make the care and keeping of marine creatures his life's work.

The next step, and one of crucial importance, was to hire a fisherman as collector. Word was sent out along the Los Angeles waterfront, to ship chandleries, fish markets, and boat works that a fisherman was needed to stock the new oceanarium. Many suggestions were offered, but one name kept turning up: "Frank Brocato," usually with the added comment, "if you can get him." Before I ever met Frank I learned that he had been "top boat" in his class for years running. With his father he had introduced the first otter trawl to the Pacific coast many years before. Together they had tapped the virgin bottom fish fauna, and had caught staggering loads of halibut, sole, and flounder. This same trawl industry is still a major fishery today. Frank left his mark on the lobster fishery, too, when he outwitted both lobsters and the other lobster fishermen by using his fathometer to locate undersea rock ledges where the lobsters hid.

During World War II, Frank fished for soupfin sharks, whose livers are a remarkably rich source of vitamin A, a substance badly needed at the time to assist in the reduction of night blindness in aviators. Before long he knew all about the sharks and had many other fisherman following him as they tried to learn his secrets. One wild night he and his young godson, "Boots" Calandrino (later the first mate under Frank at Marineland, and skipper after Frank retired), hauled aboard sharks worth more than ten thousand dollars from his cleverly set nets. Sardines, mackerel, mullet, kelp bass, and white sea bass were old adversaries, and he learned their tricks too. His fellow fishermen recommended him as a wily professional, a prodigious worker, a master net builder, and a consummate seaman.

I have never known a more remarkable man. He is one of those rare people who could have been a success at virtually any occupation that opportunity allowed. Frank's opportunities allowed him to be a fisherman, like his Sicilian ancestors for generations back, and he was a superb one.

I remember our first meeting very clearly. As I walked up to his front door and rang the bell, I wondered how I was going to put my offer to this man. I imagined him to be a stern six-and-a-half-foot ham-fisted giant who would look straight through me as his face revealed that he considered scientists and curators (especially young, inexperienced ones) a prissy, useless lot. Frank's house, a neat white stucco of a style common in California and best typified as "Early Santa Fe Railroad Station Architecture," told me nothing about the man. I had rather expected to see an array of old nets, floats, and spars around the yard, but there were none.

It would be hard to have been further off base about Frank. The man who opened the door looked like a successful used-car dealer or a certified public accountant—short and stocky, trimly dressed from shiny perforated leather shoes to conservative rimless glasses. Only the rough hands and tanned face marked him as a fisherman. The tan on his face stopped abruptly just above his glasses. Later I learned that this is because Frank never goes anywhere without his cap. Traveling with him is apt to be one continuous succession of pit stops for new caps. He has half a hundred, acquired over the years.

It wasn't long before we were deep in a discussion about every conceivable kind of creature we could hope to catch and display. Frank proved at once to be a gifted free-style talker. In addition to his voice, he talked with arms, legs, stomach, eyes, and other movable parts. He launched into an impromptu description of a basking shark running into his boat at night, and I could almost feel the thump. Later he was a bat ray, flapping along close to the rug in the best approved bat-ray style. At this point the ray became inextricably enmeshed in one of Frank Brocato's devilish nets, and then miraculously changed into Frank Brocato again, to haul himself in. Once during the conversation he was even a flying fish skimming over the water, no mean feat for a man of his proportions.

"Would we try to catch things like basking sharks?" Frank asked. The basking shark is a huge, innocuous beast reaching perhaps thirty-five feet in length. At that time I hadn't discovered the limitations of my three-hundred-foot beach seine and those fishing poles, so I enthusiastically agreed, adding that it wasn't out of the question to try for a whale someday.

"Wouldn't *that* be something—to look through a window and see a whale swimming around?" he mused, his thoughts no doubt turning pragmatically to the problems involved. "I'd really like to lock one of them up," he continued. "They've given me a lot of trouble, you know. When they migrate through, a sea bass net isn't safe in the water. They just ram through the net and keep swimming. I think it scratches their backs or something. Sometimes they'll tow a net for miles."

Frank was talking about the California gray whale, which migrates close to shore where the sea bass fishermen set their gill nets.

On and on we talked. After a while it was disclosed that Frank had promised his wife, Mary, to retire from the hard life of a commercial fisherman when he turned fifty.

"How old are you now, Frank, if you don't mind my asking?" I asked.

"Forty-nine and six months," he replied.

In later conversation with Mary, he convinced her that this collector's job would be a retirement of sorts.

Not long afterward our business manager signed a contract that gave Marineland of the Pacific Frank's trim thirty-seven-foot gill-net boat, *Geronimo,* and Frank's services for a year. The manager and I carried the check in person to Frank's house one Friday afternoon. There we ran smack into our first fisherman's taboo.

"I can't take the check on Friday," Frank said quietly. "It's bad luck, you know, to start a new job on Friday."

Mary, ogling the sizable sum stamped on the check in red numerals, said wistfully but really without hope, "Won't it be all right, Frank, if *I* take it, dear?"

"No, you'll just have to wait before you go off spending any of that money." Frank firmly pushed the check away with the palm of his hand.

The manager and I left Frank's house still in possession of the check. It was dropped in the mail the next day, to everyone's satisfaction.

During my days at Marineland I ignored the Friday taboo twice and, even though I'm still no believer in such taboos, lived to regret my action each time. Once I scheduled a fish-collecting trip to Mexico starting on Friday, and it blew a frightful gale for seven days; when we finally did catch some nondescript fish, they were eaten to the last scale by hordes of insidious little water fleas. We came home with nothing but a bag of fishbones to show for our effort. Frank said nothing about the matter, but his silence was eloquent. The next time I decreed a Friday take-off, we went after sturgeon in San Pablo Bay near San Francisco. All went well for a long time and we caught a full load. But on the way home the truck broke down on the Ridge Route. The ground around us was patchy with snow and ice when the truck began to spout live steam through a cracked block. By plying its innards with salt water from the fish tank, we limped into a garage and waited for hours, shivering in the cold pre-dawn dark before the garage man appeared and sleepily opened his doors. The ordeal was far worse than mere frostbite because I had to endure the black looks of my fishermen friends who *knew* why it had all happened. Needless to say, all the sturgeons turned on their armored sides and died from the rigors of the trip.

We signed Frank in January 1954 before the start of the white sea bass season. As the date approached when the boats would start to sea, we began to get a series of odd and plaintive phone calls from Frank's fishermen friends. The gist of them was, "Is it really true that Frank has quit us and isn't going to sea this season? How could he do a thing like this when we need him?"

Whether or not it was true, we began to get the feeling that many of the other boats relied upon Frank to figure out a solution when the fishing went sour, and that his influence extended well into the realm of superstition. Frank's shipmate on the *Geronimo* left his oilskins and boots on board until the last day before the season opened, presumably hoping that Frank didn't mean what he said and that the *Geronimo* would take to sea with the rest of the fleet.

But Frank did mean what he said, and he began converting his gear to face the unusual challenge of collecting for an ocean-arium.

Time was terrifyingly short, and all our problems lay before us. Here it was January (the buildings were well on their way to completion), and the prospective opening day for Marineland of the Pacific was May 15. Not only did we have to gather the fishes and animals but we had to beg, borrow, or build places to hold them. As it turned out, we did all three, with variations.

There simply wasn't time to catch and train a porpoise exhibit, so we contracted with Marineland, Florida, for four of their troop of Atlantic bottlenose porpoises, which were flown out just before opening day.

At first my staff and I had great hopes of housing our fish in two holding tanks at the oceanarium, each planned to be thirty-five feet in diameter. These were to be built high on the bluff on top of two old Coast Guard gun emplacements. If we could get water to them, they would hold nearly everything we would need for opening day. The suave little construction superintendent assured us they would be filled and operating by March 1. Now, if there is one piece of advice I can pass along to anyone planning to become a curator, as a distillate of my experience, it is Norris's Law: *"Never believe a construction superintendent."* All he wants to do is to get you out of his office so that he can figure out why the pipes broke under the new motel.

March 1 came and went, and no holding tanks rose on the bluff. In fact, as we peered anxiously at the old emplacements, there was hardly a hint that tanks were even planned. Wisely, my patience ran out at this point, and I decided to place no more reliance upon these mythical tanks. If they suddenly materialized, all right. Meantime, frantically, we turned our thoughts to new alternatives.

The first possibility was an abandoned aquarium in the tiny resort town of Avalon on Santa Catalina Island. This decaying establishment was composed of an old boiler with windows framed in her sides, about a dozen small cement tanks with glass fronts, and two cement pits filled with a green, stringy algal soup. The entire majestic array was serviced by an ancient pump of Da Vincian design, held together by faith and a heavy encrustation of rust, and set in a box under the main street of Avalon.

We rented the aquarium for several times its capital value and set about resurrecting it. My first task was to remove the algal soup from the cement pits. As I began bucketing out the muck, two big, famished moray eels raised their heads from the slime and snapped at my hands. How long they had been there is anybody's guess, but one thing was apparent: here was a fish we could rely upon to survive under the worst of aquarium conditions. In an animal display one grows to love and cherish these hardy souls, particularly after a few frustrating bouts with some of their prima donna relatives whose care and keeping, in many cases, are still unsolved puzzles.

Frank and some of my other men climbed into the big boiler and soon disappeared in a cloud of rust as their scrapers flew over the sides of the ancient tank.

"Be careful you don't scrape through the walls," I warned. "I'd rather have the water held in by a layer of rust than running all over Avalon."

Several days later we called on the owner of the aquarium, a happy-go-lucky deep-sea diver named Al Hansen. Al stoked up the ancient pump, and soon water began pouring into the freshly painted tanks. We watched with great satisfaction as the big boiler filled higher and higher. When it was full it would hold almost 25,000 gallons, and if we crowded it to capacity, there would be fish enough for quite a show in the big Marineland fish tank. What we didn't know was that from time to time, according to the tides, the aquarium drew its water from the salt-water fire lines of Avalon, which were serviced from a cracked, algae-choked reserve tank set high on the hill above the town.

Off to sea we went, feeling much happier now that we had a home for our fish. Frank was armed with permits which allowed us to fish in the restricted lee of Santa Catalina Island, and he happily set his traps and nets in previously forbidden grounds. As the traps came dripping over the rail, they were filled with dozens and dozens of colorful sheepshead, bass, rockfish, ocean whitefish, cabezon, and perch.

"Do you want any moray eels, Ken?" Frank asked.

"You bet I do. They're wonderful exhibit material. We could use fifty if you can catch them."

Frank turned the *Geronimo* down the coast and peered keenly at the rocky shoreline. As we cruised close along the edge of an amber-colored bed of giant kelp, he pointed down into the blue-green water and said matter-of-factly, "If I put two traps here, we'll catch your fifty eels. Inshore fifty yards we'll get lobsters instead."

I didn't want to question his knowledge of what went on below the surface of the sea, so I said, "Let's try for both, Frank. We need lobsters too."

Sure enough, next morning when we pulled the traps, there were eels in one set and lobsters in the other. The only miscalculation Frank made was that we caught sixty eels instead of the fifty I had requested. The trap was simply a cube of eels as it swung on deck. I had never seen so many eels in one place outside the pickle jars of my museum days. Later I learned that there was little point in expressing doubt about Frank's expertise in such matters. It was best just to watch and look for clues as to how he did these things. I never found out about the eels.

We became entangled in a mass of regulations with our first load of fish for the Avalon tanks. The port captain informed us that we would not be allowed to dock anywhere except at the end of the municipal wharf, and then only in the very early hours of the morning. This was so we would not interfere with the all-important tourists who emerged with their money later in the day. The port captain's edict meant that we had to use an ancient winch barely capable of lifting five hundred pounds when forced to its creaking, groaning limit. All our captives had to be handled in fifty-gallon drums. Sharks came up with their tails dangling out of the tops of these drums, and bat rays literally had to be rolled up like Dead Sea scrolls. More regulations prevented us from driving directly down the main street (the strolling Mexican orchestra used that route, though they seldom strolled at five in the morning). Instead, we had to follow a circuitous path through the back of town in our rickety flap-fendered pickup, and since we had no aeration equipment to keep the fish alive, we were forced to drive like teen-agers in a square-cornered drag race, while water splashed onto the sidewalks at every turn.

About this time the team of Frank and Boots was reunited,

when we hired Boots (Frank) Calandrino as assistant collector. Frank Brocato is Boots' godfather (*gumbah*), but Frank has been far more than that to Boots. Boots went to sea with Frank when he was thirteen years old and has been with him most of the time since then. Boots could tell how Frank was feeling a good city block away. He knew what knot Frank wanted on what trap, and under what conditions of the wind and tide, and tied it with bewildering speed and ease. I learned the hard way that the best thing to do when these two were carrying out an old, practiced operation was to make myself scarce. Otherwise there was real danger of getting my foot caught in a loop of flying Manila line, or simply of eliciting a torrential exchange in Italian, unintelligible to me, but clearly a colorful and graphic description of my landlubber tendencies. Under such circumstances I busied myself at noncontroversial tasks like doing the dishes or washing down the deck, and even here I usually received ample advice about which way to throw the dishwater or what to do with the potato peels.

Boots received his nickname because he was so thin that when he stood sideways about all you could see were his big fisherman's boots. Thin or not, Boots was tough as rawhide. He could outrow and outpull any man I knew. He could go hand over hand up the forestay of a swaying ship's mast or perch all night in a freezing wind on the masthead watching for fish. Lack of sleep seemed not to faze him, and he would spend the next day working nets or rowing without sign of fatigue.

Perhaps more important, he was Frank's complement. Frank was a fiercely proud man for whom nothing could be done half right. Every detail had to be perfect and every eventuality accounted for. In hard going this sometimes leads to frayed tempers just when they must be kept in check. At times like these, Boots would give me a poke in the ribs and say, "What the heck, let's try it again," or more often, "Watch out for *gumbah*, he's about to blow his cork."

Boots was a humorist of a special, almost indescribable kind. For example, he spent hours and hours learning the scientific names of every fish we took so that he could wander down to the fish market, stand alongside a boat that was unloading, and make comments about its catch.

"Morning, fellow," he might say. "Nice load of *Cynoscion nobilis* you got there."

"Whaaaat?" comes from one of his fisherman friends, standing hip-deep in slimy white sea bass.

"I said," Boots would explain carefully, in rather condescending tones, "nice load of *Cynoscion nobilis* you got there—only I prefer *Xiphias gladius* myself."

"*Disonorato,*" the fisherman would hiss under his breath, "looks to me like you got an overdose of those boys out at the fish factory."

At the "fish factory" construction was progressing but with many unforeseen problems, and our opening date had been moved to the end of summer. My crew and I didn't object at all, especially since those holding tanks promised by the construction superintendent still had no water.

Frank and Boots made trip after trip, and I went along when events back at the oceanarium would allow. One day we caught bat rays in the murky recesses of Catalina Harbor, the next trip we went after six- to eight-foot blue sharks in the deep azure waters of the open channel. I had never seen a live blue shark before, and it was an exciting moment for me when we came upon our first one "finning." When the sun comes out, these slender, rapacious sharks come to the surface and cruise along with their dorsal fins out of the water and the tips of their long tails lazily sculling back and forth.

"Watch this," Boots whispered. He threw the head of a mackerel and it landed with a *plop* a few yards in front of the slow-moving shark. The shark seemed startled, and then rushed swiftly at the sinking fish.

"He's ours!" shouted Boots.

I couldn't see how he was "ours," but refrained from saying so. Boots baited a hook and threw it in the general direction of the mackerel head. Moments later his heavy hand line jerked taut, and after a brief but violent struggle a seven-foot shark was swimming in the deck tank on the *Geronimo*. On other occasions

I watched Frank and Boots drive these sharks into a feeding frenzy with pieces of mackerel, and then lead them into a submerged dip net and scoop them, unhooked, from the sea.

The Avalon tanks were soon crammed with fish. We gazed at them with relief and pride, and, as it turned out, a false sense of security, for one night the ancient, rusty pump gasped its last and collapsed. Our night watchman could save only about a third of the specimens, as the water became increasingly stagnant. Wearily, we installed a new pump and began again to fill the tanks. We felt like the toad in the well who goes upward three hops and slips back two.

The tanks were refilled, but our troubles were not over. A few weeks later our Avalon caretaker, Marion Marin, watched helplessly as most of the fish mysteriously turned belly up and died, even though the water continued to pour in. The next day we found that the main city pump had broken and we had been switched to the fire line from the little reservoir on the hill. The heavy encrustation of algae annoyed one of the city officials, so he impulsively threw several pounds of an algae-killing chemical into the water. The effects on our fish were much more dramatic than on the algae, as the whole collection except for a few moray eels expired.

This time we were thoroughly alarmed. Here it was the middle of April and we had almost no fish to show for our efforts. Even though the day of opening had mercifully been moved back a couple of months because of construction delays, it was clear we could not depend wholly on the rickety old aquarium at Avalon. Diversification seemed the only answer. Even though we began to restock the old aquarium, we began also to look elsewhere for secondary storage depots.

The holding tanks at Marineland, completed by this time, were my initial hope. However, while we watched the first water gush in, we also saw it leak out at a lesser but still rapid rate. The new tank walls had not bonded to the old gun-emplacement bases upon which they had been cast. Turning my back ruefully on this sight, I addressed my thoughts once again to other plans.

"If this construction company can't make a tank hold salt water, maybe we can," I thought bitterly.

Before long we had set up a series of battered old steel sardine transport tanks on the beach below the growing oceanarium, and water was pouring into them from a couple of small pumps. This jerry-built jumble violated every construction code known, but it held fish for us right up to opening day.

Meantime it seemed to us as if we were locked in mortal battle with the contractors—they were determined that we shouldn't keep a living thing on the site until they left, and we were determined to have specimens on display the moment the oceanarium was complete. This battle was certainly mythical, since both groups were working feverishly to complete their divergent projects, but it didn't seem so at the time.

One day, for example, three members of my staff, Dave Brown, Marion Marin, Bill McFarland, and I came roaring down the dirt road to our tanks on the beach. Our fish truck was loaded with precious yellowtail, the first of this beautiful species we had caught. A paving machine was creeping up the hill, leaving a trail of hot asphalt behind it. Once these satanic monsters start breathing fire and spewing asphalt, apparently they cannot stop without putting pleats in their work, or something like that. In a few minutes we would be unable to reach our jerry-built tanks across this steaming barrier. We parked our truck, leaped out, frantically scooped the fish from the fish box, and ran to the tanks. Each time the run became longer as the clanking, smoking machine rolled inexorably up the hill. We scooped out the last fish moments before the hot asphalt was to encircle our truck and trap it too. We roared to freedom with truck doors flapping and inches to spare, but our fish were swimming safely in the sardine tanks.

Another diversification involved the rental of a receiver in Los Angeles Harbor. This is a sort of floating palace for bait fish made out of several slat boxes suspended in the water from an anchored platform. One simply dumps fish into the submerged boxes and feeds them once a day. With it one never has to worry about pumps or ruptured lines or paving machines. The water is as abundant as the bay. One thing we began to worry about, though, was small boys.

Our receiver was soon filled with a tantalizing array of pinto groupers, bright-orange garibaldis, red snappers, opaleye perch, and any other fish we could grab hold of. We simply cruised up in the *Geronimo* and dumped load after load into the slat boxes. Our fish hotel—or ghetto, if you prefer—was anchored a good twenty-minute row from shore, and we assumed it was safe. However, before long we began to have visitors. Fish were speared and hooked and scooped, even though we locked lids over the boxes and placed guards. The temptation was simply too great for the small boys in the area. Now that I can look back on the incident dispassionately, I can't say that I blame the boys too much. When I was a boy, I'd have been there too, I think, if there had been such a treasure-trove in my bay.

A great many fish did survive these commando raids, and last time I looked, some scarred veterans were still alive. One old patriarch of a Gulf red snapper lost an eye to some boy's spear in one of those boxes, and grew to enormous size in the Marineland fish tank. For years, every time I saw him, he brought back those frantic days.

The sardine tanks of Marineland's beach and the bait receiver in Los Angeles Harbor would not hold enough to assure a decent display on opening day if the Avalon aquarium failed at the crucial moment, so we settled on yet another and more grandiose scheme. We decided to net off part of a bay. The bay we chose was the magnificent Catalina Harbor, on the windward side of Santa Catalina Island. Far inside this all but landlocked natural harbor is a hooklike jetty of rocks, once used to load cattle barges. Behind this jetty is a ten-acre bay that we could barricade closed with a net about seventy-five yards long and twelve feet deep. Frank and Boots prepared a heavily tarred sardine net of the proper size, and with permission from the friendly island authorities we set off to tie it in place. First we pounded about twenty long steel pipes into the bottom of the bay as fence posts.

We tied the net above-water to the poles in such a way that it would rise and fall with the tide. Then I descended into the murk, equipped with an aqualung, and tied the net in place under water, as it swept back and forth over me with each surge. I emerged covered with tarred net marks from stem to stern.

Next we threw in the fish. Barracuda, bat rays, opaleye perch, garibaldis, and dozens of other species were brailed in throughout the weeks that followed. The harbor is isolated, and no small boys wander its shores. The water changes with each tide, and we had ten acres of it locked securely behind our stout net. At last we thought we had a fortress without a flaw.

Almost inconceivably, this was not the case. The final trouble we encountered was strictly unpredictable—*eagles*. The murky water hid our charges. We simply dumped the fish in and watched them disappear, and threw in food from time to time. It was weeks before we discovered that the lad we had stationed as a guard was spending much of his time in Avalon with a girl friend. In his absence a squadron of ospreys, or fish eagles, had stationed themselves on top of our net poles, waiting. Many of our captives, unaccustomed to living in a muddy bay, broke water from time to time as they swam aimlessly about, and this was their undoing.

Those eagles dined as they never had before or since. The devastation was so great that I half suspect as one flight became so gorged that it could not catch another fish, a new flight moved in to take up station on the poles. I assume the first flight then went off to digest and wait its turn. For all I know, the schedule might have been even more complex, with three or four flights involved. At any rate, some fish species that we had stored in large numbers were simply absent when we later seined the enclosure.

Itwas now mid-August, and in a few days Marineland would open its doors officially. The huge tanks were complete wherever the public would go, but the leaky holding tanks out back that had once been so central to our plans still didn't hold water. The battle with the construction superintendent was nearly over, but he fought on gamely to the last. To our disbelief, we heard him tell us that we were to have water in the main fish and porpoise tanks only three days before opening. All our collections, scattered over much of southern California, would have to be brought in and acclimated to their new surroundings in that short time.

Until completion papers were signed, turning the oceanarium over to us, the construction firm would have to operate it, and the cost was astronomical. Our already strained pre-opening budget could stand only three days of such wasteful operation. We would have to move with the precision of a drill team, and the fish were only part of the problem. My crew was also charged with decorating the huge display tanks. We had been allowed less than a week to build rock formations on the tank bottoms, made of great many-ton boulders, each of which was swung in place by a powerful overhead crane, and to sink a variety of underwater artifacts such as sunken boats, anchors, and thousands of pounds of coral and shells.

Finally Dave Brown, Bill McFarland, and I hastily put the finishing touches on the rockwork, climbed from the tank, and watched the water pour in—brownish green with construction dust. It bubbled up over the tops of the window, casting the inside corridors in muted greenish light, and finally leveled off at the overflow drains.

That evening the three of us stood on the rim of the oval fish tank. I gave a signal and we three jumped, landing simultaneously in the water. We were the first organisms, other than germs, to enter the newly filled tanks. The next morning the manager had a little ceremony with the press in attendance. Amid popping flashbulbs, he threw a cat shark artistically into the tank, and the reporters rushed off to write copy about "First animals enter huge oceanarium tank at Palos Verdes." We knew better.

Then began three days of noisy confusion. Trucks roared in from all directions. The winch on the top deck whined almost continuously as tank after tank of live fish was raised and placed in the display tanks. The *Geronimo* and a hired bait boat shuttled back and forth across the San Pedro Channel bringing in our precious captives. There other crews seined or scooped fish from tanks and enclosures. Frank and Boots were everywhere, doing everything. For the most part I stood in the midst of this chaos trying to comprehend it, as did the manager, who looked bewildered but pleased. And well he could be pleased. His men and women had worked magnificently with no other thought than to get the job done. Somehow it was done, and at the end of August 1954 the doors opened to 14,850 curious southern Californians.

The display wasn't the magnificent one it is today. The oval fish tank had soaked up dozens of loads of fish and still looked sparsely populated to us. Next door in the whale and porpoise pool the four Atlantic bottlenose porpoises we had flown in from Marineland, Florida, did no more than feed from their trainer's hand and occasionally poke their heads out of the water. But our doors were open, and we could stop worrying about little boys, pumps, poison, and eagles.

Meantime we were also learning to catch our own porpoises.

CHAPTER THREE

Bottlenose Porpoises

When Frank and I first began to think about catching porpoises for Marineland, we had ahead of us a long and often frustrating road before we would succeed. First I traveled to Marine Studios (now Marineland, Florida), where the curator, Forrest Wood III, introduced me to the intricacies of their smoothly functioning collecting operation. "Woody" showed me the nets they used to entangle the animals, the long canoelike skiffs that allow a skilled team of fishermen to roll a porpoise aboard without swamping, and the maze of waterways behind the oceanarium which the porpoises often frequent. Such waterways do not exist in California. Normally the closest a Pacific bottlenose porpoise comes to shore is when his school swims into crowded San Diego Bay, among aircraft carriers and tugboats, or plays in the booming surf of southern California beaches as far north as the Los Angeles area. During my days at Scripps Institution I often saw schools of bottlenose porpoises in the surf, racing along wholly inside a big wave and turning back to sea the instant it began to break. Time and time again they would return, probably just for the fun of it.

How does one catch a porpoise, either in the surf or in San

Diego Bay? Not, I ruefully concluded, by the methods that had been successful in Florida. San Diego Bay had few places where a net fisherman could work, because of boat traffic, and nowhere could one block a channel in which the porpoises swam. The open California shore was even worse. There one would have to fish right in the breakers. To trap a herd of porpoises against the beach in such a situation would require superb seamanship and split-second timing. Not only that, but it would be highly danger-ous to shoot the surf with a heavy net paying out astern. One mistake and the fishermen could come up in the net along with the porpoises, very likely drowned. I know; I tried it once, and I can conjure up the memory of the big, lethal net rubbing across my shoulders after the skiff swamped in a comber coming over the stern.

These problems turned our attention to offshore porpoises. In his fisherman days Frank Brocato had seen many porpoises off-shore, though he didn't pay much attention to them. So, shortly after he signed on as chief collector, Frank suggested that we should go hunting out in the deep water of San Pedro Channel. If we felt the animals that lived out in the open sea were good exhibit material, "perhaps," he said, "we might figure a way of catching them." "Let's go," I assented. Since we had bought the *Geronimo*, I hadn't yet sailed on her, and I was eager as a boy with a new toy. By the time my assistant, Bill MacFarland, ("Mac" to everyone) and I reached the dock, the provisions had been stowed and the coffeepot was already steaming in the gal-ley. Expertly, Frank backed the trim little vessel out of its slip amongst all the sleek yachts. I felt a bit superior being on board a real working boat, and especially one going in search of por-poises.

The sea was glassy and the sun warm on our backs. We could see for miles, or at least Frank could. About ten miles out he called out, "Porpoise off the bow!" We rushed forward, peering at the featureless sea, and could see nothing. However, a few minutes later a large school of common dolphins (*Delphinus delphis*) veered in toward our bow, leaping and splashing as they came.

We leaned over the rail to watch about a dozen of them station themselves alongside the cutwater, riding effortlessly along below the surface. They swam in tiers, one above another, their flukes almost touching our stempost. Occasionally one spun over and away from us in a graceful underwater barrel roll, to rise and "blow" a dozen yards away, outside the ship's bow wave. As quickly, another swung in to take its place. Occasionally one rose directly in front of our onrushing bow, sometimes blowing just before its smooth, shiny head broke the surface. In the instant of time its blowhole remained open, it expelled and took in a lungful of air. How, I could not conceive. All the movements of these magnificent animals showed exquisite and subtle response to the dense liquid around them. A tiny gesture of a flipper sent the animal into its spin. A movement from one of us looking down from above caused them to shy like anxious fillies. Beautiful white-bellied, brown-backed creatures they were, with striking black-and-gray snouts and eye rings like a pair of heavy dark glasses—long, slim-snouted animals, utterly smooth and glossy. To this day I never cease to be awe-struck by their ease of maneuver while swimming at eight to ten knots in front of an onrushing vessel.

We played with them for three-quarters of an hour before returning to our course. What an exhibit they would make! More beautiful by far than any porpoises now in captivity, I thought.

By midafternoon the steep hills of Santa Catalina Island loomed ahead of us. Emerald water lay quietly against them, brush-marked here and there by amber kelp beds. Jumbled rocky headlands alternated with little vest-pocket coves. Their sand and cobbles marked crescents of white between cliff and sea. While I mused contentedly over this lush scene, Frank, as usual, was looking to sea. His cry, "Porpoise!" swept away the reverie in an instant.

We turned to see him spin the wheel, veering the *Geronimo* away from shore and out toward a distant foam line, where the wind swooping over the island descended again to the sea. It all looked like distant whitecaps to us, but soon we saw a line of black-and-white objects in the roughening water. They didn't appear to be porpoises, but instead looked like a line of black-and-white squares, rolling over and over. Abruptly they disappeared together. Minutes later they reappeared, closer this time, materializing into a line of unfamiliar chunky, brilliantly black-and-white porpoises.

They moved slowly, arching their peculiar laterally flattened tails each time they submerged—hence the illusion of the rolling squares. The tails of these creatures are most unusual. They are flattened like a double-edged knife blade, and each up-and-down movement slices almost effortlessly through the water. Situated at right angles to this keel are the animal's very small black flukes. They were Dall porpoises (*Phocaenoides dalli*) and at the time were a rare find off southern California.

Suddenly a pair of these animals broke formation and rushed toward our bow. Instants later they were crisscrossing in front of us, never rising to breathe nearby. Instead, each time they needed a breath, they cut away, then rose, and as their heads plunged back into the water, they breathed inside the transitory air cavity they had created in the surface. Then, abruptly, the entire line disappeared.

Later we were to see Dall porpoises do this time and time again, and even in the smoothest seas we often lost them. We began to suspect they could swim long distances under water and then rise to breathe so gently that not a splash resulted. Without the white spray for us to see, they simply sneaked away, unnoticed in the swells.

Later I searched through the library and learned that there were only two records of Dall porpoises for southern California before our sighting. Each had been a dead animal washed ashore. Soon, however, we came to know these animals as regular winter migrants to southern California waters. With great predictability when water temperatures dropped to sixty-four degrees, the Dalls could be expected to appear. This swift, exotic, and beautiful animal was another possibility for our list of exhibits, and I felt it could be the most exciting of all.

As any fisherman knows, months of experimentation are required to develop new fishing gear. Even though Frank, Mac, diver Ted Davis, and I later developed head-netting gear that is now standard capture gear, at the time we couldn't wait for such developments. Or, that is to say, the opening-day schedule at the oceanarium couldn't wait. Besides, we didn't even know if these open-ocean species would live in captivity, or if they could be trained. So as mentioned, in order to have trained animals by opening day, we had depended upon our friends in Florida. Woody obligingly sent us four Atlantic bottlenose porpoises from his flock at Marine Studios. This, we knew, was only a temporary solution, because it was simply too expensive to fly these animals in whenever we needed to develop a new show. Even so, the Floridian foursome of Frank, Floyd, Mabel, and Myrtle were long the mainstays in the show of Marineland of the Pacific. Old troupers that they were, within a few days of their grueling flight from St. Augustine, one of them rose to take a fish from a trainer's hand, and soon they were doing their trick of plucking a fish from the trainer's teeth. Later we learned that these porpoises had seldom performed this latter trick, since they were low in the "pecking order" at Marine Studios. More lofty members of the school claimed that prerogative in the Florida tanks. Released from this social constraint, our porpoises showed they knew all the tricks of the oceanarium show. Many times since, I have seen porpoises learn complicated routines from each other in oceanarium shows.

It is commonplace nowadays for people to marvel at the intelligence of porpoises, but when the concept of oceanariums was new, no one realized what remarkable creatures they were. To Arthur McBride, the first curator at Marine Studios, they were just another possibility for a passive aquarium exhibit. In the early 1940s he began laying the first plans for their capture in the inland waterways near the new oceanarium. Bottlenose porpoises (*Tursiops truncatus*), the graceful gray fellows so familiar to us now, ran in small schools up these waterways to feed. McBride thought they could be trapped in one of the blind arms of these channels, chased into a net, entangled, and rolled into a waiting skiff. His fishermen built a net long enough to span the channels and deep enough to reach bottom everywhere, and then set out to catch their animals.

As I have since learned over and over, well-laid plans like these seldom fool porpoises. McBride and his fishermen watched as a small group swam leisurely into the still waters of a blind channel. Quietly the men slipped up behind the school and set their net across without disturbing their quarry. The fishermen then slipped upstream beyond the porpoises and began slapping their oars on the water. Predictably, the animals swam rapidly downstream toward the waiting net. Then came the surprise. Instead of rushing into the net, the animals stopped their head-long dash dozens of yards from it, turned, and swam back up the channel. No amount of disturbance served to drive them into the entangling meshes, and the effort had to be abandoned.

How could the porpoises know that the net was there? Presumably it made no sound in the still water. The water itself was amber with tannin from the surrounding swamps and, beyond a few inches, opaque to the human eye. It seemed impossible that the porpoises could have seen or heard the net. McBride at this point had the brilliant intuition that these animals might be listening to the echoes of their own sounds reflected from the net.

McBride wondered, Did the porpoises somehow emit sounds that could travel through the murk and hit the webwork of wet twine and return to the animal? Such a signal could tell them a trap lay ahead beyond the limits of vision. A wet net would not return much of an echo in air, but perhaps it could be a more effective "sound mirror" under water.

Acting on his intuition, McBride reasoned that his net was actually doing this improbable thing and was returning echoes to the porpoises. Somehow he would have to make the net less "sonically visible." This he accomplished by making the meshes of his net much larger. He reasoned that since there would be less twine to reflect sound, perhaps the echoes would be below the level of detection by a porpoise. McBride was immediately able to fool some porpoises and bring them into captivity.

His demonstration provided the first hints of "echolocation" in porpoises. It lay buried in McBride's field notes until several years later, after his death, it was discovered and published in McBride's name by William Schevill of Woods Hole Oceanographic Institution. By that time Schevill and his wife, Barbara, had performed the first definitive experiments demonstrating echolocation in these animals.

Why should a net under water reflect sound at all? A possible answer was suggested later by Schevill as a prelude to one of his pioneering experiments. He thought that the twisted twine might trap bubbles of air, each of which could act as a tiny sound resonator, thus sending back a signal if a porpoise directed sound against it. This hypothesis was supported when he found that a dry net placed in the water was easier for a porpoise to detect than a "marinated" one that had been soaked and had lost most of its trapped air bubbles.

When Frank and I decided to capture our own porpoises, we knew of none of these experiments. It would be quite a while before we were driven to similar conclusions. All we knew was that a reliable local source of animals was needed, and soon. Tempting as the offshore animals were, the inshore bottlenose porpoises seemed easier to catch. After much talk we decided we would try to circle them with a very long and heavy net, set by the *Geronimo* cruising at flank speed. We would collapse the net around them by hand and roll them out of the water into a big beamy-net skiff waiting alongside the cork line. When the net, a huge, expensive nylon affair, was completed, it was some twelve hundred feet long and twenty-five feet deep. It was piled on the stern of the *Geronimo*, and she set out down the coast to San Diego Bay. Once there, we spent more than a week just following and observing the small resident school of bottlenose porpoises.

Slowly some of the regular patterns began to appear. As is usual when observing any wild animal, everything seems random at first, but when, many weeks later, one knows the animals intimately, very little is actually random. Each bit of behavior has its function. We didn't watch long enough to pry very deeply; the needs of collecting disrupted that. What we did learn, however, was fascinating.

The animals were on a fairly regular circuit. During part of the day they could be found swimming along in the wake of the Coronado Island ferry, which at that time cut across the midriff of the bay, running from downtown San Diego to the sandspit of Coronado Island. The latter defines the outer coast of the bay and is not actually an island at all. We could not be sure why the porpoises swam behind the ferries, but our best guess was that they were feeding in the muck stirred up by the churning ship's screw. At any rate, they dove repeatedly a hundred yards or so behind these ships, following them monotonously back and forth. The relentless predictability of the ferry's return just as monotonously prevented us from trying to catch them. One has only to imagine a ferry filled with cars bearing an impatient group of commuters lying dead in the water, its screw tangled in twelve hundred feet of stoutest nylon, to know why we decided, reluctantly, to work elsewhere.

During our many frustrated passages back and forth across the channel behind the ferry, we noted that occasionally some porpoises broke off from the rigid track and went off into the deepest parts of San Diego Bay, amongst moored Navy landing craft and freighters. Also, early in the day and again near dusk, we often encountered a little school close along the north shore of Coronado Island making their way toward the bay entrance, tucked in the lee of mountainous Point Loma. Where they went beyond the bay we did not know, execpt that we occasionally encountered them in the surf along the sea coast of Coronado Island. Later fishermen told us that the porpoises followed the Navy garbage scow down the coast to Imperial Beach. This scow collects garbage from the Navy ships anchored in the bay and dumps it outside, a few miles north of the Mexican border. We confirmed this movement and came to believe that the porpoises fed not on the garbage but upon the large number of fish attracted to it. As each of these patterns revealed itself, it became apparent that the porpoises had developed a culture of

sorts, attuned to the niceties of life in a busy port. It's the sort
of thing they do in many places throughout the world, and certainly one clear indication of their flexible intelligence.

Frank selected the upper harbor as the best place for us to
try our first net set. Anchored Navy ships were about the only
craft found there, so we could safely retrieve our net before
someone ran over it. Furthermore, the water was dirty and shallow. Our net would hit bottom quickly and would be difficult
for a porpoise to see.

On a foggy January morning Frank, Boots, and I boarded the
Geronimo and cast loose her damp lines. Quietly she slid out into
the calm bay. Before long we made our way into the upper bay.
There we found three bottlenose porpoises cruising slowly between anchored landing craft. Frank watched these animals,
carefully bringing the *Geronimo* alongside them about fifty yards
off their course. They reacted nervously at first, but settled
down as Frank kept resolutely on course, not changing a turn
on the engine's speed.

"Get in the skiff, Ken," he instructed quietly. "And, Boots,
when I get ahead of them a little bit, I will give you a hand
signal, like this, and you slide the skiff off into the water. Careful, now, here we go."

The *Geronimo* inched ahead without changing course. The
hand signal came and the skiff slid quietly off its net pile into
the water. Then the idling engine came to life, flank speed, as
Frank turned the helm over and swung the ship about two hundred feet ahead of the slowly moving animals. The net, attached
to my heavy skiff, payed out in leaping folds from the stern,
sinking to its cork line in the opaque coffee-colored water. I
saw the frightened porpoises submerge, and watched their flight
toward the front of the net by the big, muddy boils of water
thrown up by their beating flukes. Around came the *Geronimo*
to meet me. She heeled over with the speed. One hundred feet
from the far side of the net the porpoises stopped, turned, and
came charging directly toward me under water. While we frantically tried to close the last few feet of opening, they raced
under my skiff and were gone. No hesitation, no searching; they

knew they were nearly trapped and instantly made for the remaining twenty-foot hole in the unclosed net. How, we wondered,
had they known? It was as if they were above-water looking down
on the whole operation.

In the weeks that followed we came to recognize some school
members, and, finally, they us. Old Scarback was hard to miss.
This old fellow seemed to have run afoul of the screw of a good-
sized ship. His dorsal fin and tail were scalloped with a regular
series of deep cuts, long since healed over and white. Scarback
once jumped over our net (a rare bit of behavior in porpoises
for some unaccountable reason), and had once rammed right
through it. Ultimately, we think, he learned to recognize our
ship, probably by some vagrant noise—a whistling stern bearing
or a characteristic-sounding auxiliary engine, for example. At
times when stalking the school, we could see Old Scarback lay
over at the surface looking at us with one eye, and usually the
school then became unapproachable.

Frank was frustrated by the growing ostracism, but gave Old
Scarback his due. "The old boy knows us, for sure, and knows
we're not playing. The only thing that can happen now, Ken, is
that it will get worse until we can't get within a country mile."

"Yeah, Frank, but maybe we're just imagining it all," I replied.

Frank's woeful expression changed to a condescending half-
smile. "No, Ken, take a look over there at that tug. In a minute
you'll see Scarback and his pals riding *their* bow like it was the
safest place in the world."

And, sure enough, we could see the gamboling porpoises in
the tug's bow wave. It didn't take many more attempts before
it was obvious even to me that our ship had worn out its welcome.

But this is getting ahead of the story a bit, because not long
after our first two or three attempts to circle the porpoise school
came the incident of the breakwater.

It was this incident that showed me what different lives the
average Anglo-Saxon and Italian lead. Working with Frank and
Boots eventually made me feel emotionally like a bowl of pablum.

The heights of elation, the depths of despair my Sicilian com-
rades could reach were well nigh incomprehensible to me. They
could cuss, enjoy, hate, love, and fight with a richness that has
my everlasting envy. They ran through most of this range when
we tried to catch the school behind the Coronado breakwater.

With weeks of frustration behind us, Frank decided the net
was simply too short, even if it was twelve hundred feet long.
We were reluctant to ask the management for more net with
so little in the way of success to show them. If we could effec-
tively lengthen ours somehow, Frank reasoned, it should work.
He thought he knew how.

At the north end of Coronado Island, a long Navy breakwater
juts out into the sea. Protected by this breakwater is a little bay
whose other shore is the lovely strand of Coronado Island. Occasionally, we knew, the porpoises came into this bay on their
return from the Imperial Beach garbage-dumping grounds. They
usually milled around awhile before skirting the breakwater and
starting into San Diego Bay proper. Frank thought that if the
Geronimo lay quietly with one end of the net attached to the
breakwater, he might wait until the porpoises passed him, going
into a cul-de-sac. Then he could run the *Geronimo* across the
bay to near the opposite beach, paying out net as he went,
and the skiff could take the last of the net ashore. We could
then handle it like a beach seine and haul the trapped porpoises
onto the smooth beach. Even Old Scarback wasn't likely to recognize us when our engines were shut down, or so the scenario
ran.

The porpoises didn't enter the little bay every day. Frank and
Boots contained their frustration remarkably well as day followed
day with no porpoises. Finally, patience was rewarded as several
unsuspecting big gray fellows came gamboling past the quietly
riding *Geronimo*. Frank started the engine and began to move
cautiously across the bay, meanwhile watching the unsuspecting
animals swim deeper and deeper into the trap. Elation swept
over the two collectors. "It's going to work!! We've got 'em this
time, for sure!" "There's no way they can beat us this time,"
they crowed.

By this time the *Geronimo* was ready to launch the skiff, and only a few yards of water lay between our crew and success. The surf was low and so even that seemed no special problem. Plenty of net remained piled in the stern.

Just then the porpoises startled, as if they had sensed our dreaded sound. To everyone's surprise, the animals didn't turn as usual and head for the ever-closing opening but, as Frank and Boots watched unbelieving, they began to race toward the stony barrier of the breakwater. The joy of the moment before turned to anger and then frustration and despair as, one after another, the porpoises raced to a low spot in the breakwater and lunged part way out of water and over into the deep water on the other side. It was mid-tide, and the channel, where some stones had rolled away, was just adequate for passage. They obviously knew it well.

Once on the other side, they slowed and began a lazy, mocking mill. From Frank and Boots came rapid-fire, high-volume Sicilian. I'm sure it rose to the sky and blackened the underside of Heaven. True coherence about the event for my men didn't return for some time, and even now, when they recall it, voices and the cadence of conversation go up a little.

After this incident, I decided that the mental health of my crew could stand no more. Perhaps Mexican porpoises were not so educated to the ways of nets as these. We knew, from earlier fishing trips, that the upper Gulf of California harbored very large schools of bottlenose porpoises. Many of these were fat old patriarchs, ten to twelve feet long and weighing eight hundred pounds or more. We knew, too, that they played around the shrimp trawlers, waiting for the trash fish from the nets to be shoveled overboard. Our hope was to catch them napping in the midst of such a free meal and, using a chartered boat, to set out net around both them and the trawler. The net would be pinched in the middle and the trawler set free, while the porpoises remained in the other half. Another neat plot had been hatched awaiting porpoise ratification or veto.

Working in Mexico is always an adventure, especially at the border, and especially when one can't pass as a tourist. That's

hard to do when arriving in a big truck piled with nets and
gear. Ultimately, however, Frank and Boots found a "genuine
dago" in the guise of a border guard, and all launched into rapid
Italian while white "X"s signifying acceptability were scrawled
on our cargo boxes in chalk. Off we went. The sleepy little fishing
port of San Felipe, 120 miles south, was our base of operations.
Shore camp was established in the "St. Francis Hotel," a roof-
less abandoned refrigerator plant. Once these amenities were out
of the way, the three of us trudged along the dusty streets to
the fisherman's cooperative. There we hired the *San Luis,* an
ancient trawler shot through with dry rot and held together by
faith alone. Most important to us was her Yaqui Indian skipper,
an old friend, Fortunato Valencia.

For a seaman the Gulf of California is a capricious place. It
can be calm and glassy but within minutes can be whipped by
winds into a maelstrom. Fortunato read the sky, the tides, and
the swell, and knew well his boat's foibles and capabilities as a
good skipper should. Years ago Fortunato had rowed across the
gulf for six days and nights in an open canoe from Guaymas,
Sonora. He had only a little food and wine bottles of water but
hoped for greater opportunity in the growing port of San Felipe.
Once his judgment and skill became recognized, he had risen
to the considerable eminence of skipper in the ragtag navy of
the cooperative. We found him a gentle, almost childlike man,
quick to break into a grand, radiant smile at the little things of
life, and as impervious to its stresses. At first glance the *norte-*
americano would see only the high-cheekboned and fierce mien
of the Yaqui and note the deep scar on his forehead that had
healed untended, but from other trips we had grown to know
and cherish him.

There was no pier at San Felipe, so all our gear was piled into
an old surplus amphibious DUKW and driven across the shallow
high-tide flats to the *San Luis* anchored far offshore. It seemed
like a long way, but six hours later, when the twenty-foot tide of
San Felipe receded, she was nearly on the beach.

Boots presented Olayo, the cook, with some food from our
stores, including a canned ham, some chocolate, and canned

goods. Olayo, who had twelve children, had, we felt, become a cook more to avoid the rigors of family life ashore than from a love of good cooking. Olayo wasn't used to canned hams, but once we were at sea he attacked the can with a butcher knife and extracted it whole. Olayo worked under some difficulty in his galley. It had no deck, only a gaping hole leading down into the engine room directly over the throbbing engine. So when Olayo cooked, he had to grasp thin railings on either side of this chasm with his bare, semiprehensile toes. The ham was slippery with gelatin and wouldn't stand still when Olayo tried to slice it. Boots happened to be walking by during this event. It wasn't until after our lunch of fried ham and potatoes that he told us how Olayo had solved his dilemma. By propping the ham in a corner against the bulkhead and grasping it firmly with the toes of one foot, he was able to slice off chunks while maintaining his balance in the rolling ship at the same time. If you don't enjoy ham cooked under these circumstances, collecting in Mexico is not for you.

Suffice it to say that Mexican bottlenose porpoises are quite as wise as those in San Diego Bay. The *San Luis* made seven and a half knots wide open, and the porpoises seemed to wait until the last frustrating moment before slipping smoothly out of our trap, not even considering the effort worthy of great haste.

We noticed that the big porpoises came very close to the after railings of the shrimp trawlers, sometimes within four or five feet. This seemed like an opportunity for capture, so we went aboard a trawler to observe.

The bottom of the northern Gulf of California is mostly flat, featureless mud. The trawlers simply pay out the long net, release the otter boards, or tables, that spread and sink the net, and tow it for three or four hours, scraping slowly along the bottom. Then the winch rolls up the tow cable and the net is lifted in over the afterdeck with the boom. The cod end of the net usually bulges with a potpourri of marine animals: sponges; starfish with arms sticking out through the mesh; dozens of species of little fish; small, translucent squids; and, with luck, several bushels of big, tasty Gulf shrimp.

Day and night mean little to the trawlermen, since they have only a short season during which they are permitted to fish. So we found ourselves creeping along in the darkness, a circle of light cast on the stern and out over the surrounding water from a boom light. Our net came aboard filled, and when the pucker rope was released, a four-foot mound of dripping muddy bottom life cascaded on deck. We watched the crew sort it, picking out the shrimp. One fisherman then began to shovel the remainder over the side. Porpoises appeared magically and began to swim through the circle of light, snapping up the floating fish. Some came so close we could almost have touched them. But how were we to catch them? One of the crewmen said it was easy. "Just use a hook and line," he said, and promptly went below, returning with a heavy two-inch hook.

While we watched, he attached this to a roll of Frank's heavy nylon net twine, baited it with a half-pound Gulf croaker, and tossed it into the midst of the feeding porpoises. Moments later a huge, looming whitish shape rose under the bait, and a pair of porpoise jaws appeared above the surface engulfing the fish. Our intrepid fisherman set the hook with a yank, which was instantly returned to him tenfold. At the last instant before going over the side, he let the line free and regained his balance while it screamed through his hands. It was too much even for his toughened fisherman's hands, and he stood there ruefully looking at the crisscrossed burns on his palms while the line leaped into the water behind him.

Frank sprang into action, grabbing the bitter end and securing it to the cleat of a skiff tied alongside. "In!" he commanded Boots and me. The fisherman jumped into the skiff too, moments before the line snapped taut and took the full force of a several-hundred-pound porpoise maddened by the painful hook set in his jaw.

We were spirited up out of the circle of the boom light with a jerk that nearly sent me sprawling. Fortunately, Frank had a flashlight in his pocket, and it became our only communication with the trawler as we raced across the middle of the gulf, miles from land, powered only by an almost unseen but obviously huge and healthy porpoise. The trawler followed behind us as our whole crazy retinue raced through the night. In and out of the lights of slowly moving trawlers we went, their crews watching us fly by, incredulity written on their faces. We hoped the porpoise wouldn't foul himself with a trawl cable, and later, as the hours went by and our animal showed few signs of weakening, we hoped he would. It was midnight when we started, and the first streaks of dawn tinted the calm gulf when the four of us finally wore that animal down enough to bring him alongside. I think he must have weighed eight hundred to a thousand pounds. He was nearly as long as our fourteen-foot skiff.

The approved fashion for boating such animals is to station two or three men along one rail of a beamy skiff, each reaching into the water around the animal, leaning backwards, and bringing it on top into the skiff. Once this is done, everyone wriggles out from under the animal, wipes off the salt water, and heads for home. I had middle position, and when I reached down around the fatigued animal, it was like putting my arms around a barrel, but one so large that my hands could not touch. All four of us strained and puffed, and the animal was so tired he didn't resist much, but we could not bring him aboard. Then the hook fell free from the corner of the porpoise's mouth. We felt him slide inexorably from our enfeebled grasp. He shook himself and swam slowly off as we watched, all of us absolutely drained of strength and emotion. We wearily turned and headed for the trawler a mile or so away. There must be a better way, we thought.

As we made our way homeward across the Baja California desert, Frank, Boots, and I thought and talked of ways we might succeed. A longer net might do the trick, but I was still reluctant to ask for the extra money. Then Frank squinted, pointing an index finger at me, and said, "If you're right, Ken, I know how we can do it." He was referring to a speculation I had made back in San Diego. I, too, after a much more extended and agonizing preparatory period than McBride, had concluded that porpoises must be able to echolocate.

Frank went on, "Every day those porpoises in San Diego

Bay swim right along the north shore of Coronado Island, a few yards from the beach. We'll set the net like a beach seine, parallel to shore, but far enough out so they'll swim inside it. As they approach, all their sonar will be able to detect will be the end of the net, and it won't look like a net to them. Once they're inside it, we'll pull the ends in and we'll have them."

For once, a plan involving porpoises worked to perfection. John Prescott, my assistant curator, who had gone along in my stead, came in with a truck full of porpoises. He wearily told me they had caught the whole school, including Old Scarback. They settled for three young adults and let the rest go, but even so, it was all they could do to bring them in. "It's not," John said emphatically, "the way I want to catch them every day."

~~~~~~~~~~~~~~~~~~~~~~~~~

CHAPTER FOUR

Pilot Whales

With the hectic pre-opening days behind us and with our por-poise supply assured, Frank and I began to think more and more about capturing a live whale. There was nothing much to go on. Years earlier Marineland, Florida, had kept a pilot whale for a few months, but they hadn't caught it. It came ashore in one of those unexplained mass suicides in which entire schools simply swim resolutely onto a beach and die when they strand and drown in the surf. Evidently it wasn't sick at the time, since it adjusted to captivity nicely and became a fine exhibit animal.

On an early fishing trip Frank had introduced me to my first live pilot whales. We were on board the *Geronimo,* heading for Santa Barbara Island, on one of those stormy afternoons when the northwest wind howls in from the open sea and the sky is a leaden gray. The wind had been blowing for three days, rais-ing restless lines of slaty swells that lifted the little vessel high on their shoulders and dropped her again into deep troughs, obliterating the gray bulk of the island ahead. Wind gusts clutched the watery slopes, whipping white spume trails across the surface and over our tossing vessel. Frank peered through the momentary clear patches on the windshield swept clean by the big wiper blade.

"Not much lee behind Santa Barbara," he volunteered. "Might be better to head back for Catalina."

That suited me fine. I sat braced in the galley corner, filled with awful bleakness, wondering if the next lurch of the *Geronimo* would destroy my nonchalance and send me stumbling for the rail.

Frank skillfully brought the little ship around, high on the crest of a huge swell, and within moments she stabilized with the sea to her stern. Not long afterward I, too, stabilized somewhat and rose to stand alongside Frank at the helm.

"Feeling better?" Frank asked, having understood my problem all along.

"I'll say so," I replied a bit sheepishly.

Frank looked intently ahead through the now clear cabin port. "Look out there, Ken," he said, changing the subject. "I think I saw spouts." It didn't seem possible that a spout could exist in that wind, but I moved closer to the glass and scanned the gray-and-white sea. Sure enough, far off the bow, now and then I could see puffs of vapor that were quickly swept away. Soon flashes of dark gray came into focus under the spume. "Pilot whales," Frank said with certainty. "They're what we Italian fishermen call *monaco,* or monk, because sometimes they stand upright in the water just like a stump. You have to see it to believe it. I haven't any idea why they do it, but their black color makes them look like a monk standing out there in the water in his robes."

The *Geronimo* closed slowly on the animals ahead, since we were both going in the same direction. I could now see about twenty long black animals. They swam as a rank, rolled to the surface in unison, and dove almost as one. Later, when we came abreast of the school, I could see that a couple of them were huge old fellows, perhaps twenty feet long, while many smaller animals were also in the school. Two babies bucked along, each beside an accompanying adult, throwing their heads free of the water in coltish exuberance each time they rose. They weren't much more than five feet long, I guessed.

As the *Geronimo* came abeam of the school, I braced myself

in the galley door and watched the entire school body-surf down the foreslope of the great sea swell on which we also rode. The animals slipped down the face, inside the gray-green swell, with only fins cutting above the water. Then they were gone.

That vignette stayed with me when Frank and I began serious discussions about catching a whale. The pilot whale was the animal we should learn to catch, I felt, not the huge gray whale Frank first had in mind. Not only were gray whales protected by international law, but adults were forty-five feet long and weighed many tons. Even in my more colorful flights of fancy I couldn't come to grips with the problems we would meet in subduing such an animal. But a pilot whale, even a twenty-footer, seemed possible, even if it seemed a quantum jump upward in difficulty compared to a porpoise.

The new Marineland general manager, Bill Monahan, was delighted when we suggested a whale capture, as he, too, wanted whales as a part of the exhibit. No other oceanarium had a whale at that time, and having one, possibly trained, would unquestionably draw visitors from all over the world. Bill endorsed our project and told us to see him when we needed help from the upper office. So the dream suddenly jelled into a task we were required to perform. Dreams without responsibility are one thing, but the reality of whale capture in the open sea is quite another. So, in dead earnest now, we laid our plans.

As with the porpoises, we would first learn to know our animals, and somewhere in that process we expected to come upon the key that would allow us to capture one alive. Frank knew from his commercial fishing days that they were abundant on the southern California coast in winter. He also knew that they came because the sea at that time of year thronged with countless tons of squid that spawned and died in the submarine canyons nearshore.

Winter had come, and just as Frank predicted, so did the pilot whales. We sometimes found school after school on a single cruise.

They were deceptively easy to approach. Frank tested them, bringing the *Geronimo* up slowly behind schools without changing engine speed so that no new sound would alert them. We were able to slide up until their broad, dark flukes nearly touched the *Geronimo*'s cutwater. At other times Frank maneuvered ahead of a school, cut the engine, and drifted, rocking on the smooth sea, waiting. At their usual lazy pace of about two knots, the whales came by, often gliding within a few yards of the rail, rolling now and then on their sides to look up at us. It seemed as if our major problem would not be approaching them but instead figuring out what to do about their vast strength and bulk once we had one on a line.

These pilot whales seemed ungainly, with their bulbous foreheads, barrel chests, and large, hooked dorsal fins. The slim tail protruding behind seemed much too long for the animal. In adults the pectoral flippers are long and sickle-shaped, and as the animals grow their rounded foreheads protrude more and more until the upper jaw becomes well hidden beneath. The sexes, we found, are very different in size: females reach fifteen feet in length and weigh perhaps fifteen hundred pounds, while old males may reach a little more than twenty feet in length and four or five thousand pounds in weight. All are grayish black in color and bear a light-gray blaze mark on their chests between the pectoral flippers. On adults one may see a saddle mark of reddish gray behind the dorsal fin, a pattern mark that shifts in prominence with the angle of the light. It usually shows up best when the animals are swimming below the surface, and, in fact, may be the first thing a diver sees when the whales slip by him at the edge of visibility.

As we watched, the behavior of these whale schools came slowly into focus. Particularly touching to the human observer, we found, is the behavior of adults toward their young, yet there is, at the same time, a streak of rigidity about this behavior which is hard to put in proper context. An example will help to explain what I mean. Once when we were pursuing pilot whales off the west end of Santa Catalina Island, Boots sighted a school coming resolutely toward us. We cut the engine and lay still in the water to see how close they would come. The bulbous foreheads broke the water more or less in unison, each advancing animal splashing a sizable bow wave in front of it. We noticed one medium-sized adult whose head appeared pure white. By watching closely each time it broke water, we could finally see that it held something white in its jaws. Its forehead, too, was white, as if smeared with zinc oxide. I trained my binoculars on the animal. To my surprise I discovered that it was carrying a dead baby pilot whale, so decomposed that all its black skin had sloughed off and its grease had smeared the adult's forehead, or "melon," with white. I could also see that the big whale held the baby by its pectoral flipper, and so flaccid was the tattered corpse that ripples passed unimpeded through it as the adult carried it along. This baby had probably been carried in this way for a week and a half, or days and days past the time when the solicitude of the adult might be of use. Later I found that this was no isolated incident but a fairly common occurrence amongst porpoises and small whales.

Slowly we began to know our animals. Morning was usually feeding and hunting time, a period that was perhaps the tag end of a nighttime of activity. The whales were usually gathered over the flats on the windward side of Santa Catalina Island, or in pods out in deep water in the lee, diving repeatedly over the squid spawning grounds, sometimes rising with squid squirming in their jaws. On the flats they occasionally swam near us, sometimes even directly under our keel, racing after the flickering squid school, and we came to believe that the whales usually pursued their prey from above, perhaps making use of their binocular vision, which, because of the shape of their heads, is directed down and forward.

Feeding groups were very different from hunting or traveling schools. In the latter, ranks of animals were lined up side by side, differentiated into recognizable social groups, such as adults with young or groups of juveniles, with the old males usually on the fringes of the school. Young whales born in the late fall, winter, and early spring swam along within inches of an adult, usually close beneath the large whale's dorsal fin. We could tell when they were newborn not only by their length, four to five feet, but because the youngest bore a series of vertical stripes that we knew to be fetal folds formed when they had lain curled up in their mothers' bellies.

More often than not, on the wings of these ranks, which might spread for over three-quarters of a mile, we found small groups of various species of porpoises, the most common being the bottlenose porpoise (*Tursiops*) but less commonly the Pacific striped porpoise (*Lagenorhynchus*) and occasionally the peculiar elongate, finless right whale porpoise (*Lissodelphis*). When the pilot whale school dove, these adherent schools usually dove too, but seldom stayed down as long as the whales. It was as if they had run out of breath after three minutes or so, while whales routinely swam below for five minutes.

Once we watched a group of right whale porpoises from the air, and then it became clear that these "social parasite" porpoises were moving as the whales did, actually following them. My assistant curator, John Prescott, reported to me by radio from the plane that each time the whale school turned upon being harried by the *Geronimo*, the right whale porpoises turned too, even though they were hundreds of yards out from the flank of the whale school and certainly could not see them through the water. Our feeling is that the porpoises kept tabs on the whales by sound. Then, later, when we netted a whale, it was often little porpoises like these that swam resolutely with the struggling animal. They sometimes stood by until the whale was actually brought aboard the capture vessel.

Why should there be such a relationship, we wondered? The whales seemed to pay little attention to the porpoises. It was only when I thought about the barrage of clicking sounds these advancing whales made that I produced a plausible theory for the association. If the whales were scanning the sea with these sounds to locate food, there was no more efficient school shape for them. As they swam, they swept a three-quarter-mile-wide swath of sea with echoing clicks. Anywhere food was found in that broad avenue of sea would cause the whole school to gather for a meal. The little porpoises, with their far smaller numbers, might be just what we had first dubbed them—social parasites. They could not hope to be so efficient at finding food as the whales, but like sea gulls who pick up fish that slip out of a pelican's pouch, they could be there when others located lunch.

We found that these whale ranks were not easy to disrupt. Once Frank crossed such a rank several times with the *Geronimo*. Each time the whales waited until he was close behind, then threw their flukes into the air and dove deep below us as we passed overhead. Time and again they came up in the same rank, swimming in the same direction, and after an hour or so of harassment by the *Geronimo*, they dove to reappear in a single file going at right angles to our course. When we followed this file, they dove once again and reappeared in their rank, going in the same direction as before. We came to believe that these times of single-minded schooling might be our chance to approach and ensnare our whale.

It seemed possible these whales could be caught from the bow of a vessel like porpoises. The trick is to wait until the animal commits itself to breathe and then to net it as it rises to the surface. When Frank nursed the *Geronimo* up behind whales in such traveling schools, he brought us very close. But we would have to throw a net over the animal's head, and that part of the animal was well out of reach anywhere from twelve to twenty-five feet ahead of us. So Frank installed a swordfisherman's plank on the bow, a teetery timber that jutted out twenty-five feet, with a tiny basketlike cage of steel pipe at the end. On a calm day one could tightrope out on this plank, hanging on for dear life to the cables strung to either side, as a slight swell swung one up and down many feet each second. At the end one sidled into the basket and breathed a sigh of relief before wondering about the trip back. Boots, who occupied this seat of honor most often, never hesitated even in rough weather when the *Geronimo* pitched and rolled in a sickening combination of movements. Out there on that wildly moving platform the only sure way to get a rise out of him was to maneuver the ship into the swell so that the basket, and Boots with it, dipped into the cold ocean that rose over the tops of his ever-present hip boots. Then Boots would turn around, sea water cascading from him, fist shaking, as he let loose with a torrent of vintage Italian.

We soon found that however simple it had seemed to approach our quarry, the whales always seemed to maintain a margin of safety. They apparently objected to that plank projecting over them and would shy away when we came near, diving with maddening unanimity at the last instant.

We turned to other capture ideas. Perhaps, I thought, we could rig a long line from the *Geronimo*'s boom and tow a skiff from it as we circled the school, thus dragging the skiff diagonally across among the whales. At first we had no success, because the whales dove each time the skiff came near. Then we noticed that in the afternoon the pilot whales often lolled at the surface in disk-shaped groups, not going anywhere. The three of us became able to recognize these aggregations from long distances and gave them a name—loafing groups. The animals in these loafing groups seemed to be doing just that. Some would be found swimming upside down with flippers in the air. Often we saw why Frank called them *monaco:* individuals "standing up" like big black stumps projecting five or six feet in the air. Sometimes we saw the reverse; namely, a long waving tail and flukes as the animal balanced head down in the water. We saw mating in these loafing groups, too, and heard a variety of airborne noises, such as sputtering sounds, clicks, and chirps.

The loafing group seemed like a good bet for the skiff-towing trick, so one day we stationed Frank in the skiff and payed out a couple of hundred yards of nylon towrope. It soon snapped taut against the bobbing skiff as the *Geronimo* came up alongside a loafing group. Boots swung the helm over, circling ahead of the unwary whales. Frank and skiff slipped right into the group with whales milling all around him. Boots stopped the *Geronimo* and left Frank gliding along quietly. We watched as Frank stood peering over the gunwale while a big whale approached from the opposite direction, swimming on its back, eyes below the water. It thumped resoundingly into the skiff, causing Frank to drop hard onto the thwart. Frank recovered and spun around to see the surprised animal throw its flukes several feet over his head and dive. He did not, however, recover in time to get the animal.

Since we found we could tow the skiff among the whales, perhaps we could simply row in amongst them. When the next opportunity arose, we tried, and I made sure I was in the skiff to take part in the adventure. Frank silently sculled us closer and closer to a group. I could hear their calls—squeaks and pops—projected into the air and, we suppose, below the surface as well. Twenty yards away, the group took notice of us, probably from the sound of water slapping on the skiff bottom. A couple of animals rose up with their bellies toward us, peering at our skiff with their curious little brown eyes. They slipped back beneath the water and could not be approached again.

Finally, after many attempts, we decided that even though we could approach whales with the skiff, it was impossible to maneuver a net from that rocking platform. The collector was on the same plane, approximately, as the whale, and there seemed no way to slip a net over the animal's head. So we returned to experimenting with the swordfish plank. At least with that uncertain weapon the collector was ten feet or so above the whale and there was hope of getting a clear shot. Not that it proved easy. What was later to become routine seemed fraught with insurmountable difficulty. I suppose once one knows a thing can be done, like a four-minute mile, there is enough change in one's attitude for success to come much more easily. But at that time it had never been done, and we were far from sure we knew the answer. Days slipped by without success.

One foggy winter morning Frank; Boots; my assistant, Bill McFarland; my frequent field companion, the Marineland artist Don ("Moody Brown") Hackett; photographer Fred Lowe; and I tossed our duffel bags into the *Geronimo* for another try. Frank took the vessel outside the breakwater through the morning mist. Big, smooth swells welled up around the foghorn house, but there was no wind, for which I was thankful. Frank switched on the "fisherman's information service," or the citizen's band radio. With it he had instant contact with dozens of fishermen friends all ready to shoot the breeze about anything fit to put on the air. Frank picked up the hand microphone, depressed the switch, and said, "This is Whiskey Charlie 3588, the *Geronimo,* calling the *St. Francis.* Sam, do you read me? Over."

A deep voice came crackling back so quickly it was obvious

that "Sam" was waiting for conversation. Sam was Frank's cousin and known to everyone around San Pedro Harbor as "Foghorn" because of his nearly incredible vocal powers.

"This is the *St. Francis*, Charlie Baker 9673. I read you loud and clear. Caught any whales lately? Over."

"Noo, sorry to say, Sam, but we're ready to give it another try. Have you seen any, Sam? Over."

"Sure have, Frank. This morning when I was pulling nets off Salta Verde the water was full of them. Had one swim right under the skiff. The day before yesterday I anchored in the Isthmus and there must have been forty of 'em right off Bird Rock. Going north. Hope the weather holds for you, though. That's about it. I don't want to see you around Pedro this time if you don't catch one, Frank. Say hello to that skinny friend of yours. Anything else? Over."

"No, that'll do it, Sam. This is the *Geronimo*, Whiskey Charlie 3588, out and clear with the *St. Francis*."

"*St. Francis* clear."

Fog had fallen in a soft blanket around us, closing in our sounds and making them intimate. Faint shadows of the vessel and her rigging played across the vapor. We throbbed on at half speed with Boots out in the bow watching for signs of another ship. None came. Three hours later when the fog lifted to mast height, we found ourselves on course just off the jagged stacks and boulders of the west end of Santa Catalina Island. Frank cut in close, turning along the coast just outside the welling surge that rose against the rocks. I watched it suck away moments later, leaving a hundred rushing white rivers to find their way among the kelp-choked crevices. Just ahead was the big bight of windward Catalina, and, as Sam said, it proved dotted with schools of feeding whales.

For days we worked from school to school. Mostly the animals "threw their flukes" as we approached and dove before Boots swung over them. Occasionally they made a mistake, and Frank would delicately edge the *Geronimo* over the line of whales. A long, brownish shape would come to cruise directly beneath the plank. Boots followed the rising whale with the tines of his whale net, lunging down on tiptoes like a matador against the whale. A flick of the head or a quick dive pushed the net aside. Often flukes flew up under the platform, a foot or so from Boots' tiny basket, and spray obscured the detail of what had occurred. Boots found his net was too flimsy to stand the thrust into the sea ahead of a whale. Frank patiently rigged another that he had made, precisely because he thought this might happen. This one proved so heavy Boots had difficulty in following the whales as they changed course beneath him. Change followed change. Boots once had the net in place over a whale's head, but the whale, a little one, somehow stopped and literally backed free. That experience occasioned some almost imperceptible changes in the rings of the net that allowed it to slip loose more quickly.

In the evenings we turned into the snug pocket of Catalina Harbor, "dropped the pick," and put on the spaghetti sauce that Mary Brocato had put up in jars for us before the trip. Frank's friends, anchored nearby, stopped by with sacks of fish or lobster, which were ceremoniously quartered and cooked with the sauce, to be cascaded over mounds of spaghetti and downed with draughts of local sauterne or chianti. Preparing such feasts was routine for the *Geronimo*'s crew and required no concentration, so we were free to talk about the day's problems and what our next moves might be. Frank thought he saw a solution.

"Our best chances have been when I brought the *Geronimo* up slow. If I speed up at all, they get edgy and mostly sound. Tomorrow I'll take it easy and see what happens. Also, Boots, a couple of times when you missed, I thought you tried to net too soon; before we were really over the whale. Try waiting until I've got them beneath you and a little behind the basket."

Boots nodded in assent. "Yup, that'll make the net dig under their chins, and the water pressure should flip it over their heads. I'll have to stand on my head out there, though. I guess you know."

"Yeah, yeah, I know, just catch a whale, please," Frank said, his mouth full of spaghetti.

Next day a storm raged in from the southwest, blowing the

crests from the swells and making work on the plank impossible.
Each pitch plunged the plank deep into the sea. To keep that
delicate appendage from snapping, Frank headed into the lee
of the island. The only area we could work was a stretch of quiet
water lying in the shadow of the steep hills, a few miles long and
perhaps three miles wide, and all day we traversed it back and
forth without seeing whales.

Toward dusk Boots shouted from the masthead, "School of
whales ahead!" He swung down the rigging and out onto his
plank while Frank brought us up behind them. There were about
twenty, of all sizes, and they moved resolutely along in a traveling school.

"A case of beer if you net one, Boots," I said, half joking. Mac
added a carton of cigarettes to the bargain.

With the utmost delicacy, Frank crept up behind the animals,
not changing a revolution of engine speed. An eighteen-foot
animal cruised slowly just ahead, seemingly unaware. Boots shot
out the net as the animal dipped its head in startled recognition of our presence. The net fell away into the water.

"Close, close!" I shouted.

"Do I have to pay you guys if I miss?" Boots asked over his
shoulder as he made the net ready for another try.

"No, you'd be broke by now," I said sarcastically.

The school hadn't spooked as it usually did. The rank of animals
plunged slowly on. Frank brought the *Geronimo* around behind
them again, this time concentrating on a smaller animal about
twelve feet long. Closer and closer we came. Its tail was now
under the plank. We gained almost imperceptibly on it. It was
now brightly visible eight feet down in the crystal blue water.
It rose, and simultaneously Boots' net flashed out.

Everything happened at once. The whale's tail flew out of the
water, flailing a few feet below Boots' feet, and disappeared in
spray. On the flying bridge Frank cut the engine and spun the
helm over to sweep the stern away from the animal and the line.
The line popped its little string ties along the rail and ripped
astern, leaping from the carefully flaked coil. Boots tightroped

back to the deck, and he and Mac grabbed the line together while Frank started the winch engine.

"She's only a twelve-footer," Boots said breathlessly.

"We should be glad that's all," grunted Mac, who was trying to force the rigid line into a snatch block.

The fifteen-hundred-pound animal sounded into the deep water. The line was out three hundred feet, straight down. Four minutes later she rushed to surface, vented an explosive breath, and dove again. The entire school swam just in front of her, as if urging her on to greater efforts.

Frank never let her put her weight directly against the line, but played her like a game fish, now giving line, now taking it in. At times she sulked at the bottom of a dive, hundreds of feet below us, and Frank stood there holding a slack line that no one would guess was attached to a whale. Darkness came and we could no longer see the plunging whale. From the bow we could hear the breaths of the school ahead of us, and now and then make out the flashing form of our quarry in the boom light. At times rocket trails of phosphorescence told us where they were.

It was nearly midnight before the whale seemed tired enough to be brought alongside. Protesting to the last, she came into the circle of the boom light. We fought with her thrashing tail, finally slipping a noose of rope over it, bringing it up taut, and immobilizing her with the head and tail lines. As she lay alongside squirming and blowing in terror, a group of Pacific striped porpoises swept to within a few feet of us, nearly nudging against our captive, her last guard before we removed her from the sea.

She was far too big to hoist on deck, so we had come prepared with a specially constructed inflatable rubber life raft. Boots and I spread it on the surface, while Don, Mac, and Fred in the skiff outboard of the captive helped us slide it beneath her. The frightened whale whistled her apprehension as the raft slid beneath her. Two tugs at the trigger lines, and carbon dioxide gas rushed with a tinny hiss into the raft. In less than a minute the whale was dry-docked, lying inside the raft on a soft cushion of sea. Lines were rigged by weary hands for the long tow home. Gratuitously, the long fight had carried us about five miles closer to home than when the whale was netted.

We stopped our labors for a moment and looked at our captive. Then silently we looked at each other, breathed tired sighs of relief, and tried to realize that we had succeeded. We had finally caught our whale.

Miraculously, the sea had calmed. Instead of the heavy seas of the day before, we plodded along through calm waters to the Marineland pier. It was after midnight, but the pier railing was lined with excited people. The news of our capture had traveled fast, and before the next day was over would be splashed over newspapers throughout California. A heavy wooden platform was swung over the side of the pier. Expectant divers stood on it in the swashing water as the raft was brought alongside. The raft was slipped onto the platform and quickly hoisted onto a waiting truck. A few more moments and the whale was ensconced in her new home in a Marineland training tank. The tired shipboard crew, buoyed by the excitement, watched her swim quietly in tight circles.

The little whale, named Bubbles by the children who visited Marineland, was an instant success. Before long she became thoroughly acclimated to captivity and was put in training along with the porpoises. In spite of her size, she proved an apt and gentle pupil. The highlight of her performance for several years was a leap in which she rose to take a fish from the trainer's hand and fell back with a cascade of water that sometimes doused patrons dozens of feet away. Bubbles was soon followed by other whales, some as long as twenty feet. None of us who had caught Bubbles could really understand why it had been so hard the first time.

CHAPTER FIVE

Gray Whales

My second trip to Scammon's Lagoon came at the height of the whale-breeding season of 1961. I was invited as a guest observer aboard the Lockheed-California Corporation research vessel *Sea Quest*, which was to attempt penetration of the lagoon to listen for underwater sounds of both the California gray whale and the much smaller Pacific bottlenose porpoise. The latter was, of course, the same creature whose schools had greeted us at the lagoon mouth on the previous trip. Much was known about the loquacious bottlenose porpoise by then, but a scientific controversy existed among cetologists concerning the gray whale. Some said they were mute except for the low, cavernous rumble of respiration, and devoid of vocal cords; others claimed to have recorded simple "pinging" sounds from them, like those produced by a fathometer. Our job was to resolve this question if possible, since the sounds of the sea have become very important in this electronic age when submarines and surface ships must use sound for navigation. A submariner's most useful sense is not sight but hearing, and he must know who or what is making the sounds his sensitive transistorized underwater "ears" pick up.

The deck lockers of the *Sea Quest* were crammed with heaps of heavy black waterproof cable and the latest hydrophone listening gear. Inside the deckhouse, banks of high-speed, high-fidelity tape recorders stood bolted securely to the bulkheads. Bill Evans, the able Lockheed bioacoustician and later my colleague on a number of experiments, explained to me that we would try to locate a channel inside the lagoon that was a passageway for whales. We would then set the hydrophones (underwater microphones) out on heavy steel tripods, which would, he hoped, sink part way into the bottom ooze and stand firm against the strong tidal currents, while the *Sea Quest* went on what Evans called "silent ship." The *Sea Quest* had been specially rigged so that every engine and motor could be shut down, leaving her bobbing silent as a ghost, her vital functions supplied by banks of batteries, while inside her technicians listened for voices in the surrounding sea.

We would also try to set out a long fence of air-filled aluminum pipes in the water, across a whale pathway. We knew that the bottlenose porpoises could spot such a barrier from a long distance away, and would begin to emit whistles of various kinds and long trains of their peculiar clicking echolocation signals. The air columns inside our hollow pipes would act as near-perfect resonating chambers, allowing the porpoises to detect them by echoes of their own sounds as surely as if they could see through the murky water. What the gray whales would do we did not know, but if they could locate the fence by emitting sounds, we should be able to pick the sounds up and record them on our tapes.

Bob Eberhardt, Lockheed's biological oceanographer, who was in operational charge of the expedition, told us as we left the dock at San Diego that we would pull into Ensenada to pick up an observer sent by the Mexican government, presumably to see what we were doing. I can understand such governmental curiosity, since our mission was clearly a bit odd and we could not possibly expect to explain our reasons to Mexican officialdom in our meager Spanish. As it turned out, our uprooted observer couldn't have cared less about whale talk. Jorge Lagos Kuntze, a tall, muscular, curly-headed young executive officer of a Mexican corvette, boarded us from a flea-bitten water taxi half submerged in Ensenada Harbor, tossing ahead of him a canvas ditty bag full of hair lotion, several brands of soap, and an assorted collection of towels and washcloths, brushes and combs. Jorge was just what we scientists needed. He danced the mambo for us, taking both the male and female parts, as we fiddled with our electronic gear. He sang and recorded "Pecos Bill" in Spanish on our whale tapes, accompanying himself with a broken-down guitar, and spent hours each day currying his curly hair and anointing it with several kinds of aromatic oil. Always in good humor, Jorge later became my hiking companion and spent hours on the beaches with me searching for whale bones. And when we needed a translator to reason with outraged officials, Jorge took over with telling effect, in their own idiom.

A day later, as the *Sea Quest* cut her speed in the dim light of dawn several miles east of the entrance to Scammon's, I could make out a long string of spar buoys stretching out from shore, and the gray bulk of a grotesque-looking ship near the beach. A huge pipe jutted from her side, spewing a 150-foot stream of water into the sea. It was the dredge of the giant saltworks that had been built in Black Warrior Lagoon, a shallow bay whose headwaters were just confluent with Scammon's to the west. I felt a wave of sadness at the sight. After a hundred years Scammon's was now a place where you could hike fifteen miles and buy a cold beer or sit in an air-conditioned prefab company house while the huge salt harvesters clawed along outside through the evaporating pans, loading fifty-ton diesel salt trucks. Progress, I suppose, but Scammon's would never again be the same for me. The ever-present undercurrent of apprehension that made us protect our skiff and engine like the Kohinoor diamond on the previous trip would be absent. The danger of being alone and without hope of help had passed.

With these lugubrious thoughts in mind, I climbed to the flying bridge to watch the skipper attempt to bring the *Sea Quest* through the narrow entrance channel that had been so dangerous for Captain Scammon. Hal Moody, our captain, was a retired Navy skipper, and a cautious man. Good seamen are all cautious, for they know the sea for what she is, often somnolent, but secretly capricious and dangerous. Moody had studied the charts and had sifted all the information he could get so that he knew a great deal before the *Sea Quest* ever slipped into the channel mouth. He waited patiently until the tide turned and began to flow into the lagoon before heading in between the offshore bar and the beach. This would give us a safety factor if we ran aground on the passage in, for the water would continue to rise and allow us precious moments for escape. The flashing red neon of the fathometer told us when we finally crossed the entrance bar with a few feet of water under our keel and were safely in the inner channel, which steadily deepened beneath us. It had been easy because the sea was once again quite calm. Only a smooth, low swell and a gentle morning breeze swept in from Sebastián Vizcaíno Bay. The swell was sufficient to pour over the outer bar in a low line of breakers, but these only marked out the path for us. I felt grateful for our easy passage and, as usual, wondered ahead to the time when we must return.

The porpoise greeters were there in force. By this time I had made the acquaintance of several porpoises at the oceanarium at Marineland of the Pacific, and watched with pleasure and a sort of interordinal comradeship as they veered and cavorted around our prow. After a few minutes they left us to return to their station at the entrance, waiting for the next ship to come.

Gray whales were everywhere. We could see them broaching nearly free of the water far off at sea behind us, and in the fairly narrow neck of the entrance they surfaced and blew their steamy breaths on both sides of us, surprisingly close aboard, seemingly oblivious of our presence. Moody looked furtively from left to right, apprehensive that the whales might get aggressive notions about our little ship, which was only ten feet longer than the longest of them. He had heard stories of whales charging skiffs or tossing them out of the water with their flukes. One particularly pertinent tale told of a whale and a whaling ship that had become jammed in the entrance as they tried to negotiate the channel together. Moody didn't see how this could happen, in view of the several hundred yards of deep water that comprised the channel at its narrowest, but he was forewarned.

Fortunately, the whales seemed to be concerned with other things. They paid not the slightest attention to us, even though we were often so close that we could see the barnacles on their backs, and were able to watch them glide to the surface, protrude their double nostrils, and blast out a breath of hot, fetid air that condensed in a thin spout. The best and biggest spouts are probably a combination of this condensed vapor and sea water, caused when a whale "blows" an instant before his nostrils are free of the water. It is often downright nauseating to travel downwind of a blowing whale. The stench is staggering even from fifty yards out. Probably some of their invertebrate food becomes tangled in their baleen and simply rots there.

As we passed the sandy headland where I had beached our skiff ten years before, the air fell calm and all that marked the glassy waters were the roily marks of tide rips that defined the deep channels for us. From our vantage point atop the flying bridge, I could see that on our previous trip we had barely entered the lagoon. Far ahead of us, indenting into the barren desert, was a vast arm of the sea, penciled here and there by low, brownish rocky islands. Our little shell sand bar lay to our port, only a few hundred yards out of the main entrance channel, and was soon left behind.

Our first glimpse of the age-old events taking place in this lagoon came a few minutes later when Bob spotted a group of sea gulls, which seemed to be standing placidly on the water ahead of us. As we neared them, it became apparent that they were atop a hugh discoidal whale placenta and umbilical cord that had been cast off by a mother sometime after the wrenching moment of birth. We wondered how the baby breaks free of this cord and placenta. It can't be bitten free by its mother, since gray whales have no teeth. Probably, we thought, the cord simply breaks at a predetermined point under the stress of twisting and turning as the baby gasps to the surface for its first breath of air. We learned later from an examination of stranded babies that the job is neatly done within an inch or so of the baby's abdomen.

The moment of birth must be filled with danger for both mother and young; we discovered that Scammon's Lagoon is the home of large predatory sharks that rip and tear at baby whales unlucky enough to strand, and these rapacious creatures are probably attracted during birth when the surrounding waters are filled with the odor of blood and body fluids. Perhaps, however, the fluids contain a shark repellent to protect the baby during birth. No one knows.

Late in the afternoon Captain Moody piloted his way among the sand bars and weedy shallows and brought the *Sea Quest* up close along the low, rocky shores of Piedras Island (also called Gilmore Island, in honor of a well-known cetologist, Raymond Gilmore), which lies directly athwart the main channel of the lagoon. Our quiet, competent engineer, Wendell Tripp, dropped the anchor over the bow.

I could hardly wait to go ashore for an exploration hike. There is nothing quite like setting foot on a remote uninhabited island. An island, any island, holds a unique and powerful fascination. Cut off from the world, it becames a kingdom to be explored, and each of its tiny marvels becomes a personal secret. The most minute and prosaic coves and headlands demand that names be given them. Piedras Island might deserve to be ignored on many counts. It is small, low, and barren, clothed here and there with patches of low lichen-covered cactus and ocotillo. It is only four or five hundred yards from the mainland. It does not stand ruggedly against the open sea, but is tucked far back in a placid lagoon a couple of miles from the nearest pounding breaker. Still, I fidgeted with anticipation, and much to my pleasure, I found that Evans and Eberhardt were also "island explorers." So after badgering the skipper, who had hoped to rig up his fishing gear, we were ferried ashore and left to fend for ourselves.

Piedras Island had been the home base for the Douglas–National Geographic Expedition that had attempted to record the heartbeat of a whale for the famous heart specialist, Dr. Paul Dudley White. We found the remains of their camp, the boat-launching ramp, and abandoned oil drums. We also found tell-tale signs of another famous visitor to this remote spot. The single tracks of a small motorcycle told us that the mystery writer, Erle Stanley Gardner, had explored Piedras before us. Gardner was a true explorer of the remote back country of Baja California. His camp on the beach dunes of Scammon's Lagoon had been pointed out to us on our passage into the lagoon. He often rode a rugged little rough-country motorcycle called a Pak Jak, and the tracks were unmistakably his, or those of one of his party.

At the far side of the island Bob, Bill, and I rested on the windrows of sea grass that were piled five feet deep on the beach. Once we were quiet, we began to hear gray whales. Deep, resonant exhalations and low snores came from far across the still channel. At first we could see no whales, but soon Bob pointed out a thin black line on the water a quarter of a mile away. The noises continued, and we began to see whales "spy hop" occasionally near the opposite shore. A spy-hopping gray whale rises more or less vertically out of the water past the level of its front flippers, and peers around before slipping back into the water tailfirst. No one really knows why they act in this manner. It is thought by some that they are simply looking around out of curiosity, or feeding, and others feel this behavior is for navigational purposes.

The black line moved slowly with the tide, and before long we saw a flipper swing up into the air as the whale rolled over in the water. In half an hour we saw several more whales simply drifting along, all but submerged. A ten-foot-long black line was all we could see of a twenty-five-ton whale. Their exhalations made only sound, since we noted no spouts from those lolling giants.

Later, as the tide receded, I sloshed out on the long, partly exposed sandspit at the south end of the island to look at the flocks of shore birds feeding there. Grotesque, gawky curlews stalked near the water's edge, probing deep in the soft mud. Dowitchers, sanderlings, and willets flooded away in dense, nervous little packs as I advanced upon them, leaving a moving no man's land between me and the birds. Far ahead, a skittish flock of gun-wary black brant rose into the desert air, their

white wing specula flashing in unison as the birds tipped and
wheeled in flight, to settle in a rush of water far away on the
still surface.

I walked along, musing about invading the birds' normally
safe retreat and about my evident unpopularity, and uncon-
sciously wandered close to the main channel's edge. Suddenly,
not thirty yards from me, a whale thrust its head straight up
in a spy hop. It rose about twenty-five feet into the air. The
creature had a fixed smirk, and a little pig eye, surrounded by
wrinkly, protruding eyelids, and it seemed to look straight at me
until the whole unbelievable beast sank quietly below the surface again. It was absolutely encrusted with barnacles and
blotched over with gray-and-white patches and scars. The sand
bar upon which I stood seemed to shelve out gradually, and
for a moment I thought the whale must have risen from water
two or three feet deep. Undoubtedly, however, there was a
deep enough channel there to support and float all that blubber,
bone, and muscle. Startled by the sight, I had frozen stock-still,
but after the whale disappeared, I trained my camera over the
vacant water. To no avail. The creature rose no more, and finally
I turned and slogged back across the bar through the rising tide
to the island and the *Sea Quest.*

When we boarded the ship, Wendell and the skipper agitatedly
cornered us and said that a monstrous bulky five-foot fish had
gobbled up their bait, whereupon it turned ponderously at the
surface and simply swam off with all their gear. Jorge looked on
knowingly and said, *"Mero."* Now, *mero* is the Mexican word
for grouper, and Jorge then told us that we were anchored in a
famous grouper hole, well known to the Baja fishermen. What
a day for giants!

That evening Bob decided that we should penetrate deeper
into the lagoon to look for a narrow channel in which to test
both our hydrophones and the pole fence. On the old chart
we found one channel that looked particularly good. It was
narrow and blind, and was named the "Nursery" because it was
allegedly the stretch of water where the pregnant female whales
went to give birth. Next morning at low tide, all of us except

the skipper, who piloted from the flying bridge, hoisted the anchor and stacked the chain. Soon the *Sea Quest* began to make her careful way among the sand bars out into the several-fathoms-deep channel, headed for the deepest recesses of Scammon's.

Bob and I were keeping a weather eye out for stranded whales, since we wished to obtain certain measurements and tissue samples from as many as possible. Soon we both noticed a black object three or four hundred yards to port. I didn't think it was a whale, but Bob persisted, peering intently through his field glasses. "Hey!" he said, using the tone of someone who has just made a minor discovery, "I think I see a sea gull, and it seems to be pecking at that black thing." More peering, and then Bob burst out, "That black thing is alive, but I still can't make out what it is. It seems to be splashing at the gull." He thrust his glasses into my hand, but I could do no more than confirm his findings. It was enough, however, and Bob asked the skipper to stop the *Sea Quest* while we investigated.

Bob and I jumped into the little ship's dinghy and set off toward the object. Very soon it gathered itself into focus and we could make out a sea gull walking up and down on the back of a frantic baby gray whale, stranded on the sand bar. The gull would peck, sinking its bill into the little whale's back, and each time this happened, the whale thrashed and rolled in an effort to chase away its air-borne tormentor. When the flippers passed too near, the gull fluttered lightly into the air, like a big cinder in a chimney, feet still extended, and landed again as the whale subsided helplessly.

When our skiff ran aground on the shallow mud bottom, I leaped over the side and pulled it toward the whale by the bow painter. As we reached the whale's side, the gull flew up, circling and squawking its harsh cry. One look at the baby showed that the gull had been nipping three-quarter-inch-long mouthfuls of blubber and skin with every peck. The whale's back was a mass of peck marks, and was still oozing blood over a wide area. It was very likely that many gulls had been feeding upon the living whale that morning. My first thought was "How cruel," but of course no such moral value concerned the birds. It is not a matter of cruelty but of survival for the gulls, or for an eagle swooping on its daily food, or a rattlesnake striking a mouse at night. Use the tools you have to survive the weather and your neighbors, and if you succeed today, use them again tomorrow.

The whale had wallowed out a broad hole in the soft, muddy bar and was lying on its side, stranded in the receding tide. The animal was a male, about fourteen feet long, and we guessed its weight as a little over a thousand pounds. He was newly born, as we could tell from the short umbilical cord, still oozing blood. I felt no trepidation at approaching or handling him, except for his tail flukes, which he might still be able to use in the manner of his parents. In an adult, the toothless gray whale's most formidable weapon is its tail, which can be swung up and down or from side to side, cutting through the water with tremendous force. On one such encounter in the open sea, an adult female gray whale had lifted our heavy net skiff two or three feet on a frothy wave with a near-miss from her flukes. So even with the baby whale I stayed carefully near his head.

Surprisingly, baby gray whales are born with quite a supply of hairs. A few, around the upper lips and the double blowholes, are retained by adults, but this newborn animal had a regular mosaic of them over its entire head, each springing as a long, coarse white hair from a deep indentation in the soft, rubbery skin. The over-all effect was as if the little whale's head had been quilted. While looking at these, I noticed that the obese fetal skin of the animal was folded into long vertical wrinkles and that each contained a thriving colony of the peculiar crustacean called a whale louse. Here was an animal, not long born, but covered with parasites. Some of the hitchhikers on his mother must have jumped ship at the time of the whale's birth, or during nursing time later on. There were no barnacles that I could see on the young animal, even though adults are encrusted with them.

This animal undoubtedly was still nursing. I decided to see if I could understand how such a creature as this whale could grasp its mother's nipples, which lie buried in the mammary slits along the ventral surface of her abdomen. I lifted the head of the little whale and could see the lower lips rise up on either side of the lower jaws and envelop the jaws above. I then inserted my hand into the whale's mouth, directly from the front. The whale, perhaps very hungry, grasped my hand, and I could feel a definite suction upon it, produced by his tongue, which had wrapped around my hand from below. These huge babies must receive large amounts of milk in the few moments' time it takes for an underwater nursing session. This probably is accomplished by a combination of the prodding snout of the baby pressing against the large milk sinuses of the mother, the suction just mentioned, and the contraction of muscles possessed by the mother which may help eject a stream of milk. Nursing must be very frequent, since the babies grow at a prodigious rate, perhaps two hundred to four hundred pounds per week.

Measurements were taken, as best we could on the thrashing animal. Then we attempted to push the pitiful newborn into deeper water, where he might have a chance for survival. We thought we might have seen his mother in the opposite channel, repeatedly spy-hopping. At any rate, there was a large, barnacle-encrusted adult that rose from the water every few minutes, so we steered the baby in that direction. We heaved and hauled on his flippers and finally edged him into about three feet of water. He took a few frantic strokes with his broad flukes, which caused him to charge along in the murky water. At the end of such a flurry he invariably attempted to sound by turning on his side, pointing his head downward, and unceremoniously ramming it in the mud. After this he lapsed again into helpless inactivity while we watched in exasperation. Finally he reached deeper water, and I leaped aboard the skiff.

Bob found he could steer the whale, more or less, by running up near his head with the outboard and rapidly turning, thus directing the full blast of sound and water to the side of the animal's head. The whale, however, repeatedly frustrated us by heading again into the shallows.

We had particularly little desire to engage a possibly irate female who might blame us for her baby's troubles. So as the water became deeper, we became more and more uncertain and worried. Finally, after an hour of maneuvering, we abandoned our efforts. By now the young animal was in six or seven feet of water and heading rapidly for shoal water to the north. On our last view of him, we could see him turn on his side and sound helplessly, but with enough water for recovery. We believe we found his dead body later, stranded on the north shore of Piedras Island, but identification was difficult.

Judging by the number of stranded dead babies we found later, the plight of this one was not an isolated incident but a very real and devastating problem for newborn whales in Scammon's. Probably they simply become cut off from their mothers by shallow sand bars and, as the tide falls, strand and die of exposure, from wounds inflicted by gulls or sharks, or from sheer fright.

The depredations of sharks upon these babies was graphically depicted by one carcass we found. Clearly, as this newborn animal felt the tide dropping around it, it frantically sought to swim, and the movements of its flukes drove it aground, head-first. The flukes and tail, which remained in the water, were cruelly mangled by shark bites. We could even guess at the size of the sharks from a few clear bite marks where a shark with jaws six inches across had left a semilunar incision in the whale's flank. One can understand why a baby whale seldom leaves its mother's side in this placid lagoon, and why the mothers have gained a reputation for ferocity. The open sea may be a more inhospitable place for birth to occur, but the deceptively peaceful lagoon itself is obviously full of hazards.

We pushed on toward the very head of Scammon's, miles from the open sea, where the Nursery lies tucked in a fold of sandy hills and low bluffs. It is an avenue of water perhaps a half mile across at its mouth but quite shallow for most of this distance. Only two deep channels enter it from the main lagoon. The one our ship traversed cuts in behind a long sand bar and heads directly up the middle of the passage. We found it to be a highway for whales, some with babies and some without. Since we saw young animals and evidence of birth throughout the lagoon, we took little stock in the whaler's story that this avenue

The *Geronimo* scouts for bottlenose porpoises in San Diego Bay. *Below*, An early photo of Marineland of the Pacific from the air. MLP PHOTO

Boots Calandrino rigging whale-catching gear on the *Geronimo*. A twenty-five-foot plank was set up, with a tiny basketlike cage at the end. *Right,* The trick was to net a whale as it rose to the surface to breathe. Here, Boots, in the moment of truth. *Below,* Frank Brocato, skipper of the *Geronimo* and consummate seaman.

A pilot whale comes alongside. Boots attaches a tail rope. *Below,* Bubbles being hoisted to her tank at Marineland of the Pacific. Over twelve feet long and weighing fifteen hundred pounds, she was the first live pilot whale to be captured. MLP PHOTO

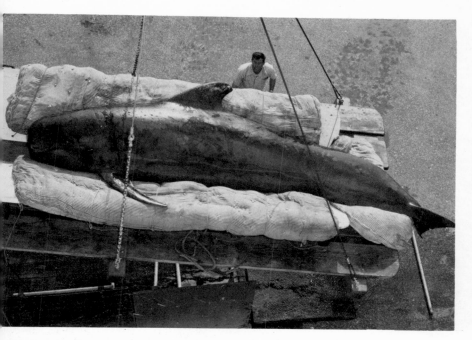

Keiki, whose name in Hawaiian means "child." He was the first porpoise to be trained, released in the open sea, and then brought back into captivity. PHOTO BY BOB HOOPER, OCEANIC INSTITUTE

Coconut Island, Hawaii. Keiki arrives for his speed trials.

Left, In spite of her size, Bubbles was an apt and gentle pupil, and became the star at the Whale Stadium. MLP PHOTO

Two views of Keiki in his cage at sea. At first he refused to venture into the unknown beyond the cage. CAMERA HAWAII

Speed trials at sea. Keiki leaps alongside the pacing boat. CAMERA HAWAII

Sherm Warner and Ken Norris check Keiki's speed from atop Manana Island. CAMERA HAWAII

Keiki begs for his reward, and receives a pat from Karen Pryor. CAMERA
HAWAII

was really a nursery. Nevertheless, it proved an optimum spot for our experiment with the air-filled aluminum poles, since we could build a barrier that would almost completely block one deep-water channel. The poles were rigged with heavy nylon line and towed into place across the channel and then anchored carefully at each end. The barrier looked as if a whale could hit it and not break it.

Once this task was complete, the hydrophone tripods were lowered over the side of the *Sea Quest*, and Bill Evans set about tuning and calibrating his beloved recording gear. We were ready, but where were the whales? All of us watched the mirrorlike surface, both up the channel and out in the main lagoon. Then, while standing on the stern of the silent ship, I noticed the dorsal fins of four bottlenose porpoises cutting lazily through the water, coming up the same channel we had used for the *Sea Quest's* entry. Bill quickly turned on the recording gear, clapped a pair of monitoring earphones over his head, and listened. Soon he whispered, "I can hear them clicking once in a while." The porpoises were now about five hundred yards away, approaching our stern as they swung up the channel. The clicking increased, and long before the porpoises reached the barrier they turned back and swam away from us out into the lagoon.

On another occasion, an approaching group of bottlenose porpoises sent a scout animal ahead, toward the barrier. After this animal had run along the length of the fence, it returned to the school, and amid much whistling and clicking, they all swam carefully between the poles.

Still no gray whales appeared. Finally Jorge and I went ashore to walk the beaches in search of whale ear bones. These ivorylike conch-shaped bones resist the erosion of sand and water longer than any other part of a whale skeleton, and seemed to be present throughout the lagoon. An hour or so later, when we were walking along the strand nearest to the pole barrier, I saw the black shapes of a mother whale and her calf rise slowly to the surface astern of the *Sea Quest*. We knew the men on board saw them too, as we could see Bill racing into the instrument house to turn on the recording gear, while Bob took station topside. Jorge and I sat down on some grassy hummocks at the edge of the strand and watched the scene. The whales passed close to the *Sea Quest*, and we wondered what, if anything, Bill Evans had heard. The whales cruised unconcernedly toward the pole barrier and were already far closer than the porpoises had been when these small animals had first given evidence of detecting the resonant air columns. As we watched, fascinated, the pair barged right into the barrier with a metallic clatter of poles. Frightened, they surged ahead, thrashing the water with their flukes. Our supposedly strong line snapped like a piece of uncooked spaghetti as the whales raced through. Now, in their fright, they turned and raced back through the broken barrier again, but not through the opening they had previously made. Instead they broke the barrier again in their frenzy to reach the deep water of the main lagoon. When we last saw them, they were plunging along at flank speed out the Nursery entrance. Bill reported that he had heard not a sound from the pair.

Once the tattered pole barrier had been retrieved, we hauled up the anchor and moved down the lagoon to the broad channel just inside Piedras Island. This watery path was full of whales; we could usually see a half dozen or so, lazing at the surface, floating passively with the tide. At night, when our ship lay silent and probably almost undetectable to the big whales, many passed within a few yards. Occasionally we could look out and see their incredible bulk directly alongside. Some "blew" while they were several feet under water, and this exhaled breath rose in a single bubble to boil at the surface. On the listening gear we could hear the release of these bubbles as a deeply resonant *blooop——blooop–blooop–bloop-bloop,* starting at a low note and rising with the final trickle of bubbles. Their exhalations at the surface could be heard through our listening gear, too. They produced a deep, rushing sibilance made of a mixture of high-pitched sounds like those produced by air shrieking at high pressure through a valve, combined with the low rumble of a man calling in a storm drain. Our conclusion, from hours of listening and watching, was that, so far as we could tell, the big whales emitted nothing like a true echolocation signal, and that at best they might be sophisticated passive listeners, who navigated by listening to sounds from their environment, which are legion. The breathing sounds could serve to notify them of the presence of other whales, but seem unlikely to give any refined navigational assistance.

With some regret, we left the lagoon for home. It may be bleak and forbidding, but it houses one of nature's grandest spectacles and is consequently a place of great fascination. The people of Mexico have now realized the uniqueness of this desert sea-full-of-whales, and have designated it as a nature preserve. Those of us who know the lagoon are deeply grateful for this action. It is a somber thought indeed to think that "progress" might one day populate the shores of this lagoon with houses and its waters with motorboats and water skiers, for the whales would surely leave, just as they have from San Diego Bay, California, which was also once their home. They deserve a better fate, and so do those many people who would like to observe the whale lagoon in its untrammeled state.

CHAPTER SIX

Kathy

Once the notion that porpoises might echolocate came to me, I began to dig around in the scientific literature, and to my surprise, there it was. The Schevills' experiments had shown high-frequency hearing, ranging up to about ten times the upper limit of human hearing, and their later work indicated that an animal could navigate in murky water, finding its way around a net barrier for food hung silently in the water, all the while emitting "rusty hinge" noises. Winthrop Kellogg and his associates at Florida State University had described the clicks of porpoises, which were in some ways reminiscent of the sounds of bats and in others like the "pinging" of a fathometer. Kellogg also observed high-frequency hearing by watching the fright responses of captive porpoises exposed to high-frequency sounds at Marine Studios. Both the Schevills and Kellogg had speculated that animal sonar existed in these animals.

The difficulties of experimenting with porpoises are rather formidable in some ways, and none of these experiments had the classic simplicity and finality of some of the studies on bats. For instance, in none of the work was vision eliminated, and conceivably it could have played a part in the behavior which resulted. To be sure, a human being could not see very far under the conditions of some of the tests, and it seemed unlikely that a porpoise could either. But we did not know this. This may sound like carping to the layman, but it is not. One must know that vision was eliminated to be sure it was not involved. Further, in none of the tests was either sound reception or transmission interfered with. If one could somehow block a porpoise's sound-sending apparatus, the animal should no longer be able to navigate in the absence of sight if, indeed, he did echolocate. Or, conversely, if I could somehow interfere with his sound reception, the same thing should happen.

The earliest work on bat echolocation had these attributes. Lazzaro Spallanzani, an Italian scientist who lived in the unenlightened era of the 1700s, was one of those rare men in any age who saw nature with uncommon clarity, and who tested it with the purest scientific method. He was curious about widely divergent parts of his world, from volcanoes to bats. His experiments with bats were classically incisive. Blinded bats, he found, could fly as well as those whose sight was unimpaired. Then, following the experiments of a French surgeon named Jurine, he plugged the ears of his bats with wax and observed that they crashed into obstacles and were completely unable to navigate. Perhaps these plugs were painful, or produced some unknown effect on his bats, other than blocking the path of sound, he reasoned. So he pierced the wax plugs with tiny brass tubes. When these pierced plugs were placed in the ears of his bats, their navigation ability returned at once. He could reach no other conclusion but that his bats were somehow able to navigate by listening; to what he never learned. But as a final commentary on his excellence as a scientist, he knew that he could not refute his carefully repeated experiments, and that he must accept them, however irrational their results seemed at the time.

I wanted to try some experiments along these lines, but could find no opportunity. The problem was simply that while oceanariums maintain a stable of porpoises, the animals work in the shows and are not readily available for consecutive experimentation of this sort. The more enlightened oceanariums, nowadays, know that trained porpoises need vacations from their work, perhaps even more than human beings do from theirs, and there are often shifts of porpoises, those resting and socializing, and those working at the routine of public shows. However, in 1957 this sophistication was not part of our thinking at Marineland of the Pacific, and I had no porpoise at my disposal. Besides, the housekeeping for a porpoise is expensive; their tanks must be kept clean and supplied with running sea water, and they eat a dozen or more pounds of fish every day, so it is wasteful to have nonproductive porpoises at an oceanarium.

My chance for the experiments came about two years later, when Michael Sklar, producer of the highly respected CBS science TV series "Conquest," called on us. He wanted to know if we would be willing to help with a show on porpoise communication. I told him that if communication—porpoise language and that sort of thing—was the subject he had firmly decided upon, he should consult some of the scientists working in that area. But if he would be satisfied with a show on navigation by a blindfolded porpoise, I would try to oblige. I would even set up a real experiment for him whose outcome was unknown.

After some discussion of why we should hope that a blindfolded porpoise could navigate, Mike was convinced. We marched up to Bill Monahan, the general manager, and Bill readily agreed to the attempt and gave us the encouragement, space, and funds for the animal we needed. Nationwide shows are valuable publicity for Marineland, and this one was of the highest caliber.

What was clearly needed at this juncture was to apply Spallanzani's ingenious tests to a porpoise. The first step would be to devise a porpoise blindfold. This was much easier said than done. Forrest Wood, at Marine Studios, had been the first to try, working with one of his tame performing porpoises. He tested endless kinds of blindfolds, but nothing would stay in place. Each time they slipped quickly from the porpoise's slick head or were shortly shaken off by the animal. One day he noticed a television advertisement for a certain brand of adhesive tape. This tape, according to the glib copy writer, would stick to anything, even an egg submerged in a glass of water. Woody tried the tape, but even if it would lift eggs, it would not stick to the slick skin of his experimental subjects, the skin of which is like the texture of a wet inner tube. After this final frustration, Woody's many other duties caused him to drop his search for a blindfold into his inactive list of projects.

I believe, though I can no longer be sure, that Woody had told me about his numerous blindfold attempts two or three years before the idea occurred, seemingly *de novo,* to me. This sort of passive and partial recall of ideas, without good recollection of their sources, sometimes leads to scientists' bickering with one another about "who got the idea first." In this case, however, when I told Woody that I hoped to blindfold a porpoise, he just shrugged resignedly, wished me luck, and filled me in about the adhesive tape and the non-eggheaded porpoise.

Our porpoise was a young subadult female Atlantic bottlenose porpoise named Kathy. She was a sleek, gray animal about seven and a half feet long, and possessed a peppery sense of humor, combined incongruously with a blind and friendly attitude toward humans, as seems generally to be the case with this species. Kathy had been slightly trained before being flown out to us from Marine Studios. We housed her in one of the circular cement holding tanks in the Marineland service yard.

The task of blindfolding this animal fell to me and to my assistant curator, John Prescott. John is a quiet person of great determination, with a sharp and unusually orderly mind. He is also an avid diver and was soon spending much time each week in the tank with Kathy, watching her and making her acquaintance. Together we laid out a program that we hoped would end with a blindfold successfully in place over Kathy's eyes.

It was early July of 1959. A month should suffice, we decided naïvely. Neither John nor I could then have been classed either as an animal psychologist or as a practical animal trainer. At any rate, undaunted by our ignorance, and possibly aided by it, we plunged in.

We planned to use two main techniques to assist our training, both learned from the professional trainers at Marineland. The first is called the "bridging stimulus." This consisted simply of training Kathy by repetition that when she heard a blast from a police whistle, she had done a correct act, and thus an act for which she would gain a reward. This allowed us to tell her, "Yes, Kathy, that was right," wherever she was in the tank. Also, by withholding the whistle or food, we could tell her, "No, Kathy, you'll not get rewarded for *that* sloppy job."

The second technique is what is sometimes called the "process of multiple approximations." This bit of jargon means that when you wish a porpoise to perform a complicated or difficult act on cue, you start toward the ultimate end simply and build up to it slowly, step by step. The trick is to divide your ultimate request into small, easily comprehensible parts, starting with the simplest possible approximation of the final act.

I must mention one other thing in connection with training porpoises—or any other animal, for that matter—before I describe what John and I did. This last item is empathy. A trainer will get simply nowhere with a sensitive and intelligent creature like a porpoise unless he develops a real feeling for its moods. A heavy-handed person who fails to develop this automatic unspoken communication with his charge might just as well leave and get a job selling hot dogs or insurance. He'll never get off the ground.

John and I started out with Kathy by getting to know her. Very shortly she would take food fish from our hands. We made every effort to stroke and pet her, both in the water and out. At first she was skittish and flinched from our advances. But soon she would let us rub our hands over her flippers and sides with apparent enjoyment.

We knew that soon we would be requiring Kathy to perform many specific bits of behavior many times a day. This meant that we had to teach her to take small bites of food rather than whole fish each time she was rewarded for doing something correctly, or else she would be full when halfway through our daily plan of training. It was nearly two weeks before she condescended to feed freely on little chunks of mackerel. After she had lived on this fragmented fare for a month, Kathy had become so used to it that she sometimes temporarily refused whole fish that were thrown to her.

With this basic bit of learning out of the way, we started at once to break her to a blindfold, or at least to our conception of what the blindfold was going to be. Here the process of multiple approximations came into play. Our plan was ultimately to cover her eyes with a sort of giant economy-sized pair of "eye muffs." They were to be held in place by a spring steel loop circling over her head. The simplest approximation of this grotesque gadget was simply to require Kathy to allow our fingers to rest for a few seconds on the tip of her snout. This was accomplished readily enough. Next, we began to slide one hand down the side of her head tiny step by tiny step, toward one eye. As we came closer to the eye, Kathy became skittish. She resented this invasion of her person, and besides her eyes were sensitive areas, not to be poked by human fingers. She showed her distaste about this time by lurking repeatedly at the far side of the tank until we came to the tank edge and turned our backs to her, usually when we were deep in conversation about her progress. Then she would flash across the thirty-five-foot pool, do a great sliding aquatic Brody turn, and send a green sheet of water out of the pool and over our unsuspecting heads. John and I literally had to stop all training while we trained this antisocial but understandable action out of her repertoire. We didn't completely eradicate it for a long time, though. It would pop up now and then after Kathy had undergone a particularly harrowing day at our hands. For some reason she seemed to wait until one of us, or a guest, appeared in a clean, pressed suit, a rare enough event in the curator's department. Then would come the sly observation period and then the rush, the wall of water, and the shocked stream of curatorial epithets from us.

At any rate, once we had this bit of righteous indignation contained, we returned to the former approximations. Soon Kathy would let us hold our cupped hand over one eye for fifteen to twenty seconds at a time.

The next approximation began about August 1, which, as you may remember, was our original estimated date for completion of training. We began to slide the other hand down while the first was in place over one eye. Kathy looked up at us when we started this new tack, rolled her eyes until the whites showed, and raced off around the tank at full tilt. This showing of the eye whites seems to signal anger or agitation both in porpoises and in whales. She refused to come near us for the rest of the day, speeding by us as we called her, slapping her tail on the water in pique. "No performance, no lunch," was our silent reply.

The next morning she was more tractable but only allowed us to touch her snout with both hands. We began from there and gradually worked both hands down toward her eyes. Things went faster this time because Kathy now knew what we wanted. She simply didn't like the whole idea and insisted that she be approached with the proper degree of delicacy. Soon, however, we could call her with a special underwater sound generator and place both hands over her eyes, and she would stay virtually motionless for nearly half a minute until we blew the reward whistle.

Kathy really registered her objections when we tried the next approximation. To simulate the actual blindfolds, we decided to cover our hands with a foreign substance and then cup them over her eyes. In this case we simply donned a pair of canvas work gloves. Kathy rolled onto her side, just out of reach, and looked suspiciously at us. John dipped his gloved hands into the water and slapped the tank wall for Kathy to come. She came warily to him, but with the first touch of the gloves on her head she shook away from his outstretched hands, whirled in the water, and raced around the tank. Each time she swished past, she turned her head and leered at us from beneath the surface. All day long she remained firm in her refusal to submit to this new indignity. At the end of the day she had not performed and thus had not received any rewards from us.

Again, no work, no fish. We looked at her in frustration, fed her about two-thirds of her daily ration to make sure this training wouldn't harm her, and waved goodbye to her for the day as she sped around the tank, well out of reach. It passed across my mind many times during our training sessions with Kathy that if we didn't have this ironclad control over her food, there would be little question who would win in a battle of wills—porpoise or man.

As a matter of fact, even though Kathy had all the cards stacked against her, she sometimes tricked us. On several occasions it actually came to the point where she was training us. Her method was so subtle that we didn't realize we were being trained. An example of this cetacean counterattack came at about the time we broke her to cloth gloves. Each time we called her with a slap on the tank wall, she came docilely enough, but day by day we had to reach a little farther out to put our gloved hands over her eyes. I don't believe the rate at which she retreated could have been more than an inch a day. Then one day, a week or so later, I stopped abruptly with a silly feeling of embarrassment, realizing that I was all but ready to fall, face first, into the water each time I tried to touch her. As for Kathy, she sculled there in the water with apparent docility, that sly smile on her face. Perhaps she was calculating the retreat length for the next day's operation, and wondering when John or I would lose his balance.

Next we approximated the spring steel loop by running a length of plastic tubing down into the thumb of one glove while we were wearing it, up in an arc, and into the other glove thumb. Then, with our hands thus bridged together, we repeated the old performance. Kathy took this well enough after a day or so, but fled in apparent terror each time the tubing touched the top of her head. In a week she had steadied to the point where we could try our first blindfold.

The construction of the first blindfold caused a degree of confusion in the Marineland accounting department. John puzzled over materials for the blindfolds. After some deep thought, he hit upon a brilliant solution. What could be better, he surmised, than to make the actual eye cup of that gay human deceiver, the all-American falsie? So, forthwith, a requisition went through channels for one set of junior-teen-sized falsies. From what we heard, the accounting department was buzzing with speculation about what John, or the curator's department in general, was to do with these items. The imagined story was probably better than the real one, we thought, so we let the matter remain a mystery.

At any rate, the blindfold didn't work. In each attempt Kathy accepted the rakish creation with good grace, retreated from our hands, and shook her head violently from side to side until it was swept free. What was worse, Kathy refused to breathe as long as the loop remained over her head. This, we felt, was a rather severe limitation of the method, so we turned our thoughts toward other possible solutions. John and I toyed with blindfolds that would attach with a harness over Kathy's dorsal fin. We thought about reversing the loop blindfold so that the spring steel loop ran under her head rather than over it, and we watched the TV ads for possible improvements on the egg-lifting tape, but none appeared. It was mid-September by this time. Mike Sklar and his cohorts on the "Conquest" show called us dispiritedly from time to time, and the best we could report was that we were not yet ready to give up.

One morning I was in the Louvre (the Marineland artists' room) plaguing the artists because of some misspellings in one of their displays, when my eye fell on a latex model of a white shark. An open jar of the raw casting latex stood alongside the model. I absent-mindedly stuck a finger into it. Then, forgetting the misspellings, I picked up the jar and rushed to the lab. Soon John and I were deeply involved in the production of suction cups. Mine were low, streamlined models made in the hollow of a photoflash reflector. John's were of a deeper, more sturdy design, with undeniable junior-teen affinities. We set our creations out to dry.

The next morning I was called to a meeting with manager Monahan. He wanted to know how we were coming on the blindfold project. Kathy was a valuable show animal, he pointed out, and we had had her for more than twice the estimated time. "When," he wanted to know, "will you be through with her?"

There was no question that he had been more patient than I had any right to expect, so I pleaded, "Bill, give me two weeks more with her, and either I will prove to you we can blindfold her, or you take her and put her back into regular show training."

"It's a deal," he said, smiling. I departed, fully convinced that our relationship with Kathy was almost at an end.

As I sat telling Muriel Johnson, my secretary, about this latest development in our long series of frustrations with blindfolds, John stepped quietly into the office.

"They work," he said matter-of-factly.

"What works?" I asked uncomprehendingly.

"The suction cups. Kathy let me put them on and then swam off around the tank without so much as shaking her head."

I burst in, "You don't mean . . . ?"

"Wait a minute." John held up his hand. "Kathy *wore* the suction cups, left my hands and *swam* around the tank a couple of times without so much as coming *near* the wall, and then, *listen to this, returned to me when I slapped the wall,* and I took them off."

"We did it—we did it—we did it!!!!" I shouted, jumping out of my seat and waving my hands.

"Come see," John said. I did and he was right. Kathy navigated beautifully, totally without sight, and returned to his hands when he gave the signal. It was an uncanny performance and one I will never forget, even though it became commonplace later on. In fact, it wasn't long before I had to remind myself that this swift-swimming, maneuverable animal was actually doing her antics with her eyes closed under thick latex suction cups (John's models).

I called Bill Monahan about an hour after I had left his office, and told him that we had succeeded. He took the news a bit warily, perhaps wondering what kind of game I was playing with my two-week time limit.

Then John and I got to work. We called Mike Sklar across the country in his New York office. His initial resigned tone changed at once into enthusiasm, plans, and schedules. Next I contacted Paul Asa-Dorian, a friend who is a civilian Navy psychologist and acoustic specialist. He listened to my tale quietly for a time but was soon rattling off a rapid-fire list of mythical-sounding recording and listening gear he planned to haul up to Kathy's tank so we could take down her supposed echolocation signals.

"I'll get a multichannel PQM set," he told me (or something like that).

"Good, good," I replied, "be sure you don't forget," not comprehending in the slightest what he was talking about.

"Oh, yes, and if you think we need it, I can get a wide-band sound vibralizer," he added. This sounded to me a little like a machine for reducing one's waistline but I withheld further comment.

When he appeared a week later, the majestic array of acoustic gear was far more confusing to me than it had sounded over the phone. I've since achieved a sort of wary acceptance of such machines, but I doubt if we will ever be close friends. Paul brought with him a tall Navy chief who tinkered with a lot of colored wires. He was Paul Perkins, Asa-Dorian's right-hand man and confidant in matters acoustical, and was known to everyone as Perk. Perk seemed utterly dedicated to doing what he could to solve the Navy's acoustical problems. If a man listening inside a virtually sightless submarine cruising under the dark sea heard a strange noise, Perk felt it was his personal responsibility to be able to tell who or what was making the racket. It was partly for this reason, I suspect, that Perk wanted to listen to Kathy, and, perhaps, partly because she was a kindred soul using something similar to the Navy's sonar system. In any case, the noises Kathy produced proved fascinating to Perk. Sometimes we had to steer him forcibly away from his amplifiers as darkness and chilling winds told us lesser mortals that it was time to go home and sit around the warm fireplace with a beer.

While listening and recording devices were being rigged and tested, John and I trained Kathy to swim to a target suspended in the water across the tank from her. Soon, while blindfolded, she located this target with almost unerring accuracy, swam to it, and pressed it with the tip of her snout, causing a bell to ring. This signaled success to her. Then she returned to our hands for a reward. To our amazement Kathy could locate a target as small as an inch in diameter apparently from across the entire thirty-five-foot width of the tank, without sight.

This simple test allowed us to direct Kathy straight toward a submerged hydrophone. We merely had to put the hydrophone behind the target, or drop the reward fish near another hydrophone on our side of the tank.

The two Pauls then swung into action. Their early recordings confirmed that the rusty-hinge sounds were the ones used by these porpoises during their blind navigation. As the Schevills and Professor Kellogg had found, each of these creaks of the rusty hinge was composed of hundreds of tiny clicks, each about a thousandth of a second long. While we could detect a small fraction of them with our limited human hearing, nearly all of the noise in each click was far above human hearing.

As Kathy zeroed in on a reward fish dropped near a hydrophone, she made her clicks in a rather regular fashion. At the first splash of the fish, she wheeled around in the water and headed directly for the splash, giving out trains of clicks at the same time. We felt that this initial location of the target was accomplished by the use of two capabilities. First, Kathy seemed to possess a remarkable ability to localize the position of the splash, simply by using her extremely acute directional hearing. Then, when she was headed in approximately the right direction, she began to pick up the echoes of her clicks as they bounced off the sinking fish. These brief, but intense, clicks began to come faster as she swam toward her target. By the time she picked up the tidbit, we could detect as many as 416 clicks per second. There was another interesting thing we noticed; Kathy waggled her head up and down and around in circles just before she snapped up a sinking fish. If she temporarily lost the fish, or if we dropped it an inch or two from the hydrophone, these head waggles became extreme. At the same time the hydrophone picked up a tremendous concentration of clicks. It seemed obvious to us that she was trying to find her fish with these clicks, and to discriminate it from the nearby hydrophone. She looked for all the world like a miner peering into the crevices of a mine shaft with his head lamp.

Our next step was to devise a maze for Kathy to swim through. Two lines of air-filled metal poles were suspended from clotheslines stretched across the middle of the tank. By giving Kathy a task on the opposite side of the tank, we could require her to swim through this maze, and each time she negotiated it, we tugged on one line or another to get a new alignment of the poles, thereby producing a new maze. Kathy became so adept that she flashed through the forest of metal poles without any hesitation, and without touching a one. We tested her further by dropping chunks of fish near the poles of the maze. She located them easily, swam over, and very delicately picked up the fish without touching the pole, even though the morsel might have been sinking only an inch from the metal.

I wondered whether Kathy could discriminate between different kinds of solid objects by sound, and so we cut the solid muscle of mackerel into pieces about an inch long, the same size and shape as gelatin capsules used by veterinarians for doctoring large animals. When the capsules were filled with water and both fish and capsule were tossed to blindfolded Kathy, she buzzed up, waggling her head, and snapped up the fish, ignoring the capsule.

As the experiment progressed, I noticed an unusual item in Kathy's behavior. Sometimes she would lose her reward, even though it drifted very close to her jaws. We peered down into the water and the temptation was to say, "It's right beneath your snout, Kathy." This happened so often that I began to suspect she was unable to detect a fish in this position. We tried a simple test to see if my assumption was correct. Kathy was stationed blindfolded near the wall, with her head virtually motionless as she sculled quietly with her tail. I blew the reward whistle and slid fragments of fish into the water around her in various positions relative to her head. Sure enough, she always failed to find those fragments that drifted below the level of her upper jaws, even though they might be only an inch away. However, any fish that drifted above her jaws she snapped up at once. All the while we could hear her making her rusty-hinge noises. Porpoises have no sense of smell, and Kathy could not see, so we were forced to conclude that her actions were the result of her echolocation ability. If so, she seemed either to be putting out a beam of sound from her fatty forehead (called the "melon" by whalers), or was receiving echoes there, or perhaps both. This was all very peculiar, since Kathy's larynx was located well below her eyes in her throat region, and this was where, intuitively, we expected her to make her sounds, even though a porpoise has no vocal cords.

Later the two Pauls and I placed paired hydrophones in the water, several feet apart. We then blew the reward whistle and directed Kathy to run in toward one of the hydrophones. By watching the sound levels of both hydrophones, we could tell that Kathy's rusty-hinge noises were far louder in the hydrophone toward which she pointed her head, even if she passed close by the other but did not direct her head at it. Thus, we came to believe that she was emitting a beam or cone of sounds that seemed to emanate from her head above the line of the mouth. This strange conclusion was hard to accept at the time. However, recent work using hydrophones pressed against a clicking porpoise's forehead and upper jaws by both Navy scientist William Evans and my own lab confirm it.

We still can't be sure that Kathy was not producing her clicks in her larynx and somehow beaming them from her forehead, or simply producing the sounds somewhere inside her forehead. Twice when we had pilot whales lying on the deck of the *Geronimo,* I had knelt down and put my ear against the melon on their foreheads. Each time I heard squeaking sounds being produced, apparently within the aft part of the melon, and felt the melon swell during sound production. The inflation probably took place in the complicated air sacs associated with the internal nasal passages of the animals. These observations increased my feeling that the sounds were made inside the tissues of the forehead and upper nasal passages, and that the cycling of air was somehow involved in sound production. Very likely there was a system which allowed the porpoise or toothed whale to reuse its small air supply over and over. In this way they could produce sounds far below the sea surface during long dives.

Through all this experimentation we had not performed the complementary experiment—the one akin to Spallanzani's plugging his bat's ears with wax. We had shown that the porpoise *could* navigate without sight, but we had not shown that she *could not* navigate blindfolded without either hearing or sound emission. Thus, while we knew Kathy was producing sounds during blind navigation, we did not have ironclad evidence that she was really using them as a means of navigation.

It's one thing to plug a bat ear with wax and another to prevent sound from entering a porpoise ear. Sound will travel almost unimpeded from water through the blubber of a swimming animal. If we blocked the tiny ear canals of our porpoise with wax, we could expect no results. Kathy's ear canals were about the diameter of a fine pencil lead, and if blocked, sound almost certainly could penetrate around the wax and into her middle and inner ears.

While sound traveling in water will pass easily through blubber, it is stopped and reflected almost completely by any sort of air barrier. That is one reason why fathometers and sonar sets often pick up schools of fish. The sound pulses from these machines bounce off the fishes' gas-filled swim bladders located just under the backbones of many species, and clear echoes will return. For this reason we decided we must devise an air barrier to block Kathy's echoes at some point. After several attempts we settled on a mask made of foam neoprene rubber sheeting like that used for diving suits, which would cover Kathy's entire melon and upper jaw. This rubber is filled with myriad tiny gas bubbles and is an excellent sound barrier in water.

The mask was a grotesque-looking object, equipped with several small suction cups to hold it in place on Kathy's melon (we were thoroughly hooked on suction cups by this time), and rubber bands to hold it onto her jaws. From the first day we tried to cajole Kathy into wearing this weird-looking mask, she politely but adamantly refused. From time to time we did get everything in place and the bands over her jaws, but each time she backed away a few yards and began to shake her head violently. After a few seconds she always shook the mask loose. Two months later, after having used every training trick we could conjure, we had made utterly no progress. Kathy's refusal was, perhaps, all we could expect from an intelligent animal faced with the loss of sight and hearing.

John and I made our last attempt during the filming of the TV show "Conquest." We succeeded in getting everything in place, and true to the old and by now time-honored pattern, Kathy backed away from the tank wall and began to shake her head. Seconds later the mask floated to the surface. Then to everyone's amazement, *Kathy swam over to the hated creation, picked it up in her jaws, swam to John, and gave it to him.* She was obviously willing to cooperate with us and let us fasten the miserable mask on her head. That part of the game was all right with Kathy. She was ready for us to do it again, but there was never any question, apparently either in her mind or ours, that she would continue to shake it loose every time we put it on her.

This one incident sums up as well as any I know the kind of personality porpoises have, and why trainers and scientists become deeply attached to their charges. It also explains why scientists working with these animals are apt to fill their writings with emotional terms. I, personally, am sure that porpoises have emotions of some sort.

The TV show was filmed and Kathy was needed for her long-overdue show duties, so our experiments came to a halt. They were good experiments and great fun. They were everything experiments should be. At the start they were full of hard work and uncertainty. Then came the drama of a breakthrough; and when we were done, many tantalizing puzzles were left for the next investigation.

CHAPTER SEVEN

Alice

Dear Alice, old, shy Alice, old maddening Alice, whom we often called stupid in our frustration. For all her faults, she was a key figure in letting us learn. At first she was a "loaner" porpoise, borrowed from the Navy, a sort of U-drive porpoise, whom we had to return when our contract was up. But later, out of a resigned fondness for her, built out of the mutual frustrations of the road we had traversed together, I bought her outright. Then I *owned* Alice, and if you have never owned a porpoise, you can scarcely appreciate what this means. Such ownership is a contract for life of even greater solemnity than the ones we humans exchange with each other. It means not only that you must care for her every day, weekends, Labor Day, Christmas, and all, but that you must see to it that the pump to her tank doesn't falter, that the fish dealer who supplies her lunch doesn't slip in bad fish, and that her tank is cleaned twice a week. My ultimate folly becomes evident if you realize that when I bought her I had nothing but a set of Esther Williams plastic swimming pools on the UCLA campus in which to house her and that my colleagues and I had to *make* new sea water every two weeks to replace that she had soiled. The memory of us hauling two and a half tons of salt each fortnight to mix a new batch makes my shoulders ache.

For all her foibles, Alice was my companion during the time when many of the magnificent adaptations of porpoises became evident to me. Just by being there she helped me learn. Especially she helped us look with something akin to awe at the subtle and magnificent ways in which she was adapted to living in the sea. She also helped us to imagine the long process by which she came to be. I had joined the zoology faculty at UCLA by that time and was beginning to pursue porpoise research in earnest.

Every wild animal like Alice is a history book. Its tissues, behavior, blood, and bone are made of past adaptations, reworked, and miraculously melded into a modern creature. In all modern animals some traces of the evolutionary past, mostly in the molecular machinery of cells, probably go back two and a half billion years. The features we think of when we call an animal a "mammal" are comparatively new. A mere eighty to a hundred million years ago the mammalian plan began to assemble and to elbow its way into the living world. The plan proved exceptionally good, and a thousand evolutionary experiments began, each challenging most living things around it. Contented old dinosaurs awoke from complacent slumbers to find the proxies collected and a new board of directors elected. They shuffled off to early retirement. One group, bearing many resemblances to modern hoofed animals, pocketed its "certified mammal papers" and started off toward the rivers, swamps, and estuaries. To its evolutionary delight, the papers opened doors as if by miracle and the race proliferated. But probably none of this was dramatic at first, for early fossils are few.

Only much later, when the new tribe reached an accommodation with the water, did it spread in great numbers, littering the accumulating sediments with the bones from which we now read its history. At first the water must have been grossly foreign, probably to be invaded only briefly for food. The running legs of a land mammal were awkward in water, and the buoyancy of lungs made the animal teeter like a badly laden skiff as it searched for sustenance beneath the surface. Its hair became wet, and cool waters swept away its body heat, causing it to retreat to land, shivering in the seeping cold. Each time the animal ducked below the surface, it was as if someone had clapped a pair of ear muffs over its head. Sounds were instantly deadened, as aerial ears responded imperfectly beneath the water. Even though the water cascaded with sound, the animal heard little but the faint hiss of its own neural circuitry. What other sounds the animal did hear were, at first, unclassified, and hence not understood.

An animal out of kilter but bearing one trump card, like our floundering, shivering mammal, is superb foil for change. With it much evolutionary work needs to be done, but the basic plan is sound. Probably the closer the animal is to disaster, the faster the pace of change we can expect. It's no wonder, then, that these early experiments seldom leave traces. In time legs became diving planes or retreated beneath a newly smooth body surface to serve only as attachment for a set of obscure internal muscles. Hair and subcutaneous fat engaged in evolutionary debate over which could become more useful. The fat won and became the blanket of blubber encasing modern cetaceans, while the hair remains only in fetal porpoises and whales, or in adults as a sparse sprinkling on their upper lips and heads.

But evolution is a vastly more complicated process than this. No feature of an animal evolves alone, though it seems simplest to think that way. In fact, all life evolves together in one incredibly complicated interlocking system, driven ultimately by the forces that regulate the energy streaming from the sun, by showers of high-energy particles from interstellar space, by magnetic forces, by internal events within the earth, and by cosmic dust drifting through the atmosphere, to sift in time into the chemistry of organisms. Truly, it is *systems* that evolve, the totality of organisms plus environment, that are engaged in change. Our pre-porpoises, tentatively poking their maladapted feet into the water, are a tiny fraction of this scheme, and ultimately cannot be separated from it.

So, to understand how porpoises came to be, we will be closer to the truth if our conception is not of an animal that plunged hellbent-for-leather into a lake or sea but, instead, of an animal superbly adapted to one domain that tentatively probed another and came up mostly, but not completely, wanting. Its initial forays into water must have been short, while its reservoir of strength remained as a land animal. Gradually, gradually, the water became familiar, and most such adjustments of body or mind that allowed such familiarity subtracted something from its adjustments to land. Like the otter, who swims with fluid grace but bears its young deep in an earthen burrow, every creature-in-transition may come to a point of no return where it teeters on a knife-edge—neither a land animal nor a creature of the water.

Its reservoir of survival craft, which once lay in such land adaptations as fleetness and the ability to sort out the faintest hint of a telltale odor from other vastly stronger smells, became blunted. New priorities of danger had to be classified and understood from the swelling and diminishing shoals of sound coming from far beyond the limits of vision. Our animal had to learn which sounds told only of the ordinary thermal layering in the sea that scattered and jumbled sounds like light streaming through wavy glass, and which ones told a more relevant story. It learned to feel nuances of pressure in the passing water. It eventually was able to adjust effortlessly to the great and changing weight of water as it dove, and its body became terete and delicately balanced in the yielding fluid. Perhaps it also learned to taste its world, for its nostrils proved of little use at sea. Perhaps the porpoise came to understand the molecular hints that flowed past its tongue and that might tell in acridity that a great shark had just passed. The envelope of water through which the shark slipped might carry away a part of the shark's substance to be beat by the sweep of its tail into a wavering molecular trail. That story is still unknown, since no one has as yet unraveled the story of cetacean chemical sense. However, it is now sure that the acoustic sophistication of porpoises is exceeded by no other animal, and Alice helped us understand this.

Alice was a timeless old gal, her youth but a dim memory even when I first met her. Her dorsal fin was frayed at the edges and streaked with scars, as was her lumpy old body. Perhaps because so many of her years had been spent at sea before she began her life with humans, she never really became used to us. Alice's problem, and our problem, was that she was so shy that any new request from us was apt to throw her into a tizzy. Sometimes these snits lasted for days.

For example, one time when we were working with her at Sea Life Park in Hawaii, she was in a training tank with several other porpoises. We wanted to run all the porpoises into a connecting tank so the first could be cleaned. In general, porpoises hate to go through gates, especially into another tank that they have not visited before. One may have to force them at first with a net, but usually after three or four such pursuits they become accustomed to the act and will swim rapidly through of their own accord. Not Alice. *Never* Alice. Even though we had switched her in this fashion many times before, she always refused in obvious terror. So the net was brought out and swept up behind her, forcing her closer and closer to that awful eight-foot-wide entrance. She lay on her side whistling piteously as the net dragged her closer and closer to the broad square of water through which she could see the other porpoises milling slowly and calmly. The moment came when she would be forced through, and she lunged back in hysteria, becoming tangled in the net six feet below the water. If a porpoise takes in a lungful of water, it will drown in moments, so I knew she was in great danger. Without waiting to strip down, I jumped in and forced her four-hundred-pound bulk to the surface. She gasped and sputtered as she drew in a frightened breath. In my arms I then pushed her, whistling in terror, through the gate. This sequence so unnerved her that it was two days before she began, skittishly, to work again.

All through our studies with Alice she behaved this way, and the loss of experimental time is something I'd rather not think about. A bright, adventurous, young porpoise might have done the work in a third the time Alice required. Yet every morning when we went to her tank, she turned on her side, cocked one eye up at us, and greeted us with a cheery, two-parted squeak. We sighed in resignation. She seemed to know she was a trial to us, and would do her best, even if it was a fraction of what another animal might do.

The tasks we designed for Alice were attempts to look back in time at her ancestors to see how they had solved certain acoustic problems. Since originally they were land animals, they had certainly come to the water with ears adapted to air, and, like us, this should have all but incapacitated their hearing. Sounds act very differently in water than in air. For example, they travel nearly five times as fast. If porpoises had made no adjustments for this during their long history of invading the sea, their ability to discriminate between two sounds close together should be only about one-fifth as good as that of the ancestral land mammal. Thus, the basic question we asked Alice was: Had her ancestors somehow compensated for this reduced capability, and if so, how much had they achieved?

Another peculiar acoustic problem faces an invader of the aquatic world. In air we receive sound only at our ears. It is funneled into our heads by our external ears and passes through the paper-thin tympanic membrane, or eardrum. Once inside the middle ear, it sets the air of that cavity in motion, causing the tiny ear bones to move. They, in turn, conduct sound inward, and thus we hear. Everywhere else on our bodies nearly all sound is reflected back into the air or absorbed by our clothing and does not enter our bodies to any great degree. This is not the case in water. Much water-borne sound penetrates not only sea creatures and seaweeds but also the silts and muds of the sea bottom. In general, the nearer a submerged object is to the density of water, the more sound energy enters. Porpoise fat is acoustically much like water, and hence sound penetrates it easily. It seemed to us that a porpoise should receive sound everywhere on its blubber coat. If so, how did Alice localize sounds? Wouldn't sounds enter her ears from a variety of directions? We suspected that somehow Alice and her ancestors had solved these problems. Kathy had convinced us of that. When she cruised her tank blindfolded and picked up fragments of fish, we knew porpoise acoustic capabilities were great.

My associate on our first work with Alice was an extremely bright young psychologist, Dr. Ronald Turner. He knew to perfection what is often called "Skinnerian psychology," or the techniques and theory of conditioned response learning. Simply put, this is a vastly more sophisticated version of the training techniques and their underlying ideas that we had used on Kathy. Ron was able to lead both Alice and me along a very difficult experimental path. Our start was my simple-seeming question: How fine a discrimination can a porpoise make using sound alone? We huddled in my UCLA office to explore where my simple question might lead, and how we could attack it. At length we decided to train Alice to make a discrimination between two spheres of different sizes. We would ask her to tell us, while blindfolded, which sphere was larger by pressing levers hung in the tank. She would be asked to choose the lever on the side of the largest sphere. By switching the position of the spheres in a random fashion, we might be able to build up a history of choices great enough to tell us whether she was just guessing or actually could tell them apart. In other words, if she was right, say, 85 percent of the time, we would know it couldn't be chance. Then, if she came close to 100 percent success with the first pair, we could substitute another pair closer together in size and try again. Eventually we should reach a size disparity where Alice would fail; where her choice would become random, no matter how long or hard we tried to train her further.

The first step was to get our apparatus assembled. We devised a pair of levers that hung in the water which Alice could press with her snout. We planned to hang our spheres about two feet behind them. Alice could direct her clicks at the spheres, and then if she could tell the difference, she had only to press the lever on the side of the largest sphere to indicate her choice.

Modern psychological experimentation is often highly automated, and for good reason. Such automation removes the chance of unconscious bias by the experimenter. For instance, Alice

might learn to press both levers in a tentative way, and the observer would be forced to make a personal decision about whether
she had chosen correctly or not. Since the experimenter knew
the answer, he might give it away by some unconscious action.
In this way she might fool us into making the decision for
her. Ron reasoned that by putting tiny switches on the levers
and automating our feedings, he could remove such human decisions from the experiment. Thus, either Alice pushed the proper
lever hard enough to throw the switch or she didn't, and we
weren't directly involved in the decision.

So, before long, Alice's plastic tank became a maze of wires,
levers, and switches. On the far side of the tank we installed
an automatic porpoise feeder. It looked like a wheel whose
spokes were slots for fish. When the proper electrical signal
reached it, an arm equipped with a shaving brush at its end
swept around, pushing a fresh fish out of a slot into the water. The wheel then rotated to the next slot, waiting for another
electrical signal to dispense the next fish. During experiments,
Ron and I sat in a little tin shack at tankside surrounded by
panels, counters, and wires. These allowed us to set up, from
what is called a table of random numbers, the order in which
the largest sphere would be presented on the right or left side.
The table might dictate, for example, that the largest sphere
be shown to Alice on the right side first, then the left side,
left side again, then right, then right, and so forth. Because the
table was mathematically random, no one, including Alice, could
divine on which side the large sphere would appear next except
by directly measuring the spheres.

Finding the proper spheres was a real problem. The decision
was crucial, because any irregularities of shape could produce
a distinctive echo, regardless of size, that might allow Alice to
select a single sphere from others we thought were identical.
Thus, if we were not careful, Alice could learn to give us answers that might fool us into thinking she was discriminating between spheres of two different sizes when actually she was only
listening to some peculiarity of echo produced by, say, a wrinkle
on the sphere's surface.

Glass or plastic spheres that were uniform enough simply couldn't be found, but I finally came up with the answer—ball bearings. They were homogeneous and machined as perfectly as could be asked. We scoured Los Angeles for ball bearings and finally located a supplier of assorted sizes up to huge ones two and a half inches in diameter. I prepared an order for a series, two of each size. The supplier, who generally sold them by the gross to machinery companies, listened to our unlikely tale and, shaking his head, laid out our series for us.

We began to train Alice. She had been loafing, warily watching as the gadgets accumulated around her tank. First she learned to accept blindfolds, as Kathy had done much earlier. If anything, she was more reluctant than Kathy. Repeatedly she shied away from Ron as he held the blindfolds cupped in his hands. It was then that I learned how a true experimental psychologist hands out discipline. I found it elegant and wonder why it seems so little used on obstreperous children, overbearing bosses, and other troublesome types. This is what Ron did.

When Alice balked at receiving the blindfolds, Ron and I turned our backs and walked away from the tank. At the same time Ron started his stopwatch. Then, after walking out of Alice's sight, we peered out at the tank from behind our little building. We waited until Alice spontaneously began to search for us, which we usually knew precisely, because she would stand bolt upright in the water, looking anxiously over the rim to see where we had gone. With a click of the stopwatch, Ron noted the time. Then for that day he added twenty seconds or so to the time she had taken to begin looking for us, and used it as punishment. Thus, each time she balked, Ron would say, "Time out," and we both walked out of sight and stayed away for the length of time we knew made Alice anxious plus the additional twenty seconds. Usually, when we returned, she then settled down to work. The frustration had been too much for her.

Haltingly, Alice built up the sequence of behavior needed to perform our experiment. A year after we started, Alice finally settled into a routine, and since we introduced no further unsettling requests, she performed many days without a hitch. In the morning Ron called her to tankside, after she had given us her little greeting. She swam docilely between his hands, receiving the blindfolds. Then, when a sound signal was produced under water, Alice began to swim in a big circle ending in a traverse directly toward the levers, behind and between which the ball bearing pair hung suspended in the water. At about midtank she rose for a breath of air, then she submerged and swam directly toward the levers, emitting a train of clicks as she went. A bit less than a yard from the levers she made her decision of which one to press, as she either swam directly to the one in her path or broke for the opposite one. From her breath at midtank to this point of decision she required from two to four seconds. Then, with a sideways swipe of her snout, she pressed the lever. If she was wrong, the switch did not click and no sound signal was given under water. She petulantly jerked away to begin the circle again. If she was right, she could hear the click of the automatic feeder across the tank. Then, with an enthusiastic start, she raced toward the splash where her reward fish had fallen into the water, emitting a whining series of clicks given so fast they made a high-pitched buzz.

At the same time she swam toward her reward fish and while her back was turned, the spheres were lifted from the water and rotated to the next position on the random list. We took care that this action should always sound the same, no matter what the ultimate position of the spheres might be. If our way of placing the big spheres on the right, for example, produced a sound somewhat different from placement on the left, Alice might learn this and fool us into thinking her echolocation had told her the right answer. In fact, such "secondary cues" are the bane of the behaviorist's existence, and animals will learn the most subtle and unlikely things to confound the investigator. There is no other pitfall so subtle or so difficult to avoid. Even automation is not always successful in avoiding the production of such cues. Two switches, for instance, may produce different sounds when they are actuated, and may provide simple cues for an animal that is being asked quite a different question. It's a little like the porpoises in San Diego Bay learning to know the *Geronimo* by some vagrant underwater signal she produced.

We used a very large and a very small sphere for the early tests. Once Alice had mastered this test and performed without error, we exchanged the small sphere for one slightly larger. Usually this caused her to make errors anew. So we worked with her until she could answer infallibly.

As this tedious testing proceeded, Alice's capability grew more and more amazing. After a year and a half she was giving us long unerring runs of responses when presented with ball bearings of 2 1/8 inches diameter versus 2 1/2 inches diameter, and she was making her decision with as little as 1.5 seconds' worth of clicks from a minimum distance of about four and a half feet away. I pondered, with some wonder, that this would be a relatively difficult feat for a person to perform visually in that length of time. We shifted the spheres closer in size, pairing a 2 1/4-inch and a 2 1/2-inch sphere. Here Alice seemed to falter again but was soon giving us runs whose success level (77 percent success) was well above chance.

Alice, you remarkable old beast! we thought. How could she so nonchalantly tell us the difference between those spheres in such a short time, using only those insignificant-seeming clicks of sound? How could she conceivably perform in this way when we, with our vaunted visual capability would probably make more errors than she did?

Parenthetically, we wondered if a spunky young porpoise might not do even better than geriatric Alice. It was as if one of us had glanced for a second over his shoulder at those spheres, swung his head back, and said, "Oh, of course, the big one's on the right."

When we were forced to terminate the test (the Navy needed its animal), Alice was still improving very slowly. I think we were close to the level where she would have failed completely, but there is no way now of being sure. She had told us enough to prove beyond doubt that her ancestors had somehow solved these problems they had faced when first entering the sea.

All this was interesting and exciting to us, but as is so often true of science, we were in for an unexpected jolt that shook our predetermined notions. Several times Ron presented Alice with an identical pair of two-and-a-half-inch spheres. She began her run in and then stopped and turned away without pressing the levers at all. It was as if she had said, "That's an impossible problem; why do you ask me to tell you the difference?" How could she tell an impossible problem from a merely difficult one? If echo strength alone was telling her which sphere was larger, she should simply make errors at random when presented with identical spheres. It was obvious that she knew the spheres were identical. How?

To help us try to understand this perplexing problem, Bill Evans joined us, making recordings of Alice's sounds as she made her discrimination runs. Alice had told the spheres apart by using long trains of clicks, each about one-thousandth of a second long. Each such click contained some sound frequencies our human ears could hear. Much of each sound, however, was far above our upper hearing capability. We analyzed the sound recordings in various ways. We counted the number of clicks made as Alice closed on her target, we looked at their frequency content, we determined how Alice changed the rate at which she emitted clicks as she came in, and what her sounds were like as she turned away from the levers to go after her reward fish. Finally, we looked for changes as she was given more and more difficult problems to solve. This is what we found.

Whether the problem was easy or difficult, Alice always gave out clicks at such a rate that the echo of one would return to her before she emitted the next. It was as if she somehow was able to compare the outgoing click with its echo in the few thousandths of a second available. Toward the end of a run, before she reached the levers, the rate of click emission rose sharply and then ceased altogether for a second or so until we could hear her press the lever. Then, unexpectedly, as she turned from the lever she gave out a burst of a dozen or more intense, reverberant clicks containing much lower frequencies than any she had used in scanning the ball bearing pair. As the fish plopped on the water from the lazy Susan, she swam toward it buzzing out a long train of clicks as much as four times as rapid (over 400 per second) as those used on the spheres, and containing much more high-frequency sound.

Thus, we learned that she had quite unexpected capabilities of altering the composition of her emitted signals within incredibly short time spans. She could turn on clicks rich in high- or low-frequency sound at will. Perplexingly, the clicks she used on the spheres were of only modest frequency range. The very high sounds, reaching from four to ten times the upper level of human hearing, so often recorded from wild porpoises, were subdued or absent at this time. Of all the problems she faced in our experimental tank, none seemed to require as high frequencies or as rapid a release of clicks as finding a floating fish in the wavelets of the tank surface. And why she gave her burst of resonant lower-frequency clicks as she turned from the levers escaped us for a time.

Finally, poking into physics books, I learned some interesting things that gradually began to make these diverse facts fit together into what seemed a plausible theory.

When a porpoise click hits a solid sphere in water, the sound does not simply reflect back to the animal. Instead, it does two major things. The first arriving sound does indeed reflect back in what is called a "rigid body echo," in a fashion related only to shape and surface texture. A sphere, I found, is a remarkably poor sound reflector, since only an infinitely small face is at right angles to the incoming sound wave. The rest hits the curved surface of the sphere and reflects in a way which produces a sort of halo of decreasing sound intensity. Much of the sound energy, however, is not instantly reflected but enters the sphere and causes it to vibrate. Each material has a characteristic mode of vibration. For example, a steel sphere will "ring" with a different sound pattern from a nylon one, or even a copper one. This vibration returns to the animal as a secondary part of the echo, which may last as much as eight times as long as the original signal. Furthermore, the size of the sphere also affects the composition of this second echo. Lower frequencies simply go around little spheres without producing an echo.

Here, perhaps, was a clue to Alice's perplexing behavior with the identical spheres. Perhaps when she turned away from the identical pair, she knew they were identical and that she had been presented with an impossible problem because the spheres returned only one pattern of echo. Even a slight difference in size, we found, could produce two noticeably different echoes. Alice could have told the spheres apart simply by listening to the lowest frequencies represented in the echoes. This level in our tests varied from somewhere near the upper level of human hearing to about twice this level, all well within Alice's capability. Perhaps, if she was using this method of size estimation, she did not need the higher frequencies, and perhaps this related to her use of modest frequency ranges when solving the sphere discrimination problem. Amazing, if true, because it required Alice to have remarkable control over those 1/1000-second clicks, and the wide variety of frequencies (pitches) each contained.

Why should Alice always produce clicks at such a rate that the echo could return before another click was given? Two possibilities struck us, and both would give her a means of judging distance and the rate at which she was closing in upon an object. First, if her brain could react fast enough, she might be able to respond to both her own emitted signal and to its echo arriving back a few thousands of a second later. If she could do this sufficiently well (which the human brain cannot), she could simply measure how long such a transit took and learn the distance of the echoing object. Second, she might listen to what is called a "difference tone," or a sound whose frequency (or pitch) is dependent upon how fast short pulses or clicks of sound are repeated. We humans can and do hear such tones, a common example being the sound produced by a new tire moving slowly over pavement. At very slow speeds one can hear the click of each rib of the tread as it hits the pavement. As speed increases, these merge into a hum that rises in pitch. As

Alice swam in toward the spheres or the floating fish, her out-going click and the returning echo should arrive closer and closer together in time, producing such a rising tone. This could give her both a measure of distance between her and the echo-ing object (the frequency of the tone) and the rate at which she swam toward the target (the rate at which this tone rose in pitch).

Which of these methods porpoises use is anybody's guess, though we now know from neurophysiological studies in porpoises that they are equipped to perform the precise measurement in their brain that would allow an assessment of the time between the outgoing click and its echo, even though humans cannot. Very likely, Alice learned in her younger years along the Florida shores to take such subtle hints as these, and to combine them in a thousand ways with her "feel" for the watery world around her, emerging with a subtly coordinated use of sound, echo, and swimming that allowed her to almost "see with sound."

While our work with Alice did not prove how she performed her remarkable discrimination, it showed the rich possibilities she had for learning about her world by sound alone. Echoes allowed her to glean information about the shapes, sizes, textures, compo-sitions, and speeds of objects in her world, perhaps to a very refined degree. Her capability of shifting the kinds of outgoing signals in a few thousandths of a second gave her further power. When she emitted the powerful, low-frequency-rich signals as she turned away from the lever to get her fish, she may have been producing reverberations to obtain a general idea of her surroundings and to keep from swimming into the apparatus and the tank wall. When we hear such signals from animals at sea, are they keeping tabs on the bottom and nearby rocks, using reverberations as a navigation device? We think it likely.

Alice's clicks seemed insignificant, but she could do amazing things with them. Her clicks and ears enabled her to do many of the things that humans do with eyes and light. Indeed, she could go humans one better by actually looking into the structure of submerged objects with her clicks.

Dear old Alice had provided us with some remarkable insights into the ways in which porpoises are adapted to life in the sea. For that we willingly put up with her foibles.

As I said before, I finally bought Alice from the Navy, and took her with me to Hawaii, when I went there to direct the research at a small oceanographic station. Though we worked occasionally with her after that, mostly we just let her bask in semiretirement amongst a group of younger and harder-working porpoises. When Alice was loaded on the plane for her 2,200-mile trip from Scripps Institution of Oceanography, she was a typical pale-gray bottlenose porpoise. I was surprised to see her darken to a deep lead gray after a few weeks in Hawaii. In the crystal waters of her tank and under the bright Hawaiian sun, she, like the rest of the tourists, had developed a nice suntan. Most mornings, as I strolled by her tank, she came to the tank edge and gave me her cheery little two-noted call.

One morning, with little warning, she died in what seemed the most peaceful of ways. She just stopped swimming and sank. A salute to you, dear old girl.

CHAPTER EIGHT

Keiki

Keiki in Hawaiian means "child." This is also the name of the porpoise we captured, trained, and took back to sea with us. He was born out in the open sea somewhere, probably not far from the hazy, cloud-shrouded volcanic peaks of the Hawaiian Island chain. Such a moment of birth can only be imagined, but it must be full of danger. Day after day the school swims through the clear sea surface; at night the dozen porpoises huddle together and move slowly along. Some members close their eyes in a fitful doze, while others emit sporadic pops of sound that shoot out into the darkness and are lost in the shoreless sea. In the middle of the school a placid old female rises to the surface and in an instant blows out her warm breath, takes in a new lungful of air, and cruises on. Her sleep is fitful not so much because of the danger in the open sea—she is too old for that —but because her unborn bangs against her belly so hard.

Birth this time comes at night, which is the most dangerous time because the sharks are more active then. For the past few days the old female has been accompanied constantly by one of her adolescent offspring. This young female now moves closer, a gray shadow in the moonlight, as the school slows. The old porpoise whistles, a peculiar modulated call, and the school groups more tightly about her. The females swim around her, craning their necks in curiosity. The biggest porpoise in the school, a powerful, scarred old bull, rockets up out of the darkness, firing against her with a train of echolocation clicks. The mother's consort races between them, squealing a warning cry, claps her jaws ominously, and the bull veers away.

No other one, not even the old porpoise's other offspring, is allowed close to this parturition. The consort never leaves again as the baby begins to appear, first a tiny folded tail, as broad as two women's hands, all lopped over at the tips and limp as a piece of pliable rubber, and then more and more of the slender tail. At the same time the fetal membranes have ruptured, pouring their pints of fluid into the water. As the fluids disperse, they carry news of the event into the surrounding sea for all who might pick up the odor trail.

The constant clicking for the first time echoes back on the right side of the school. This echo is a faint sound, and softened compared to that which was snapped into the darkness by the school. The porpoises know from experience that the echo comes from about a thousand feet away and deep below the surface—maybe two hundred feet down. There is a flurry of activity in the school the instant the faint echo is heard. Staccato trains of clicks burst out, so fast that they sound like the angry buzz of a model airplane. Echoes instantly localize the object and tell the porpoises that it is moving directly toward the school.

The old female arches herself in the water as the uterine waves push and push against the baby, now almost wholly free, its umbilical cord looping below it. She seems oblivious of the tension around her. Then the newborn is free in the water amid a dark cloud of blood and fluid. A sharp twist by the old female and the umbilical cord breaks within an inch of the baby's abdomen. The consort instantly slips in beneath the little fetal-creased baby and presses urgently against its soft belly, forcing it to the surface. It takes a convulsive breath and begins to swim with rapid, ineffective little beats of its still soft flukes. In minutes the baby takes up station alongside his mother.

The school has tightened around the pair now, and the older porpoises can tell from subtle hints carried in their echoing sounds that a large shark is sculling purposefully toward them.

The baby nuzzles against his mother's side in an instinctive search for her nipples. She nudges him away, since the risks of the night have now come to command her, where the business of birth held sole importance minutes before. She speeds up, and her newborn strokes to her side with surprising strength. He positions himself alongside the tuck of her dorsal fin, where the water swirling past his mother's side sucks him in close to her and drags him along. Although he can't sense it, his mother is working harder now, her undulating flukes pushing against the sea with powerful strokes, a little faster than those of her schoolmates, for she is swimming for two, pulling her newborn along by the unseen current of water between them. She surfaces more often than her schoolmates, too, and as she does so her short-nosed baby bursts from the water in a childish leap for a gasping, not as yet wholly coordinated breath.

The swift animals on the flanks of the school continue to spray the water with percussive bursts of sound, mostly so high pitched that a human cannot hear them. Scouting members direct their beams in every direction. Their echoes tell the school that the ponderous shark coming up from the rear has paused in the wake, amid the odorous water, and has engulfed the drifting afterbirth. In a food-induced frenzy now, he turns and swims swiftly after the porpoise school and the baby who leaves a fitful odor trail from his still oozing umbilicus.

As the shark approaches, the school tightens even more, the porpoises swimming so close to one another that fins and flukes almost touch. The school moves faster and faster through the water, swimming as a precision unit, breaking free in low-angle leaps. After a few minutes the school slows, prompted by the outlying members, who sense that pursuit has stopped and that they are once again safe.

Soon the tight ranks loosen and the mother begins to scull slowly. Her baby feels the tug of water between them slacken and cease. He drifts along her belly poking gently with his snout, and under the mysterious guidance of the unlearned knowledge that is still predominant in him, he finds the two-inch slit in his mother's abdomen that conceals one of her nipples. He pokes harder now, and the nipple is forced outward, into the tip of his waiting snout. As he presses upward, she squeezes a stream of rich milk out to him for a second or two. He swallows and rises gasping to the surface. He will be fed this way for about a year before he knows the first joyous catch of a flying fish injured by one of his elder schoolmates. Even then, for eighteen months, he returns to his mother now and then, accepting a bit of milk from her, although she becomes less inclined to accept his proddings.

During these youthful days while the little porpoise clung close to his mother's side, he learned that the school was not amorphous but a structured community of which he was a very junior member. The old, scarred bull was a rough tyrant who circled and penetrated the school in almost ceaseless review. To him any new development seemed a challenge, and that was why he had come up aggressively to the little porpoise's mother during the birth.

It mattered where one slept in the school, and where one traveled as it moved along in search of food. As he grew, the little porpoise sometimes strayed a few yards away from his mother. Although he still spent the long hours when the school moved from one feeding ground to another nestled against her, partaking of her power when a fish school was detected and encircled, he would sometimes savor the moment with a coltish leap into the air. The last beats of his small tail, while his body was mostly in the air, thrust him grandly upward so that he could fall backward with a resounding crack of his body and dorsal fin against the surface. At times like these the young female who had attended his birth stayed with him, while his mother swam off in the finely honed routine of fish capture.

Gradually the little porpoise learned the tricks required to wrest a living from the impartial watery world in which he lived. Sometimes food was sensed deep below, and the entire school dove to pursue it. No slow descent was allowed, but instead the adults arched their powerful tails and stroked almost straight downward into the blackish blue below. The little porpoise, now half grown and strong enough to stay with his elders, felt the pressure on his body as the water weight bore against him, collapsing his lungs and pushing their air into the labyrinthine air passages of his skull and forehead. Once his lungs collapsed there was no longer a sensation of pressure on his body, for it was just like the water around it. As he dove, the water darkened, and soon he could see thin, ghostly flashes of pale bluish white. The canny porpoises herded the swift squid between them, moving along, keeping station with one another in the murk. A swift sideways flick of partially open jaws, a snap, and the squid was sucked in and held, before being gulped down whole.

The school had been two hundred feet below the surface for three minutes now, and vague sensations of discomfort became more insistent, until the youngest members arched upward and rose toward the glassy surface above. The school broke the surface almost as one, venting a series of explosive breaths. Not until they took several deep breaths could the school dive again.

Unlike their close relatives, the bottlenose porpoises of the California and Atlantic coasts, these Hawaiian animals never penetrated muddy waters, or narrow estuaries and shallow bays. They did swim into the winding channels of coral formations near island shores, though, and like their relatives found a variety of food to eat—octopus, crabs, and varicolored reef fishes.

From time to time as the school fed and cavorted close to shore, the rhythmic throbbing sound of an approaching fishing vessel could be heard. The school turned and raced toward the vessel, leaping in its wake and riding inside the cascading wave at its stern. The school raced deep down beneath the smooth, plunging hull, avoiding the ponderous revolving blades of the propeller, which they knew, from the dire experience of one of their scarred schoolmates, stopped for no animal. Porpoises took up station around the bow, which plunged ahead, cleaving up an arching sheet of water on either side of the stempost. There was status in who took up what position, and the half-grown porpoise was shunted aside by his mother and by the adults who were crowding in close to the sides of the bow. The big male asserted his authority and slipped in where his flukes felt and adjusted to the unseen thrust. By the most careful and instinctive adjustments of his body and flukes, the water began to push him forward. Tiny movements of his diving-plane flippers trimmed his movements just enough to maintain the precarious equilibrium, and along he raced, without so much as a beat of his tail. Others took up station below him, tucked back under the curve of the bow.

The little porpoise did not take part in these frolics while he stayed beside his mother, but finally, when he was about three-quarters grown and perhaps three years old, he began to spend more and more time with others of his own age and to respond less and less to her ministrations. He occasionally ducked in now at the bows of these ships, and caught brief rides while the old male was occupied at the choicest spot.

Keiki's young life had been something like this, as best we know, and it was about this time that we entered it, bringing these natural relationships to a sharp close and substituting a world of our own making in its place. This happened over Penguin Banks, a famous fishing ground located far out to sea between Molokai Island and Oahu Island. The collecting vessel *Imua,* of the Oceanic Institute and Sea Life Park, was prowling these waters for porpoises and had just come from an encounter with a school of about a thousand spotted porpoises, sleek speedsters known to fishermen as "leapers" because of their habit of making great high, arching leaps. Near this massive group the vessel came upon the school of bottlenose porpoises, who rushed to greet the ship with their usual alacrity.

High at the bow, riding in a perforated metal basket bolted to the stempost, was the captain, Georges Gilbert. Georges, who was a hapa haole—part Hawaiian and part French—was the most unflappable collector I ever knew, and also one of the most skillful. He watched a school of animals and noted the exact one he wished to catch. Then, with curt little hand signals, he directed his right-hand man and pure Hawaiian assistant,

Leo Kama, to take him to the desired animal. This day he set-tled on Keiki and, biding his time while the patrons of the school took their turns at the bow, waited for the moment when the young animal would swing in under him. Fifteen minutes later, Keiki grandly took up station in the prime location.

Georges stood above him, a gossamer net in his hand. The school had been lulled because Georges had made no previous lunges, and Keiki plunged on in the joy of the free ride. Then he shot upward. At the instant he broke the surface Georges lunged with the net.

Keiki dove, but too late, for he was entangled in the resilient meshes of the net. On deck Leo cut the engine, and Georges clambered from his basket to snatch up the snaking line that dipped directly downward into the blue water. Keiki whistled repeated cries of alarm and fright, to be answered by whistles and a great burst of echolocation from his schoolmates. His mother raced to him, 150 feet below the surface, and his sister who had taken such good care of him during his youth swam to the surface in a mindless frenzy of leaping, twisting jumps, the likes of which our collectors had never seen. The school butted fruitlessly against the line and squealed helpless cries to Keiki.

Nothing in their behavioral repertoire equipped them to help, and they circled in impotent fear as the porpoise was pulled closer and closer to the drifting boat. A stretcher was lowered slowly into the water at the stern of the *Imua*. Inexorably Keiki was brought closer and closer, and now a loop snaked down over his tail, securing it fast, thus spread-eagling the animal, if such can be done to an animal with no legs. In seconds he was escorted into the stretcher, and the clank of a chain could be heard as the little animal was winched on deck.

Porpoises seem to be frightened by capture in direct relation to their age. Very young porpoises with their mothers have been known to die of fright. Keiki was undoubtedly terrified by his capture, but like nearly all porpoises he lay still on his stretcher, flinching in fear only when he was touched. Later on, after he had become accustomed to humans, his fear of transport was still with him, and we occasionally gave him tranquilizers to ease his trauma.

Now, however, the two collectors happily contemplated their prize; he was a beauty, in perfect shape, and young enough to be prime training material. Several hours later the *Imua* docked at Honolulu, and Keiki was moved by hand into a waiting truck. In another twenty minutes his solicitous handlers lowered him carefully into a training tank at Sea Life Park, and began escorting him carefully around the tank to show him that a blind rush would not bring freedom. Within days Keiki was feeding, and soon after that was persuaded to take fish from his trainer's hand.

These were the first stages of one of the most exciting and challenging experiments we were to attempt with a porpoise; namely, the training of an animal that could be reliably released, free and unencumbered, in the open sea, asked to do a variety of scientific tasks, and then brought back into captivity. It was an experience we humans, at least, will never forget.
It all started because seamen on board fast ships, usually Navy vessels, kept reporting porpoises swimming with them while their ships were making as much as forty knots. Such speeds should be impossible for a porpoise unless it possesses muscular power far in excess of anything we biologists know. An alternative explanation exists. Perhaps, somehow, the drag produced by such an animal as it moves through the water is drastically reduced. The first question to be solved, I felt, was whether porpoises really do swim as fast as these observations indicate. For instance, none of the observers who had seen porpoises at the bows of fast ships could tell us how the porpoises approached their ships. If the porpoises came on an interception course from ahead of the ship, their speed could be much less than that of the ship. We knew that once they reached the bow they could ride along without moving a muscle in the pressure wave produced by the moving ship. Hence there is no mystery how they might keep up once they got there.

Dr. Thomas Lang, a tall, soft-spoken hydrodynamicist, joined forces with me to gather data on porpoise swimming speeds.

Tom had already gained some information from photographing porpoises' leaps, but this only related to the animal's ability to produce short bursts of high speed. It did not relate to long sustained, high-speed swimming such as would be used in any long dash at sea. He had also worked with a little Pacific striped porpoise in a hydrodynamic testing tank and found nothing unusual.

We both felt that a longer, more natural "race track" was needed. I suggested the long, narrow, palm-shaded lagoon that fronts the University of Hawaii Marine Station on Coconut Island, Hawaii. Permission was promptly obtained both from the university and from the accommodating Pauley family who own the upper end of the lagoon. I had a big, floatable cage made of chain-link fencing and pipe. We assembled this collapsible affair in the lagoon, and blocked off the remaining width of the channel with a net. And then we installed Keiki.

A racecourse was constructed down the length of the lagoon with electronic timers at the start and finish lines. Ultimately, after Keiki was trained, he stationed himself under a trainer's hand in his cage (often my daughter Susan). When the hand was lifted, he started for the doorway. As he crossed the gate, the experimenter watching from above pushed a button starting the timers and producing a "start signal" below water. Keiki then raced along a buoy line. A trainer stationed on a raft pressed another button the instant Keiki had crossed the finish line. If the time was satisfactory, a reward signal was given and a fish tossed to the expectant Keiki. He was then called home to his cage, using an underwater recall signal.

To develop a complicated set of interlocking trained behavior patterns such as this is an involved process. With Keiki we started at absolute rock bottom. At first, he adamantly refused to leave his cage, but instead bobbed quietly in the water near the back wall, looking nervously at all that unknown murky water beyond its safety. Like a bird who has lived its entire life in a cage, he announced he would rather stay home.

Luring him out with food didn't work. He refused to follow a swimmer. So I reluctantly strung a net across his cage, and

Keiki was literally forced out and down the lagoon, while I swam at his side to give him reassurance. Once at the other end of the lagoon, he refused to return, so the same slow process was carried out in reverse. Finally, after a number of such traverses, Keiki lost his fear and left his cage when we called him. The underwater signal we devised to call Keiki was a loud, pulsing click generated by an underwater speaker. Loud clicks were used because their regular repetition could be detected for a long distance through the more random noise usually found at sea. The sea is often a noisy place. This is especially true in shallow waters, where myriad tiny snapping shrimps may produce a crackling barrage of sharp clicking sounds. Fish, mollusks, and many other animals add to the din.

– To train Keiki to come to this sound, an underwater speaker was held within an inch or so of his snout, the sound was turned on, and when he randomly touched it, he was instantly given a reward. Next time the speaker was moved a few inches farther away, waiting for a touch from Keiki. Once he got the idea we wanted him to touch the speaker, it was a simple process to move it farther and farther away, and finally to call him from long distances. Then, when we pressed the switch turning on the sound, he came in a series of bounding leaps toward us, pressed the speaker, and stuck his head out of water, mouth open, waiting for the reward he knew he deserved.

Then began speed training. Keiki was taught that as long as he crossed the finish line (which we marked with a piece of white rope stretched across the shallow lagoon bottom) before the start signal stopped sounding, he would be rewarded. Once he understood this concept, we urged him to greater and greater speed by shortening the time it sounded. Another reward method, called a jackpot system, was started for especially fast runs. Each day before the race trials began I decided what the day's speed goal would be. If Keiki equaled or exceeded this time, he received a jackpot reward instead of his single fish. It worked just like a slot machine paying off. Trainer Matt Hinton at the finish line threw handfuls of fish into the water all around Keiki. Keiki always flinched in surprise, and then frantically began to pick up his riches, as if another porpoise was about to horn in.

Much time was wasted early in the tests by false starts. Keiki would bound out of the cage before we were ready, using up precious energy and, worse, confusing himself when he thought he had perceived a starting signal. A trainer has to be very careful when such confusion develops, as the animal's behavior is apt to become worse and worse. The animal may persist in his error until punishments pile up so often that the entire sequence begins to disintegrate.

To solve this problem, I stationed daughter Susan at the starting gate. She was required to call Keiki with a slap of her hand on the water and to develop a subtle and always uniform method of touching Keiki. When she lifted her hand just a trifle in a way that grew familiar to both of them, Keiki knew he should start for the gate as fast as he could go. Susie became very good at this, and our starting troubles disappeared, but new ones developed elsewhere in the routine. Keiki was dismayed when the sound signal stopped before he crossed the finish line. For some time we could not fathom why. Finally it dawned on us that while we had the entire routine firmly in mind, Keiki only looked at its parts. We were assuming he intuitively knew that the length of time the sound was turned on measured the time he was allowed to traverse the entire course. Actually, he knew nothing of the sort. When the sound shut off while he was swimming obediently toward the finish line as we had asked him to, he took it as a punishment for some unknown wrongdoing.

For a time the whole routine decayed. Finally Keiki trained us sufficiently well that we used the start signal only briefly to indicate his passage across the cage entrance to start the timers. Then, for only different degrees of reward, his top speed began to climb and climb. Soon he was swimming the sixty-one meter course in a single 7.5-second burst. He did this all on his side, peering at the buoy line as he raced along, wholly under water and never pausing to breathe. We could count his tail beats by the boils of water that rose to mark the sweep of his flukes. One of my colleagues calls them "whale footprints." From these runs he came back breathing hard. He beat his tail 2.5 times per second. Then his increases in speed began to level off. Apparently Keiki was going full throttle somewhere near his top capability. Surprisingly, when the speed of these runs was calculated, his record was 16.1 knots, or less than half of that required to explain the sea observations.

Happy hour at the end of the day was joyous fun for Keiki. I wanted him to have as much human contact as possible to prepare him for open-sea work, and to develop such contact into a pleasant and rewarding experience. We all jumped into the warm lagoon water and played tag with him, stroked him when he seemed to want it, and swam the length of the lagoon with him if he seemed inclined toward a leisurely turn down the channel. Keiki spontaneously decided it would be fun to jump over our arms when we held them on the surface of the water while floating. Tom and Pat Lang, Susie and Matt, all had their turns at this play. But I ruined the whole game by trying to teach him to jump over me, instead of just my arm, as I floated. To reward him while I floated, I carried the plastic bucket of reward fish between my knees. The first time Keiki flew over me, and I tossed him a reward. The next time he miscalculated and landed on me, summarily submerging me and the bucket. Reward fish floated free by the dozen, and Keiki was instantly racing happily around picking up his "jackpot" reward and waiting for the next chance to sink one of us.

About this time Karen Pryor dropped by with her son Ted. Karen, an attractive young woman who is also a magnificent animal trainer, full of innovation and insight, had developed the shows at Sea Life Park. She volunteered to act as my troubleshooter, unsnarling our shattered routines whenever our communication with Keiki failed. Together we decided that this morning was the time we should try Keiki in the open sea.

So Karen, Ted, Matt, Susie, and I piled into a big work skiff, set up the recall console on a thwart, pulled back the barrier net, and called Keiki. He hesitantly came around the net, like a dog invited into the house where he's not been welcome. We putted slowly toward the entrance channel with Keiki following along behind, dutifully coming to the speaker when we switched on the recall signal. Once the skiff was in the lagoon entrance, Keiki became perceptibly more nervous. He hung farther behind, and when we called him, he reluctantly came, but quickly retreated again into the lagoon. I stopped the engine and recalled him until he seemed to have gained a little confidence. Then we started the engine again and moved slowly out into open Kaneohe Bay.

Keiki followed us until we were three or four hundred yards from the lagoon, and then bolted suddenly, diving below the surface and out of sight. We looked anxiously in all directions. No Keiki, for dozens of seconds. A horrible sinking feeling assailed me as I thought we had lost our friendly Keiki with whom we had worked so long and happily. Then Ted and Matt spotted him, plunging swiftly along close to the reef edge, but beyond the lagoon entrance which he seemed to have sought. A glance at his lunging flight told me that he was terror-stricken. I had no idea if he could hear our signal through those hundreds of yards of water. I pushed the switch, and he stopped as if struck by a stone, turned, and came plodding back to us. When he arrived at the underwater speaker, blowing hard, his jaws were actually chattering and the whites of his eyes were showing. We knew that these signs were evidences of fear, just as they are in humans. Keiki was terrified, but he had come back to us.

"No more for today," I said with finality. We turned and gingerly led Keiki back into the lagoon. Once inside, he raced the length in a long gambol and circled with us in the confines of his cage, as delighted as we to be in his home again.

After that incident Keiki became more and more used to swimming free with us, and he even began to take strolls on his own. One early morning the phone rang in my living room, some miles from Coconut Island. It was Lester Zucharon, the skipper of the Coconut Island research vessel *Salpa*.

"What's up, Les?" I said, wondering why he should call me so early in the morning.

"Do you want your porpoise out?" he asked.

"My porpoise out? What do you mean?"

"Well, he was out all night, I think, but I've led him back in and closed the net. He followed the shore boat over to the dock in Kaneohe and came back with us. It seemed a little strange to me."

Indeed it was! Keiki had squeezed through his gate where it hadn't been tied properly, and had swum for more than a mile, unbidden and unrecalled, behind the shore boat, across open Kaneohe Bay. I wondered if perhaps he had grown overly confident in the open sea by himself, and worried lest we might see the last of him on a series of test Tom and I had planned for the open ocean near Rabbit Island.

Rabbit Island is a caldera, or partially sunken volcanic cone, set in the beautiful transparent tropical sea a mile off Makapuu Point, Hawaii. Inside it is a channel that is usually relatively calm. We planned to build a half-mile-long buoy lane, anchored securely at each end, along which Keiki would be asked to swim. Meanwhile, from a photographic station near the crest of Rabbit Island, we would photograph him as he swam by the numbered buoys. His cage would be anchored at one end of the line and would serve as his home during off hours. To prepare for the tests, his recall microphone was encapsulated in a streamlined pod suspended beneath a discarded surfboard. This we planned to tow behind a fast speedboat, calling Keiki as we went.

In this way we hoped to provide Keiki with a chance to swim in completely unrestricted waters where shallow depth could not impede him and where the course would be long enough to allow him full scope for his capabilities.

It proved a major feat of seamanship to set up the big wire cage in the swells that rolled in around Rabbit Island. Georges and Leo towed the cage around from Kaneohe Bay with the *Imua*. They then set anchors and attached a variety of cables to keep it stationary. Even so, ultimately the relentless power of the sea is not to be stopped by mere man, and we had a constant repair job on our hands, retrieving buoys that had broken loose, and repairing places where the chain link had chafed through. Keiki didn't seem to mind, though. Even though large swells moved through his home at times, and sometimes broke within it, Keiki maneuvered with effortless ease, a feat which we humans found impossible to duplicate when we swam with him.

I wondered what Keiki thought when he was left alone at night. That channel has yielded up many a large shark, and surely at times they were near the lonely little porpoise, and he was separated from them only by fencing whose strength he could not appreciate. Every morning, though, through two weeks of tests, Keiki greeted us cheerfully enough, gamboling in his cage with the divers that entered. When the gate was opened, he raced out into the clear sea toward the nearest boat and there attempted to solicit attention from the occupants by rising up in the water and peering at them. We grew so unconcerned about him that occasionally he was forgotten, and all the motorboats would cruise off and leave him. When he found himself alone, he would race for the nearest boat, where, I suspect, the apparent safety of human company lay. Being highly social animals, porpoises do not like to be alone, even if humans are their only friends.

Keiki appeared to enjoy his three- or four-hour daily outings. He willingly raced along with the speedboats, periodically jumping free in long, low leaps. He spent much time in the spilling wake of the pacing vessel, obviously using the force of the waves as a way of gaining a little extra speed.

Those who operated the pacing vessel were sure Keiki was routinely cruising at twenty to twenty-five knots, as the craft jolted along over the swells throwing spray into the air. But when the photographs were studied and precise timing determined, Keiki's top speed was only a little over fourteen knots. Thus, one lesson learned was that it is very difficult to judge boat speed at sea. Another was surely that Keiki could not be expected to keep pace with a destroyer going thirty knots. Tom Lang and Karen Pryor later studied a slimmer oceanic porpoise, the Hawaiian kiko, or spotted porpoise (*Stenella attenuata*), and found that it was a faster form than Keiki's species (*Tursiops gilli*), but even it clocked top speeds of only a little over twenty-three knots.

We feel it safe to conclude that these species and probably

most other kinds of porpoises could only hitch a ride from a fast-moving ship by intercepting it at a slower speed and then using the pressure field within the bow wave to ride relatively effortlessly along.

Keiki completed these tests apparently without thought of leaving us. Our confidence that trained animals, such as Keiki, might be useful in porpoise-human teams was greatly bolstered by this triumph, as well as by the work of the U.S. Navy porpoise, Tuffy, who was at the same time developing his skills for future work with the Sea Lab II manned undersea habitat.

Taylor A. ("Tap") Pryor, the visionary young founder and president of the Makapuu Oceanic Center built on the Oahu shore near Rabbit Island, which includes the Oceanic Institute where Keiki stayed when he wasn't working, had been developing plans of his own for a manned undersea habitat. He built and installed a small two-man habitat called "Oceanic I" nearly on the spot where Keiki's cage had been anchored. Now that Keiki had completed his speed trials, Tap pressed him into training to assist his diving teams. Keiki learned all sorts of tasks, such as carrying bottom samples to the tender vessel above, bringing new scuba gas bottles to men working on the bottom, carrying messages, and even allowing divers to hold on to his dorsal fin while he towed them to the surface.

Through all these complex maneuvers Keiki, it always seemed to me, enjoyed the experience hugely. If he was asked to carry a message to divers waiting below, he grasped the plate on which the message was scrawled, threw his flukes into the air, and descended rapidly to his contact man (the one with the fish) in the diving team working on the bottom. If, for example, he found them huddled over some fitting, Keiki would stick his snout in amongst them, peering this way and that to see what was going on. The contact diver would look up to find Keiki inches away, still holding his message. Trading the message plate for a section of fish, the diver rubbed it clean with his elbow, scrawled an answer on it in grease pencil, scratched Keiki between the flippers, and gave him back the plate. With a boyish jerk, Keiki swung around and rocketed toward the surface and the tender vessel.

Because it is often a nuisance, and sometimes dangerous (because of sharks), for a diver to carry bits of fish around with him, Karen began an ingenious bit of training. She asked Keiki to work for porpoise money—big circular plastic disks. Before long, Keiki would carry out his assigned duty, take a token in reward for it, and swim to the surface, where an inverted wire cage floated. This cage—the "Porpoise National Bank" as it came to be called—was the depository for porpoise money, so Keiki dutifully deposited the disk by floating it up into the cage. Periodically, a sound signal was played into the water that told Keiki the Porpoise National Bank was open and that he could cash in his chips for fish. He rushed over, sculling expectantly as the trainer reached in, trading a disk for a fish until the bank was empty.

What is the future of such work as Keiki has performed for us? Can we expect porpoise couriers, or porpoise sheep dogs herding in marine pastures? Not yet. In my view, we yet have much to learn, especially about our control over such animals. Why do they stay? Would Keiki have stayed if a group of wild bottlenose porpoises had come by when he was working for us? We don't know, but we do know that in some species these human-porpoise bonds may be made stronger than in others, as we shall see in a later chapter.

In many ways porpoises are difficult animals to handle. They have special health problems, such as a very high susceptibility to respiratory disease, brought on, in part at least, by inefficient mechanisms for cleaning their lungs; the porpoise apparently has no need of such a mechanism in the clean air of the open sea. Probably as a result, pneumonia can be a devastating problem in captivity. Their health must be watched constantly, and they cannot simply be left to their own devices like a pet dog. Then, because they lack walking legs, wherever they go one must provide them with some sort of pond as a home. Fresh water won't do for very long, for they soon develop skin problems, and the reduced buoyancy makes them work extra hard. They must have food as good as any human requires, and they eat a great deal, probably because constant swimming in water requires a lot of energy. All this means that work with porpoises at sea cannot be a casual affair but requires trainers, medical skill, food, housing, time, and money. These things indicate to me that the situations in which porpoises can be used as human companions and helpmates are still special ones.

But there are such special circumstances where the use of trained animals at sea provides benefits that are difficult to match by other means. Porpoises and seals can dive through great depth ranges, perhaps most species routinely going as deep as seven or eight hundred feet with ease. Human divers find that such vertical excursions are their most difficult and tiring problem. Divers living in habitats below the sea cannot go to the surface at all, upon pain of violent death, and here a porpoise can be a vital link. If the human can work at depth while the porpoise performs the courier service, human efficiency could be greatly enhanced. Then, porpoises can navigate with consummate ease at sea, a thing human divers find difficult and dangerous. Porpoises can hear incredibly well under water. Once again, humans are poorly adapted to do this. Porpoises can localize sound sources in an instant, allowing them to home in on a diver who is calling, even though the water may be murky or even black at night.

Porpoises are swift, especially when compared with man, and hydrodynamically adept. Long swims, in the roughest water, mean nothing to them.

If open-sea aquaculture becomes a viable human activity, the porpoise may well become our truly aquatic counterpart of the sheep dog. It should be a relatively simple matter to teach them to "ride fences" in search of predators or poachers, or to bring back samples from undersea pastures.

To advance these possibilities we will have to practice more, under many circumstances, and we must learn all we can about handling porpoises and, especially, about health and disease in porpoises. Porpoise doctors like Dr. Sam Ridgway and Dr. William Medway are now systematically gathering the vital data on health norms and treatment that we must have.

As a tool allowing us to learn about the porpoise itself, the use of these trained, unfettered sea animals is by far the best available way to approach some questions. For instance, what better way to learn about diving capability than to take a trained animal to sea and ask it to dive for you? It can carry appropriate instruments to tell us how far it can dive, how long it takes, what happens to its heart, brain, and kidneys during a dive, and how often it can submerge. It was with this in mind that we began work with Pono.

~~~~~~

CHAPTER NINE

Pono

In the spring of 1965, news of a strange new porpoise reached me from Hawaii. Georges Gilbert told me that several times far offshore he had seen a calico porpoise whose colors were pink and gray, but it had always eluded him. Georges then insisted that the animal was covered with pink polka dots. Since I had known Georges as an extremely acute and accurate observer, and even though, from most seamen, the story was such as to make me doubt, I had to conclude that somewhere out there in the lonely reaches of the Pacific swam a group of polka-dot porpoises.

One day the phone rang in my UCLA office. It was Karen Pryor, and she told me that they had finally caught the elusive creature and that he was alive and swimming strongly in the Sea Life Park tanks at Makapuu Point, on the island of Oahu. Karen, who also reports what she sees, said he was the most grotesque-looking porpoise she had ever seen—great goggle eyes, his body randomly covered with round pinkish spots about the diameter of a silver dollar. Furthermore, he had a ski snoot that would do credit to Bob Hope.

The latter feature struck a bell with me. I knew of an animal that had been found several times in the Atlantic Ocean, but only twice, so far as I knew, in the Pacific. Both these Pacific records were animals that had stranded on the beach—one a skull from the Galápagos Islands and the other a whole animal that had washed ashore at Stinson Beach, California, where it was picked up by my friend Dr. Bob Orr. It has a long, sloping snout that merges imperceptibly into its forehead. It is called the rough-tooth porpoise (*Steno bredanensis*) because of vertical striations or grooves found on its teeth in the Atlantic specimens.

When we checked out the new find, my surmise proved correct; Sea Life Park had the first live specimen of this peculiar animal. Many more were to follow. We soon came to know this animal as one full of surprises, one not docile to every human order, as our old friend the bottlenose porpoise is apt to be, but insisting upon a degree of dignity and equality with humans. It proved to have extraordinary manipulative capacities, being able to do such things as opening gates with its mouth, or pulling the hypodermic needle from one of its schoolmates who was being given penicillin. If handled carefully, it became the tamest of any trained porpoise. *Stenos* just simply impress one as intelligent, however you define it.

Shortly after Karen's call, I flew to Hawaii to see this exciting new acquisition. As I walked up to the edge of the training tank, the creature poked its head obligingly from the water. At that first glance and ever afterward I have been struck by the resemblance of these *Stenos* to extinct ichthyosaurs, seagoing reptiles from the age of dinosaurs. Its long snout lined with stout, pointed teeth, the big brown protruding eyes, and the reptilian head contours are part of this impression, as are the barrel-chested, chunky body and large paddle-shaped fins and flippers.

I have yet to see an uglier porpoise. The homeliness of older animals is even greater, since they tend to become obese and heavily scarred. The lips and foreheads, especially of old animals, are often white with crisscrossed scars, which I now believe to come from encounters with squid, a major part of their diet. The polka dots also proved to be scars and are much more common in old animals. Each is a slightly raised mound of pinkish-white scar tissue surrounded by the normal gray-colored skin. Occasionally in later captures we found open wounds on these animals, circular in outline, which often cut completely through the three-quarter-inch blubber to the muscle beneath. I suspect these heal, forming the polka dots.

It was clear that the life of a *Steno* is not all joyous, carefree gamboling in the open ocean, but that an unknown assailant is abundant. As I will discuss later, in connection with spinner porpoises, we now think the culprit to be a tiny and very strange shark.

It didn't take much training work with these animals to find that they were remarkable creatures in ways that didn't show on the surface. They adapted to captivity with remarkable ease, and learned our peculiar tasks so quickly it seemed they had been doing them all their lives. Here, I thought, might be the perfect animal to extend Keiki's open-ocean experiments.

Keiki's work at sea had opened exciting new vistas. We had proved to ourselves, at least, that one could work with a porpoise in the open sea and carry out complicated experiments involving trained behavior. After all, during his two months of accumulated "sea time" Keiki had worked faithfully for his dinner just as if he had been in a tank ashore. Even though schools of fish swam near him, he ignored them, coming to the tending skiff for his herring. Our control over his behavior seemed just as sure as ever, and, in fact, we began to feel that the real impediment to open-ocean work had been our own reluctance to try.

Once we realized these things, it became obvious that many kinds of experiments we could not do in tanks were now possible. For example, many questions surround the amazing ability of marine mammals to dive. No one knew how they were able to avoid the bends, or how deep they could go, and many details of their body chemistry and function during dives remained mysteries. A trained and instrumented animal diving in deep water at sea instead of in a shallow cement tank or locked inside a pressure chamber ashore should tell us a great deal.

Though, for the time being, I was interested in testing trained open-ocean porpoises as diving subjects, many other tantalizing questions seemed ripe for open-ocean work. One could envision animals carrying instruments of many kinds and returning them to the handler on command. One might gather data from inside porpoise schools, where human observers uniformly caused such disruption that nothing was likely to be natural. Perhaps one might learn in this way what wild porpoise life was really like. One might also send couriers on photographic explorations of interesting areas of sea bottom.

But for the moment our questions concerned diving, and intuitively I expected *Stenos* to be perfect material. I had a hunch that their large eyes equipped them to hunt in dim light, perhaps on dives deep below the surface into the shadowy depths inhabited by oceanic squid. Their singular barrel chest heightened this impression. It was the sort of body I imagined a diving animal should have. No more science than that—just hunches. Though, come to think of it, such hunches really underlie most scientific experiments, and we should cherish rather than avoid them. We are still no closer to knowing whether these speculations are true, but on these premises I asked for a *Steno* to work with. Karen obliged and introduced me to Pono (Hawaiian for "justice"), a creature as lumpy and Mesozoic as any *Steno*.

Our plan for Pono was to train her to work in the open sea free from any actual restraint. Once in water of a thousand feet depth or more, Pono would be required to swim down along a lengthy weighted electrical cable hung from the rail of a vessel and to press a lever suspended at its bottom end. Her press would trip a switch, sending a signal to the deck that signified she had reached the bottom of the line. On deck we were notified of this by the lighting of a small red electric bulb. The same signal that told us she had reached the end of the line would also tell us how long it had taken for her to make her dive. We could then note the time she required to ascend, and thus an over-all description of the course of her dive could be drawn. Fatefully, we also installed a waterproof doorbell at the bottom which would ring only when Pono had pressed hard enough to light the lamp on deck. The ringing would let Pono know when she had pressed hard enough.

I pondered how we could handle Pono in the open sea. This work was going to take place much farther from shore than Keiki's tests, and we would not have a floating cage to provide a nighttime home for Pono. The waves had long since battered Keiki's cage into uselessness. Finally we had cut it loose, allowing it to sink to the bottom of the sea. I didn't have money to build another such cage. The solution, I thought, would be to train Pono to swim onto a stretcher and allow herself to be hoisted free of the water. If she would let us perpetrate this indignity upon her aquatic soul, so my reasoning went, she could be asked to swim onto the stretcher at sea and be hoisted on deck for the trips to and from work. At night, we would hold her in a plastic swimming pool set on the dock.

I was bolstered in my feeling that we could train Pono to do these things by the experiences of Adolph Frohn, the world's first trainer of porpoises. He had done his early work at Marine Studios, and I remembered seeing him work with his star performer, Flippy. When I visited him in the early 1950s, Flippy occupied a tank with three other bottlenose porpoises. Adolph had taught Flippy to enter the canvas stretcher and to be cranked a couple of feet above the surface by means of a small hand winch. Flippy's tank mates were jealous of this extra attention and took out their frustrations by nipping at Flippy's exposed flukes every time he was hoisted from the water. Flippy soon learned that it behooved him to get his tail out of reach. I can see that animal yet, swimming onto the stretcher and arching his flukes and tail out of reach as Adolph strained at the creaking winch, while the other porpoises rose up, trying to plant a couple of rows of teeth into any available exposed anatomy.

At any rate, knowing of this work, I felt sure we could ask Pono to do the same. She proved incredibly adept. Within a few days she could be called by a slap of the hand against the tank wall and guided onto the sunken stretcher, where she lay immobile while we winched her, dripping and flaccid as a bagful of jelly, free of the water. As Pono grew to trust her trainer, Dotty Samson, and me, we found we could tug and haul at her with complete impunity. By this means, I taught her to lie in a relaxed position on her side as the stretcher came free of the water. Dotty went much further. She and Pono became inseparable pals. There was literally no indignity that Dotty could dish out that fazed Pono in the slightest. For example, one day Dotty called me to tankside and asked me to watch the latest. She jumped in the tank, called Pono over, and then stood on Pono's back, forcing the animal to the tank bottom. Pono simply sank down under Dotty's weight and lay there looking placidly up through the water while Dotty perched on her for what seemed an interminable length of time. They swam together, Dotty taking rides by holding on to her dorsal fin. Dotty felt free to stroke Pono all over, including the sensitive areas of her eyes and blowhole. Pono accepted all this in a spirit of complete participation and utterly without rancor.

All this was what we might expect from a very adept bottlenose porpoise, but Pono went a step further in a way that was peculiarly ingratiating to me. Pono picked and chose her human friends with care, accepting those who for one reason or another had won her trust, and rejecting those who had not. This central core of dignity, of the measure of her own rights and worth, lay deep in Pono's spirit. A male trainer who briefly took over part of the training duties never achieved the slightest rapport with Pono. He was harsh, abrupt, and insensitive to her feelings, using conditioned response training techniques in an austere manner that "turned off" Pono completely. She quickly became refractory and began to nip. Before long he could not come to tankside without Pono's rising up in an attempt to grasp him with her long, efficient rows of teeth. At length I had to relieve him of his duties, leaving the whole program to Karen, Dotty, and myself. It worked vastly better that way, as Pono, within a day, reverted to her usual docile self again.

For all Pono's bond with us, I worried lest she leave us as soon as she was taken to sea. We suspected that we could make her feel "restrained" by teaching her to wear a harness over her back to which, initially, we attached a tether rope. Later, so our plan went, we would eliminate the line and simply trust to the feeling of restraint that the harness might give her. So weeks were spent in harness design and training. Ultimately, Pono swam to Dotty's side, allowed the harness to be strapped on, and began her workday training on other matters.

Before long everything was ready. Pono was trained, and the "black boxes" that controlled our signaling and recording systems (designed and built by instrument designer Howard Baldwin) were working. We chose a beautiful little harbor called Pokai Bay on the lee shore of Oahu Island for the work. Most of the time the sea was calm there, and the sea bottom dropped off very rapidly into deep water. It was about a mile from the harbor to a thousand feet of water.

I decided to send Pono and the vessel from which we would work around to Pokai Bay separately. Sea voyages on the deck of a ship are very hard on porpoises. Their bodies, unsupported by water, roll with every movement of the ship, and the slow speed of vessels makes these trips very long for the animals. Accordingly, we equipped a pickup truck for Pono. Foam-rubber mattresses lined the truck bed, sheets were provided to keep the wind away, and a cover was built to keep off the sun. Uncomplaining Pono came to her stretcher and let us hoist her out of the water and carry her to the truck. There we bedded her down and dipped water over her to keep her skin moist. She rolled her big brown goggle eyes up at us in curiosity, but without the slightest show of concern.

I've taken many trips with porpoises and whales in the back of various trucks, and they are usually fun because of the reactions of pedestrians and other drivers. The Pono trip was no exception as we stopped for gas and spectators quickly gathered. "Wotcha got there, anyway? A shark?" "Is it dead?" "How come it don't bite you?" "What are you doing with it?" "How can it breathe in there without water?" On and on the questions went. Tentative fingers reached out to touch Pono's flukes (behavior we tried to suppress for her sake). The questions kept coming until the truck pulled away onto the highway. Even there interest continued as cars drove up close for a look and questions formed on people's lips.

At Pokai Bay the launching ramp was jammed with a gaggle of

little brown-skinned children, who were immeasurably excited when they realized what we were planning to do. Pono's stretcher was launched and a long leash snapped on her harness. We gingerly led her out into waist-deep water and began to take her for an aquatic stroll. As soon as she found out where she was—in the sea—she began to tug at the leash like an enthusiastic hunting dog. Far out in the bay the *Imua* lay at anchor. I wanted to test our control over Pono, so we brought her close to shore, unsnapped her, and made our way toward the distant vessel. Pono swam alongside our skiff, looking up at us. Then suddenly she broke the water in two long, joyous leaps and began circling us and swimming ahead. At the *Imua* the stretcher and other gear were not ready, so Pono was left in the water, swimming around us and coming back dutifully now and then when I sounded the underwater recall buzzer. Once she heard a passing boat and coltishly broke water and began to swim away toward it. My recall stopped her at once, and seconds later her funny old head popped up alongside the rail of the *Imua* for a reward.

Pono began to look for things to play with—probably a happy time for her after the long weeks in the austere confines of the oceanarium tank. First she dove and came up with the bologna rind tossed overboard by the crew of the *Imua* during lunch. This she pushed up into the air near the rail, as if presenting it to us. The she dove again, this time retrieving a soggy towel from the bay bottom twenty feet below.

It was getting dark, so a skiffload of us escorted Pono ashore, where we snapped on her leash and led her into the waiting stretcher. A small plastic swimming pool had been erected on the dock for her. My assistants and I carried Pono over, staggering with her weight, and slid her into the pool. It was so shallow that she lay partly on her side, her tail bent inside the little pool.

I worried for fear the curious people who flocked around the dock would harm her, so we kept close watch throughout the night. In my stint I sat there stroking Pono, who lay uncomplaining and good-natured, looking goggle-eyed and trustfully upward at me. A little boy approached and thoughtlessly poked at her with a finger, as boys will do. Nothing happened. He came close again, and Pono rose part way out of the water on one pectoral flipper, snapping. The startled boy scuttled back as Pono subsided into the water. It seemed remarkable to me how quickly she knew she had to teach that boy a lesson, and how completely docile she remained with me, even though her ire had obviously been raised.

I looked down at her, the gulf between us unbridgeable except by my imaginings about her thoughts and by the trust we had demonstrated by mutual acts of confidence over the previous weeks. What *did* she think? How had she been able to reconcile all of the incredibily bizarre (to her) happenings of the weeks just past, and yet emerge with obvious trust between us, and especially between her and Dotty? Nothing that had happened to her was within the experience of her tribe. What could we conceive to be the function of such an obvious and deep capacity for affection and trust in her world far out in the open Pacific? Didn't this tell us, even if by this most fleeting of glimpses, that the little microcosm of a porpoise school encompasses bonds between animals, a complexity of social interaction, and learning and familial ties that must far exceed the simplistic view we scientists currently hold? In some fashion, within the framework of social interaction and sensory capacity lie explanations why porpoises and their allies are such advanced, complex animals living in a world populated almost entirely by organisms of far less capacity.

Next morning Pono was launched much less ceremoniously than on the day before. We matter-of-factly cruised to the *Imua* with Pono swimming and leaping alongside our skiff. From time to time we called her to skiffside and she came to us, obedient as a trained dog. This time preparations were complete on the *Imua,* and the stretcher was rigged to bring Pono aboard.

In later experiments with other animals we abandoned the stretcher idea and used a little catamaran which supported a towable aluminum cage into which animals were placed at night. But that idea had not yet occurred to us. Dotty and I looked at each other, the notion dawning that, since Pono now played happily about the *Imua*, if we simply called her to the rail repeatedly, it would be easier on everyone, especially Pono, if we simply swam her to work. So she was left in the water, and the engines of the *Imua* started. I hoped she would have sense enough to avoid the big, churning propeller. To my horror, she stationed herself in the propeller wash, seemingly within inches of the thrashing blades, ducking from time to time to one side or the other, where she rose for a breath of air, only to return again under the stern. But, fortunately, she never touched the propeller. Like all porpoises, Pono is exquisitely aware of the flow of water around her body, and I suspect she was carried along in this way, having to exert much less energy than for a straight swim in open, undisturbed water.

A third of a mile offshore Pono found a big tuft of floating sargasso weed, which she proceeded to balance on the tip of her snout. Obviously it was a real porpoise toy. From time to time I recalled her to the rail of the ship, and each time she rushed in, losing the sargasso. After snapping up her fish reward, she turned in obvious haste, swimming back fifty to seventy-five yards to pick up her precious seaweed. Sometimes balancing it on her dorsal fin, sometimes on a flipper, or even on the leading edge of her flukes, she raced up abreast of the ship again and began pacing us out to sea.

Finally, about one and a half miles offshore, where the water is fifteen hundred feet deep, the *Imua* stopped and we began to drift. The lever with the waterproof doorbell attached was lowered over the side. Dotty then required Pono to press the lever, which she would soon do at the bottom of every dive. Pono performed just as if she were in her training tank at Oceanic Institute—as if she had no real notion she was actually in the open sea only a dozen miles from the place where she had been captured some months before.

Slowly, a few feet at a time, we began to lower the apparatus. By the time it was twenty-five feet down, Pono had sufficient swimming room to show the behavior pattern that she would exhibit during the remainder of the test. She swam to the ship's rail, pressed her snout against a small paddle, and Dotty gave her the start signal. To do this, Dotty placed her hand on Pono's forehead, and when it was taken away, Pono knew she should dive. She turned away, upended, and swam nearly vertically downward. The water was glassy clear and calm, allowing us to see her descent toward the hoop shining greenish white in the dark blue water below. Only the barrel outline of her body and the wide sweep of her flukes could be seen, so steep was her descent. Then came a wait of a few seconds, and the red light flashed on the console, indicating a successful lever press at the bottom. On deck the timer that had been started when Pono dove stopped, indicating the time required for descent. I snapped on the stopwatch to time the ascent. Down below Pono heard the buzzer and knew she would be rewarded when she reached the surface. In these shallow dives, she did not always breathe immediately after surfacing, showing us how easy the dive had been. Instead she leveled off at the surface, cruising unconcernedly around before venting a typical explosive breath. Down and down we lowered the lever—fifty, seventy-five, eighty-five, a hundred, a hundred and ten, a hundred and twenty feet.

Toward afternoon the wind picked up and little swells began to roll past us. While our work was made harder, it was obvious that Pono was delighted. Each time she returned to us, she circled out to sea fifty to seventy-five yards and came racing back, riding in the swells and body-surfing down their little foreslopes. Once in the lee of the *Imua*, she cruised directly toward us under water and then popped her head up ready for the next test.

By afternoon Pono had made more than fifty dives and seemed fresh as a daisy. Any human asked to give such a performance would have been prostrate with fatigue. Then, for reasons which at first we didn't understand, Pono began to get skittish. She made wide circles at sea, some two or three hundred yards away from us, coming in alongside the ship at points away from the diving cable. Through the chop that now ruffled the sea surface, Dotty began to notice light flashes flickering around the diving cable, deep in the water. She stared intently down at the darkening water; the rest of us continued our apprehensive watch for Pono. Dotty commented that they looked like big fish. Next came the comment that they might be sharks. This possibility brought us all scurrying to the ship's rail. Sure enough, we began to make out the light-brownish forms of four sharks, each five feet long, swimming around and around the cable. No wonder Pono was reluctant to come in to her station at the top of the cable!

At once I ordered all gear brought on board and preparations made to hoist Pono in the stretcher. In seconds the lever and the coils of wet cable lay bunched on deck. Pono, however, had become more and more nervous. She circled the *Imua*, many dozens of yards out, sometimes planing along with her head partly out of water. The recall signal failed to bring her in. On the one hand her fear seemed to have forced her away from the ship, but on the other her attachment to us was still strong.

She sped along, farther and farther at sea, only now and then appearing at the surface—a fin, misty blow, and no more. I frantically pressed and repressed the recall signal. Dotty watched silently as her friend circled away. Soon Pono was gone altogether, and I ordered the *Imua* to get under way, hoping that by moving from the area where the sharks had congregated we could bring our frightened friend to us again. Her departure had been so gradual and so involved with circling that we really had no idea which way to turn.

After a few minutes under power, I ordered the engine stopped and the recall begun again. It pulsed unheeded out into the surrounding sea. We searched until dark, but no Pono. Dotty pleaded with me to use the skiff as a search boat, since it could travel much faster than the plodding old *Imua*. I assented, and she and Howard began a series of wide circles, inspecting the vacant sea. They found nothing. But the sight of Dotty, standing in the bow steadying herself with the painter, remains with me. Her taut posture and concentrated gaze across the water told eloquently enough that for her this was not just an experiment gone awry but a wrenching separation from a dear friend. Whatever Pono felt, she was nowhere to be found.

She was gone. We hoped to bring her back next day, but that, too, failed. We could only hope that she would find her schoolmates again offshore.

Later I learned the probable answer to why the sharks had congregated around the instrument cable. Some remarkable experiments in Florida had shown that sharks are strongly attracted to pulsing low-frequency sounds. The buzzer we had required Pono to press made just such a noise. Thus each time she signaled a successful dive to us she also gathered sharks from the surrounding sea and insured the fate of our tests!

Porpoises sense each other with remarkable ease over long distances at sea, so we had hope that Pono would regain her old school. Fortunately, she was not wearing her harness when she departed. She was unencumbered and could hope to keep up with a fast-moving wild school. We wondered apprehensively whether the soft life of captivity had reduced her stamina.

A day later a Pokai Bay fisherman called us at the Oceanic Institute. He had been fishing off Makaha a few miles west of our study area when a lone porpoise had circled his craft. It poked its head from the water and looked at him, and after a few minutes disappeared. This odd behavior, unlike anything one sees from wild porpoises, made us sure it was Pono.

Another fruitless search followed. I wondered how long a lone porpoise could survive at sea, bereft of the protection afforded by schoolmates. How long could a single animal evade the stealthy pursuit of the abundant sharks in the area when it could rely only on its own senses and not the summed awareness of its school?

More than a month later, I was on board the *Imua* far off the lee shore of Oahu, twenty miles from Pokai Bay. A big school of *Stenos* was sighted. In the long swells group after group appeared "finning" low in the water. I quickly went below and rigged the recall signal device. I pressed the key as the *Imua* bucked her way slowly in the heft and fall of the sea. We came near a small group of perhaps eight *Stenos*, and one swam abruptly toward us, coming to the rail near the pulsing recall signal. It raised its spotted head free of the water along the ship's waist. The animal looked up at us, subsiding again into the water, making its way leisurely forward under our bow and then cutting back to the waiting group of animals moving slowly a dozen yards abeam. Then we were sure Pono was home.

Though we had tried hard to find and recapture Pono, in retrospect our work with her was the best kind of experimental interlude. We had caught her, brought her into our world, and learned much from her. And then, before these relationships could settle into a humdrum and tedious affair, she took her leave and returned to the school where all her old ties existed. My night on the dock with her convinced me that these ties must be strong. I hope she's out there yet, living out her days in the fashion of her ancestors.

CHAPTER TEN

The Semisubmersible Seasick Machine

More than any other mammals, porpoises and whales are truly creatures of the water. Even though they leap into the air and can be maintained out of water for fairly long periods, obviously they do not belong to the above-water world. Ninety percent of their lives is spent feeding and socializing below the surface. The problems of the naturalist who tries to observe them are many. Some porpoise species will ride a ship's bow, but many are shy creatures who flee from surface craft and thus remain almost unknown to science. Porpoises are nearly always on the move. A large number of species (there are about eighty known) live in seas or rivers where the water is dirty, and thus even observation from above is difficult.

As I learned more of these animals, I came to treasure the scattered and brief moments at sea when an animal revealed a fragment of his real life to me. I pondered how one could ex-

pand these vignettes into a more comprehensive picture of porpoises as they really are. Watching porpoises in an oceanarium
simply would not do. We had learned a good deal from such
captives, but the nagging certainty that little of their behavior
was natural always remained.

In captivity usually two or more species are thrown together
into unnatural assemblages that seldom or never exist in nature.
Confinement compresses a porpoise's activity, no matter how
large the tank. The difference is between forty to sixty miles
of daily travel and movement in a tank two hundred feet in
diameter. The difference is the chance to dive out of sight of the
surface—perhaps to over a thousand feet for some porpoises—
versus perhaps twenty-five feet in captivity. The difference is a
limitless world where aggression and fear can reorder social structure within and between schools and a world where these forces
are contained by cement walls. In captivity shy porpoises can't
move far away from aggressive ones. In fact, confinement compresses natural activity so tightly that it may be distorted virtually beyond recognition. The captive porpoise forms unnatural
life patterns, like the antelope in the zoo, used to ranging many
miles a day, who comes to promenade in a stereotyped figure
eight around his cage until the single track is rutted a foot below
the surrounding soil.

Rigid daily regimes such as show routines are especially stress-
ful. The wise oceanarium manager gives his porpoises vacations,
for otherwise they will die. Such performing porpoise schools
seem never to reproduce; the only oceanarium births occur in
relatively undisturbed groups not required to conform to an intricate show routine. This is the case even though much of the
daily activity of show porpoises may be sexual, sometimes to
the distress of trainers who have to contend with love-making
porpoises when the script calls for a high jump.

How could I watch wild porpoises? How could they be made
to stand still? Georges Gilbert gave me the crucial information.
As Georges collected around the Oahu coast, he learned that he
could predict where porpoises could be found. He came to recognize individual animals, just as we had earlier learned to know

Old Scarback in San Diego Bay. Animals with scars and peculiar patterns were sighted from the *Imua's* bow. For instance, one bizarre spinner porpoise with two dorsal fins made its appearance from time to time when the *Imua* cruised between Barbers Point and Diamond Head. The forward fin was a normal one, with a small, withered, and deformed fin behind.

Georges was able to say that five schools of kiko and spinner porpoises had divided the Oahu shore into sectors which they seldom seemed to leave. Spinner porpoises, slim, delicate creatures which habitually take glorious spinning leaps into the air, formed one group of discrete schools nearshore, while the kikos, or jumping porpoises, usually remained farther at sea. Just as Frank and Boots and I had been boycotted by the San Diego bottlenose porpoises, who came to avoid the *Geronimo* like poison, Georges received the same cold shoulder from one of the spinner schools. After he had captured half a dozen animals from the school, he could no longer approach it. Good fisherman that he was, Georges reasoned that they recognized the sound of the *Imua's* engines, so next time he approached with the engine revved up, and sure enough, he netted another animal. But that was all. High or low speed, it made no difference after that. The school stayed away and could not be approached for more than a year. This frightened school was seen only between Kaena Point and Barbers Point, a twenty-four-mile stretch of shoreline. All the while, the Waikiki school remained friendly, until harassment by other collectors ultimately caused it to reject all contact with ships.

One school Georges could locate with special ease was a group of perhaps two hundred and fifty kiko porpoises that frequented the lee coast of Oahu. We found that about 60 percent of the time we could cruise offshore from Pokai Bay and find this school. One reason for our continued success, I suspect, was that kikos are not especially good show animals. They are skittish and difficult to train as compared to some of their more tractable relatives, like the bottlenose porpoise. This meant that the school had not been pursued to the same degree as other groups. Here,

I thought, might be a group of porpoises that could be studied in nature. At least, we could usually find them, and that was saying a lot.

The next question was: How could I see what the animals were doing? The vantage point from a ship was out. One could never learn much of social groupings or other behavior from a ship that intruded so much and where one could see so little. A ship coming into a porpoise school entrains that school so that all visible behavior is performed in relation to the boat. The normal day's activity for the porpoise doesn't begin again until the boat leaves and the animals subside back into whatever it is they do, and whatever is the matrix within which their impressive intelligence is functional.

I thought about a helicopter (too noisy and awfully expensive), gliders, and hot-air balloons (too dangerous at low elevations at sea). I recalled that in our early attempts at whale capture we had been able to tow a skiff into a whale school. The view from the skiff wasn't very good, but maybe that could be improved. Perhaps I could sit down in the keel of a little craft and look out after having been towed into the kiko school. Maybe, if the craft was unobtrusive enough, the porpoises would behave normally. Maybe, with patience, they would even become so used to me that I could obtain an intimate look into their lives.

When I had dreams like this involving mechanical things, my first reaction was to go see my friend Jimmie Okudara, the proprietor of a Honolulu machine shop. Jimmie is one of those rare souls who know, without benefit of slide rule, what will and will not work at sea. Jimmie also likes far-out projects like this one, so before I had even settled in my own mind on this approach, Jimmie had begun forays into the local Honolulu junk yards for parts. He came back with a couple of big aluminum auxiliary fuel tanks from jet planes, some big aluminum hatches whose origin still escapes me, and piles of other nameless parts. I thought I needed a catamaran with a personnel capsule between the hulls, but Jimmie hardly bothered to consider that idea. He was building a craft that would pass for one of those two-man subs used in World War II. An aluminum hatch would pierce one of his fuel tanks as a sort of inverted conning tower. The tank would serve as the hull. I would sit well below the water line in the upside-down conning tower surrounded by a band of nice big Plexiglas windows, and in a comfortable swivel chair with about two thousand pounds of lead beneath my feet for ballast.

The ship that emerged from Jimmie's welding torch was a little boy's dream (both his and mine). It was a fantastic craft in which a junior-grade Captain Nemo could explore beneath the sea. Without ever having cruised in it, I fell in love with the ridiculous craft. Since then it has been a slightly rocky love affair, but worth the pain and trouble.

The MOC (mobile observation chamber—the formal name for the craft) was launched in Kewalo Basin a few months after Jimmie began work. Later, others who worked with her in the open sea irreverently dubbed her "Norris's Nausea Machine," or the "Semisubmersible Seasick Machine." She floated there at dockside just like a little sub, which, in fact, nearly everyone thought she was. I jumped onto her slippery cigar-shaped eighteen-foot hull, opened the hatch, and descended ten feet down the conning tower. At the bottom I took my place in the padded swivel chair and peered out through the 360-degree band of windows into the murk of the harbor. Beneath my hands was a small metal desk where I could write or record sounds with a tape recorder. On the deck below were pedals that controlled two diving planes fixed on the hull outside. These would let me cant the craft over to look downward. Amidships and in front of me a metal wheel adjusted a big rudder behind the observation capsule. This allowed me to sweep the craft out to the side of the tow vessel by as much as two hundred feet, thus avoiding the wake. At about face level Jimmie had provided a blower. Above, a tall aluminum snorkel tube sucked in air, increasing the craft's resemblance to a submarine. An antenna ran up another pipe, allowing communication with the tow vessel by walkie-talkie radio.

I slammed the hatch closed over my head, flipped on the

blower switch, and asked the towing craft to make for the harbor entrance. The water cleared, and before long I saw familiar reef fishes—bright-yellow flashes of lovely yellow tangs, a black-and-yellow striped Moorish idol who flirted into view and was gone, tiny puffer fishes fanning their busy bumblebee ways who came curiously along the windows and were swept away as we picked up speed.

Nobody knew how the SSSM would handle and thus it was with some apprehension that I felt her buck into the swells that marked the entrance to the harbor. Here, in rough weather, entering or departing craft must go very close to breaking water. This strong swell would be our first test.

I felt the craft heave upward and sink softly into the waves. Ahead I could see the tow cable cut through the water, leaving a trail of bubbles, and then lift free as the little ship pitched. I tried the rudder. She answered with a swing to port, as I could see by watching the towing cable cut at an increasing angle to the bow. Far out to one side, I spun the wheel and she cut obediently across the wake of the *Imua,* bucking as she passed the turbulence. Outside the windows all I could see was a cloud of opaque silver bubbles streaming past, which dissipated into clear turquoise blue. I looked up at the surface some five feet above my head. It was an undulating mirror of bluish silver. Only very near me could I see through it. Out beyond, it faded into the blue of the distant sea.

This, I thought, is what a porpoise sees. Day in and day out he swims in a world bounded by the dark blue of the depths below, a silver mirror above, and on every side the impalpable fading of vision into blue. Not very far away either, even in the clearest water. At best he can see two hundred feet laterally before objects fade and finally disappear in a subtlety of shading and the play of sunlight down through the moving water.

The SSSM rode like a dream—softly heaving and heeling as she rushed along. I called for more speed. Five and a half knots. I learned quickly to judge my speed by the streaming bubbles on the attitude vanes. More speed. How would she take it? I tried the pedals. She heeled and remained steady. The angle

was so sharp that I braced myself with elbows against the cool
metal walls. A long way from capsizing, I thought. More speed.
Seven knots. I could feel the SSSM grasp at the towing cable,
restraining sharply. Above, the cable snapped and vibrated, taut
as a bowstring, whipping from the water as the swells rushed
past. She became a trifle unruly as I worked the pedals. A
whorl of bubbles, generated by a vane as it cut into the rushing
clear ginlike water, twisted and steamed away and the little
craft heeled. A lovely twisting vortex, I thought, as I watched it
form, stream, twist, and fragment into occasional puffs of bubbles jetted into the passing water. Together the SSSM and I
leaned far over, and I looked down into the blue beneath, a
trifle apprehensively, I must admit. But she righted and heeled
to the other side, only to come back again.

My confidence returned as I became used to the motion of
the craft. More speed. This time we hit eight and a half knots.
The water fairly boiled past me, a constant bubbling stream,
with whirlpools starting from every sharp surface. The keeper on
the rudder assembly spawned its own little stream, the rudders
trailed lovely twisting skeins on either side, and as the bow
bucked up and down a swirling mass beat into the sea and
swept past me.

I gingerly tried the rudders. Like an unruly colt, she cut to
the side, heeled, and swung back against the orders of her planes.
I spun the wheel, hoping to meet her, but I never knew whether
I had or not as she zigzagged back and forth through the wake
bubbles. I tried the pedals. She leaned and leaned and seemed
uncertain whether to come back. The two thousand pounds beneath my feet pulled toward the center of the earth, but her
forward force was such that it almost overcame the counter-
weight below. Close enough, I thought, and so slowed her into
what instantly became perfectly acceptable degrees of motion,
even though, moments before, I had felt a tingle of fear from
them.

Then I began to notice another feature. The air became close,
even though Jimmie's blower puffed its hardest in my face. It

only puffed mechanical air, air passed through a machine and made acrid and unrefreshing by it. The motion of the SSSM was no longer lost in the excitement of speed. My stomach constricted, my bowels writhed. I gulped for air and felt frantic at the closeness and at the locked hatch above.

Uncertainly, I looked up into the darkness of the closed conning tower, a lump that felt as though it might not recede in any decent way rising in my throat. I rose unsteadily, bracing myself, croaked a command for four knots into the walkie-talkie, and clawed my way up into the darkness. At the top the latch defeated me temporarily, bringing the impending catastrophe so close it was almost not to be brooked. Without thought, my fingers clawed at the latch and forced it free. I threw back the hatch with a slam and gulped the passing stream of cool air like a fish returned to the water. Rejuvenated, I waved at the towing vessel nonchalantly, as if I had surfaced from a wholly routine experience. Soon I was alongside, leaping onto the deck while another unsuspecting comrade took my place in that at once sainted and cursed seat below the air-water surface.

We scheduled our first operation with the kiko school for a week after launching. Georges towed the SSSM around to Pokai Bay, our base of operations for the effort. Bill Evans, now a civilian scientist with the Navy, had come over from the mainland to see what an SSSM looked like. He was almost unable to come, since Navy personnel are not allowed on experimental submarines, but he finally convinced the officials that this one, it was hoped, did not go entirely below the surface.

As luck would have it, the day was calm and balmy, and within twenty minutes we sighted the kikos leaping and splashing off Makaha Beach, the famed surfing area of Oahu. They came toward us, perhaps two hundred strong, many clearing the surface by four or five feet, in clean, rainbow leaps. I jumped into the skiff and was soon transferred to the slippery curved hull of the SSSM. At that time it was something of an athletic feat to board the craft from the moving skiff, as there was no deck or railing, though we later added them.

I slid below into that wonderful world of water where every-thing is tinged with blue. Bill's voice blatted over the radio say-ing that we were almost in the school. Georges was circling, trying to put me ahead of the traveling animals. I should be seeing them at any moment. Far off at the gossamer limits of vision, I thought I could see dark patches. In seconds they came into focus as distant porpoises. With consummate ease, a group of five animals cut toward me, their formation a liquid assem-blage that broke up as the animals swirled around the capsule. They had rocketed in out of the murk, barely showing them-selves above the water. Before long I was to appreciate how little time a wild porpoise spends at the surface. No wonder we had so much trouble observing them from shipboard.

The porpoises were not at all shy of my little craft, but cruised over within feet, and even rode the pressure wave in front of the capsule, their flukes within a foot of my nose. They were curious about me as I sat there peering out of my Plexiglas box at them. From time to time one would slice by, cock his head to look at me, and then, with a flirt of flukes and body, race away. Much of the time that I was in the school, I could see animals close to the capsule, often below it with just portions of dorsal fins or flukes showing.

My voyage didn't last long. I had just come off the land, where I had spent the previous few months behind my desk. One of those awful waves of nausea soon swept over me, driving me up the conning tower and out the hatch into the blessed stream of cool air unencumbered by pipes or fans. Bill Evans, who seems never to feel motion sickness, took my place, staying down for hours photographing the school. He then went back to Point Mugu and started the wheels rolling to build another larger and grander (and more stable) craft, the SEESEA. It is now working at a variety of tasks for the Navy, including observa-tions of wild porpoises at sea. It features a Plexiglas sphere in which observers look in all directions, suspended between the two hulls of a catamaran.

We worked many weeks with the SSSM. As with all observa-tion of wild animals, the first views may seem random and meaningless, but as time passes, one learns to read the movements of the animal, and little things fall into place. Usually, if the observer is persistent enough, nearly every movement, however small, takes on meaning. The tiny twist of the pectoral flipper can be seen to send a rapidly moving animal spiraling away, the showing of the whites of the eyes means anger, and so forth. I learned these things whenever we took the SSSM to sea.

In 1965 we had tagged a kiko by placing a plastic tag through its dorsal fin. The operation was simple and quick and seemed to cause the animal only a twinge of discomfort. In a very short while the connective tissue of the fin grew around the plastic tag shaft, holding it tightly in place. Two little plaques dangled from each side, bearing numbers that told us when and where the animal was tagged. Thus it was with a wave of excitement that I thought I saw this animal swimming far in the murk to the side of the capsule. Sure enough, the animal came to within inches of my face, so close I could see that the numbers were partially obscured by a growth of trailing algae. Three and a half years later the tag looked good as new. We have seen that animal several times since then, always in the same kiko school. Such taggings told us that the kikos are residents for sure, their chosen ground a portion of the Oahu coast. We've designed new tags now with cutout figures that algae cannot obscure. We hope these will allow us to recognize individual animals either from the SSSM or from the surface with binoculars.

We began to understand a little of the lives of wild kikos. It is immediately evident that they use the dimension of depth in ways lost to captive animals. I watched the kikos feeding, probably on squid caught far down in the dark water below me. They peeled off in pairs, in threes and fours, diving nearly straight down and disappearing in the dark azure. The limits of my vision were probably between a hundred and fifty and two hundred feet in that crystal water, but I could see no hesitation on their part as they became small torpedolike shapes and disappeared. They surfaced near me a couple of minutes later, coming up in small groups much the way they went down. To my surprise, they showed how little such a prodigious dive meant to them by leveling off a few feet below the surface and cruising laterally for a time before nonchalantly rising to blow, just as Pono had done from shallower dives. How deep they went I do not know, but we have records for porpoises seen on sonar gear down around seven hundred feet, trained porpoises have reached nearly a thousand feet, and we suspect that some forms may dive even farther—not so far, however, as their relatives the pilot whales, the beaked whales, or the sperm whales.

Sex is inextricably wrapped up in the signaling and play of porpoises, as it is in many animals, including people. In porpoises this is especially true. At the Oceanic Institute the noted theoretical biologist Gregory Bateson studied a captive school that included kikos. He learned that such apparent reproductive acts are involved in the intricate hierarchy of schoolmates and may often be homosexual. The signaling thus carried on may have little or nothing to do with the actual reproductive act, but instead can carry a variety of other meanings. Thus, when we have seen matings or sex play from the windows of the SSSM, which has been often, we are cautioned about interpreting what we see. It could be true sexual behavior, but it could also be play or the determination of dominance patterns in the school.

We soon learned from the SSSM that an intricate structure exists in porpoise schools. Individual pairs are seen again and again, and though they may merge with other groups from time to time, the same pair may often sort itself out from the rest. Larger groups exist, too. These groups were especially evident when we watched diving animals. The school, as a whole, dove in a sort of rough rotation, and no more than half of it was at the surface at any one time.

Some small groups included three-foot baby kikos, looking like sleek little tuna. They swam near their mothers' sides, just as we had long before seen the bottlenose porpoise babies do. Mother tended to keep between me and the little one, and seldom came as close as other adults. This paralleled what we had seen many times from the bow of collecting ships. Mothers seldom let their little ones risk playing at the bow. Usually these family groups skirted me, out seventy-five feet or so, a mixture of adults and two or three young, with eight to ten animals in a group.

The hydrobatics of porpoises are nothing short of incredible. We once watched an underwater arabesque including six or eight animals that twisted in a complicated spiral as the animals rose through the water. Another time, while observing rough-tooth porpoises far out in the bucking sea twenty miles from Oahu, I watched in amazement as a pair of these awkward-looking animals swam repeatedly by me. Every visible nuance of motion of one was reflected instantly in the other. They swam as a team, not outdone by the Blue Angels.

For many minutes the pair cruised effortlessly around my cap-sule, diving and spiraling, sometimes flicking at the tow cable with their flukes as they passed. Then they cut away into the distance. The water was so clear I could easily see the hull of the *Imua*, which was towing us, two hundred feet ahead. From that great distance I could see the porpoises turn and come to-ward me, a pair of cylindrical shapes perfectly mirroring each other. A few yards from the capsule the pair flicked and turned instantly together and curved in an effortlessly graceful arcing dive down and under my seat. They were weightless, and every thrust of their flukes sent them rocketing along. The pair often glided together, keeping pace with me for several seconds with-out so much as a tremor of flukes or flippers, until they beat their flukes in simultaneity and were off on some intricate maneuver. I, an earthling, hampered by grotesque hands and feet only use-ful in air, watched with envy but could imagine something of the kinesthetic joy they must feel at such magnificent command of themselves and their world—a little, I suppose, like the joy a skier feels racing down a snowy slope.

One bright day we cruised the lee shore of Oahu on the *Imua*, the SSSM in tow behind. The fluted green cliffs of the Waianae Mountains rose bright and sparkling, their crests nuz-zling the clouds. Against that dark backdrop I spotted several white spouts that rose and lingered in the air for a few seconds before fading. They were tall plumes, maybe twenty feet high, and they rose half a mile from shore. They were vented straight up into the air, rather than at an angle. This meant whales, and they were almost certainly humpbacks. No other large whale comes so close to the Hawaii shore, except occasionally a sperm whale, and its spout is slanted forward. The humpbacks swim down to Hawaii in the winter from northern seas. They bear their young near the Islands. We often see them rolling and leaping, and I have occasionally even heard their peculiar wailing cries and moans as I swam with snorkel and face plate, my head under water.

Out of water the humpback is the most grotesque of whales, a close-coupled obese animal forty to fifty feet long, shaped like a big grooved tadpole, his head all covered with knuckles and lumps, a pair of elongate, lumpy, straplike flippers, brilliant white in color as if the animal wore elbow-length white gloves, and all this followed by a great, powerful tail and flukes. From all appearances when one sees a humpback stranded on land, the creature should be a hydrodynamic monstrosity, but I have learned to mistrust such land-born opinions of aquatic adaptation. Seals and sea lions are awkward on land, but in the water they epitomize fluid grace. Perhaps the humpback could show me such a surprise. At any rate, I immediately asked Georges to give chase.

The *Imua* began to pick up speed, with the SSSM cleaving along behind, a mass of boiling water sliding up her hull and around the base of the conning tower. I clambered down to the deck from the bridge and jumped in the skiff with Leo Kama. Leo expertly landed me on the round, slippery deck of the SSSM, where I quickly unlatched the conning tower door and went below, slamming it shut with an echoing clang over my head.

The blue world raced by as I sat rocking slowly in the comfortable seat of the upside-down conning tower listening to the hiss and bubble of rushing water. For a very long time no animal appeared. By radio I learned that the whales were going nearly as fast as we were, and that they were heading for Barbers Point and the rough water off Waikiki.

Leo's voice crackled over the set. "Ken, do you hear me? The whales are abeam now, and we will try to swing you over near them. Hold on and get your camera ready."

Moments later the SSSM began to veer and tilt. I braced myself, elbows against the cool, sweating metal walls, and tried to adjust the tilt planes while concentrating on the gauzy border where vision fades into blue. For a few seconds part of this shadowy border became blacker, and I could make out the shapes of two great whales moving effortlessly along off to one side of me. The animals arched their tails together, their long flippers light blue against their blackish bodies, and dove down into the dark water below and disappeared.

That was all we saw that day; the whales never let us close again, but the long ride had other rewards. From time to time I have wondered what cues tell an animal such as a whale when he is near a shore. Is it the sound of breakers or of water welling against the rocks? Perhaps, in part, but sometimes animals seem to shy away from shore too far out to have heard the waves. To my surprise, I found that I could tell with some accuracy the depth of the water and the closeness of shore simply by looking out the ports. Even though the bottom lay out of sight below me, when we were in two to three hundred feet of water light shone back from the depths, making the sea light blue. Only when we slipped over a shelf into deeper water did the water below turn darker ultramarine, and only in very deep water did it assume the dark inky blue so characteristic of deep sea.

Our whales seemed to cruise along a bottom contour, avoiding headlands and subsurface reefs, staying in about two to three hundred feet of water, though I suspect they never dove within visual contact of the bottom. As this track swept us closer and farther from shore, I knew at once where we were, even though my head, like those of the whales, was below water. Every time we approached shore, the water became clouded with particles and floating plankton. Many times since then I have observed this halo of living things that surrounds Oahu and other islands. Salps and jellyfish, ctenophores and fish larvae, algal fragments and detritus from shore cloud the nearshore water, especially off the lee of an island.

This chance to go below water where one can look at the subsurface world is certainly a major scientific value of the SSSM. No amount of above-surface speculation can substitute for a short time spent actually observing below the sea surface. I, for one, cannot do this very well in diving gear. Only a truly expert diver seems able to divorce himself sufficiently from the problems of fright and concern with his gear to make decent observations below water. The SSSM, on the other hand, allows me to take a bubble of air, like a diving spider, down below the surface, where I can peer out from the vantage point of the living-room rocker, so to speak, and for the first time observe and think beyond myself.

I had never before conceived what waves look like from below or how animals might use them. From below, the sea surface is a hazy blue mirror, and as waves sweep across it, they are, of course, the mirror images of the wave one sees above. Big waves form big moving folds in the mirror, and as they move overhead, one can glimpse up into them. As the great hill of water rolls past, one can see less and less until, not very far away, the angle of sight leaves the surface only a mirror through which one cannot see. The wave moves on, an invisible hummock of water, rising above the mirror. To my complete surprise and delight, I found some species of fishes to be wave dwellers, spending much of their lives in these wrinkles and using them as retreats.

One such wave dweller, for example, is the needlefish, a common predatory species in Hawaii—a slim, silver-bellied, green-backed fish armed with an elongate snout margined with dozens of needle-sharp teeth. Off Oahu I have seen many cruising the wave folds as all but invisible gray shapes flitting down these upside-down canyons of water. The mirrors of their bellies match the mirrors of the wave walls, and the darker bluish green of their backs countershades them from above so that only the vaguest of outlines tells the observer where they are.

Most such wave dwellers, like the needlefish, have a bright

silvery band, usually brighter even than their belly, along both sides of their bodies. These bands, I suspect, serve to obscure the curving contours of the animal when seen from below. The edge of the animal is lost in a halo of light that merges into the mirrors around him. The needlefish are gray ghosts, living in silvery indentations, from which moving redoubts they can dart out to capture their prey. The barracuda is a similar species, and the peculiar halfbeaks and flying fish are also wave dwellers.

The ocean sailor is exquisitely aware of the state of the sea surface, because it tosses and sometimes threatens his craft. How, I wondered, does the ocean-dwelling animal feel, looking up from below? The SSSM does not allow a completely dispassionate answer to this question, locked as it is to the surface, with its encapsulated observer feeling quite as strongly about the sea state as those on board the towing vessel. But with a modicum of fortitude or, preferably, a week's adaptation to the movements of the craft, one can learn to ignore the movement pretty well, and begin to look around with interest at things other than the escape hatch.

As the sea becomes rougher, I found, it seems to pose utterly no problem to either fish or porpoise. Indeed, as we have seen in Pono's case, porpoises probably delight in the moving mountains and ridges of water that rough seas bring. Even with sea breaking a foot or so overhead, porpoises may glide along with no apparent motion of flukes or flippers, hanging like puppets on strings, moving up and down in the orbital motion of the passing wave. The breaking swells blow swirls of silvery spherical bubbles into the clear water, but otherwise the world below shows little visual sign of what may be a storm above. It must be easy for a porpoise to select from below a position on a wave where he may surface and breathe, without the expectation of inhaling much spray. I have long been curious about this question, but I found that if I had been a porpoise, I could have done it too, watching the rippling mirror for flat places on the faces of the swells.

We were curious to look at the subsurface world at night, so

Bill Evans rigged a powerful submarine light and we anchored the SSSM off the stern of the *Imua*. As darkness came, we started the portable generator on deck which flooded the water with a bright greenish halo. Soon the brilliant light began to attract tiny phototactic organisms by the tens of thousands.

A gently undulating parade of floating or weakly swimming creatures passed the windows. Little swimming worms zipped by, busybodies in the midst of their languorous neighbors. Most creatures were made of crystal. A little fish, a larval goby, moved by, its body essentially transparent, only the black eye capsules showing. It hung head up, a rapid undulating wave moving down the faintly visible fins that margined each side of its body. A grotesque larval stage of the crab partly swam and partly floated into view, illuminated as refracted light paths showed it to be there. One knew that to pick up some of these sea creatures, many with long, trailing filaments, was to destroy them.

Later, coming back from long trips at sea, I sometimes rode in the SSSM after dark. These were experiences I shall never forget. As usual, the floating life increased in quantity as one neared the island. With no lights of my own, I watched as animals illuminated themselves—with the ghostly pale light of bioluminescence. The ctenophores, or comb jelly fish, which by day are crystalline nut-sized globs, now became eerie floating lanterns, dimly illuminated against the darkness. They danced in slow undulation as my craft approached and passed them. Hundreds of nameless creatures buffeted against the windows or control surfaces of the SSSM, flashing into angry light with the impact, trailing off behind and winking out into darkness again. As the bow of the little craft pitched into the swell, it dashed a whirlpool of lighted flecks in the water, which swirled wildly in eddies, then faded. Every now and then the darting flashes of a frightened fish school exploded in all directions, leaving trails like so many pale and cold underwater skyrockets.

But all joys like these vignettes are fleeting things, to be savored at the moment and perhaps cast into words for future reminiscence. Ultimately, it simply became too expensive of time and effort to work with the SSSM in the Oahu kiko school, and my observations there became sporadic as ship-time budgets fluctuated and other requirements intruded on my time. I began to understand that if I was ever to learn about wild porpoise life, it would have to be elsewhere, where animals could more predictably be found. Thus it was that I began to search for a porpoise school that lived not so far to sea as the kikos, traveled less each day, and had a true home nearshore. My attention finally descended upon "Captain Cook's porpoises."

CHAPTER ELEVEN

Captain Cook's Porpoises

"Spin, spin, spin, head over tail, nose out, spin," Tom chanted faster than I could write. To take notes, I made up a kind of instant shorthand on the spot. Tom Dohl, my colleague on this project, was watching a school of Hawaiian spinner porpoises that played forty yards off the bow of the SSSM, close to the cliffs of Kealakekua Bay, Hawaii. His ever-present pipe in hand and his angular body folded up on the little seat over the conning tower, Tom called out the different kinds of aerial behavior to me below deck, where I sat taking notes and watching them below water.

The porpoises, all thirty of them, had just shaken off a sort of midday doldrums. Minutes before they had been spending nearly all of their time under water, surfacing quietly for three or four quick breaths before diving for up to four minutes. Their school had been a tightly packed mobile amoeba of porpoises, with some animals so close they seemed actually to be touching. They had been in this formation for four hours and not a porpoise had jumped. Now, suddenly, they rocketed out of the calm sea in their peculiar spins, one after another. Often two or three were in the air at once.

"Sleepy time is all over, Tom," I said. During weeks of watching we had begun to feel that this midday quiescence was what passed for sleep. After the rest period came what we called "zigzag swimming." Once the porpoises began to leap, the entire school raced back and forth, sometimes in and out from the cliff, and sometimes taking long traverses back and forth parallel to the coast. Always it was a strenuous affair with much leaping, and usually any time one looked, one or two animals were slapping the water with repeated blows of their flukes—"tail slapping," we called it.

Sometimes the whole school seemed to decide upon a course and moved rapidly from the bay and out to sea. I once watched such a movement from our cliff-top camp. There, at the brink of the five-hundred-foot lava escarpment overlooking the mile-wide, almost semicircular bay, I watched the school leave, passing the little fishing villages of Napoopoo and Keei, past Palemano Point at the southern tip of the bay, and swimming straight out to sea. The day was calm, as it usually is on the Kona coast of Hawaii. As far as we could see them with binoculars, the school plunged along. Animals out on the flanks spun and fell back amid spreading masses of foam that marked their path with white splotches on the flat sea. At last sighting they were about two miles beyond Palemano, or four miles from our perch, leaving tiny blips of white against the steel-gray water. Then they were lost amid the wandering breeze trails and slicks.

More often the porpoise school turned south around Palemano Point, hugging the rugged lava-bluff coast. The school then moved in procession, many animals so close to the bluffs that the rising swell lifted them high as the water surged up against the jagged black rocks. Somewhere near the fabled ancient Hawaiian City of Refuge the porpoises turned and retraced their path, only this time crossing Kealakekua Bay at its mouth and going northward. We came to believe this maneuver allowed the school to gather in little subschools that had been resting at various points along the coast, for the school obviously grew in numbers until, at dusk, it numbered about a hundred animals and spread over half a mile of water.

These Kealakekua porpoises represented one of those rare opportunities a naturalist occasionally encounters. Sometimes a rare or difficult-to-observe species presents, at some special place or time, an unparalleled chance to look into its life patterns. The trouble with watching porpoises is that they are shy and fast-moving. One may spend the greatest part of his time simply trying to find his animals, as we had done off Oahu. These Kealakekua Bay porpoises came in virtually every day to rest, and equally important, they did so in a limpid bay that is usually flat calm. We could watch to our heart's content without getting seasick.

The local fishermen knew about the porpoises, but they didn't harass them, so the animals were not frightened of people or boats. Here, it seemed, was a chance to look at the ways of life into which the mysterious intelligence of the porpoise presumably fits. Here, if we looked hard enough, lay the uses of the remarkable sound systems of Kathy or Alice or the learning capability of Pono or Keiki. Here the affection and trust of Pono had its place. A school like this *was* the world of a porpoise, if we could only have the wit to understand it.

My frustrations with the Oahu school made me decide to check on repeated stories about the porpoises of Kealakekua Bay, which were said to be tame and to live all year in the bay. One young man even told me he had fed these porpoises by hand while swimming in the water with them. Another told of the porpoises lining up around him as he treaded water, so close he could touch them. Later I came to doubt these stories, but at the time they were intriguing.

So Tom packed the SSSM aboard an interisland barge, while I scheduled the *Westward*, the Oceanic Institute's ninety-foot brigantine. At the little port of Kawaihae the SSSM was reassembled and slipped into the water. The *Westward* took her in tow for Kealakekua, sixty miles distant.

At first it was choppy and progress was slow. Once we had passed the great, spreading lava fan of Keahole Point, the water turned calm and the great volcanoes of Hawaii rose along the shore. A few miles farther, where the vast, coalescing lava slopes of Mauna Loa and Hualalai volcanoes had long ago flowed together, was the mile-wide indentation of Kealakekua Bay. It is a snug, crescent-shaped jewel of sparkling blue water, of bright reef fish, and of history. For centuries a procession of thousands of lava flows had poured down the slopes of the two great mountains. Their crests were now, as almost always, shrouded in clouds. The flows met at this point to form a precipitous five-hundred-foot, layered black cliff that drops abruptly into the sea at the back of the bay. Two smaller flows, just above sea level, spread out from either end of the cliff to define the cusps of the cove.

The dark cliff is pierced by dozens of lava tubes, each of which once sluiced lava into the sea in a fury of steam, smoke, and light. They have long been cool. Aboriginal Hawaiians used their cool interiors to bury their dead. Even today, we are told, some Hawaiians scale this cliff at night and go through the old ceremony of reburial of the carefully cleaned bones. At any rate, deep in the dusty cave recesses, sometimes hundreds of feet above the water, the sacred bones of the dead still lie wrapped in ancient tapa, the pounded bark of the paper mulberry tree, bound in palm fiber or sennit. Mummies of babies, we are told, are held in tiny wooden cradles whose pieces are also lashed together with sennit. The modern Hawaiians are quick to tell you of the spirits that abound in the place, guarding the bones of the ancients. Disturbance of the bones, they say, means the marching of the dead. Legions of giant Hawaiian ghosts will then be heard in the night, pounding their drums. Especially sacred are the bones of Kamehameha I, the first conqueror of the Hawaiian Islands, which are said to lie buried somewhere near here in a cave whose entrance was once marked by a single sandalwood tree.

A temple to Lono—a heiau, or stone platform, built by hand of

large lava blocks with almost unbelievable expenditure of energy—rises above the beach next to Napoopoo. Its priests were
repositories of the secrets of the god Lono. They said Lono
would one day return to the Islands borne on white wings. In
1787 Captain James Cook came here and, because of the white
sails of his ship *Resolution,* he was understandably thought to
be Lono. Cook was treated as befits a god, but on a later return
trip he met disaster. The throngs who at first came to see and
worship him turned ugly. The signs were wrong and Cook could
not be Lono. When a Hawaiian was killed by others in the Cook
party, they turned on the Captain, spearing him and dashing
his brains out in the shallows of Kaawaloa, the village that once
occupied the north limb of the bay.

From the deck of the *Westward* we could look up the hill
above our anchorage and see the small stone temple where Cook
was ritually dismembered, cooked, and, in part, eaten. With
Cook were two other famous figures in Pacific exploration: William Bligh, whose exploits would lead to mutiny on his ship,
Bounty, and the incredible saga of his seamanship in successfully crossing half the Pacific in a longboat; and George Van-
couver, who would later explore much of the Pacific coast of
North America. All these events, these historical figures, and the
natural beauty and calm combine to make a visit to the bay
a powerful experience for most people. I felt its aura each time
we dropped anchor off the beach at Kaawaloa.

Our first porpoises were gamboling along the shore about two
miles north of the bay. They flirted briefly with our bow and
left us. So we continued into the deep arc of Kealakekua,
dropped anchor, and began to ready the SSSM. As Tom and
I watched from her meager deck, the porpoises rounded Cook
Point and came toward us. They began the patterns we would
only begin to understand months later.

These patterns and the Kona porpoise schools are probably
historically very old, certainly antedating the advent of white
men. The burials, the coming of Cook, and perhaps even the
fiery formation of the bay itself must have occurred with a

complement of porpoises in attendance. Some hint of this antiquity can be gained back down the coast, near Keahole Point, where there lives another spinner school. The ancient Hawaiian name for the ground to which they come to sleep is Nai'a Ke'e, or "the place to which porpoises are drawn." The Nai'a Ke'e is formed in old lavas that flowed into place several hundred years ago, but I suspect the porpoises come not because it is old but because, as we shall see, its coves have the proper shape. Mark Twain, when he passed through Hawaii a little more than a hundred years ago, noted of our Kealakekua school:

> . . . we dashed boldly into the midst of a school of huge, beastly porpoises engaged at their eternal game of arching over a wave and disappearing, and then doing it over again and keeping it up—always circling over, in that way, like so many well-submerged wheels . . .

Every fisherman now living on the coast has seen them as long as he can remember.

Tom and I, not thinking about history, were merely elated to find porpoises so easily. We watched quietly as the porpoises swam into the shadow of the cliff, a dozen yards from its base. A fortuitous gift, for one day we would look down at the porpoises from a vantage point five hundred feet above, on the cliff rim.

Even though our attention was riveted on the porpoises, I had time to muse with pleasure about the calm ride I was getting in the SSSM. The ungainly craft slipped through the still cove with scarcely any of its usual movement. This is more like it, I thought. I knew I could watch for hours in this place with no discomfort.

The triangular fins of the school lazily cut the water close under the cliff, less than two hundred yards away. The animals came willingly to our bow and cut back and forth ahead of us, showing no signs of the skittishness that had become the hallmark of the Oahu animals. From my seat in the observation chamber I looked out on a mother and baby. The three-and-a-

half-foot-long young had a broken upper beak, bent to the side
three or four inches back from the tip. We named him Little
Cross Beak and were later to see him many times ahead of the
SSSM windows, always swimming close to the flanks of a big
female, who was probably his mother.

Little Cross Beak became a personality to us, showing us some
of the subtle details of life between mother and child in the porpoise world. We saw her discipline him with a petulant slap of
her flukes, and we saw him slip back along her side, his little
flipper touching her undulating tail stock, and come to rest with
his tiny flukes on top of hers, passively following the beat as
she propelled them both along. In spite of his grievous injury,
he was sleek and full-bodied. We wondered how he managed
to nurse, but never saw him try. And we wondered what would
happen to him when the time came to be weaned. By that time,
a month or more away, he might have learned to catch fish
and squid with his partial beak and thus to make his way.

The outcome, however, is clouded. Three months after we
first sighted him, Little Cross Beak disappeared, and we never
saw him again. He could have perished, as we might expect
him to, considering his injury. But he may simply have joined
one of the juvenile groups we could recognize from the surface. Their little rounded fins revealed their age and we saw them
often. But always they were shy and refused to come in to play
at the SSSM. So there remains the hope that we may see him
again when he emerges into adulthood.

Little Cross Beak was not the only injured animal in the school.
In fact, so many animals bore the scars of past injury that Tom
and I were able to compile a dictionary of scars and marks that
came to include more than fifty animals. Many bore distinctive
circular scars, like those that caused us to call *Steno* the "polka-
dot porpoise" and that are now suspected to be the work of an
insidious little fish we have called the "cookie-cutter shark"
(*Isistius brasiliensis*). Everet C. Jones of the National Marine
Fisheries Service discovered that this strange eighteen-inch shark
is remarkably adapted to bite into the bodies of fish and porpoises, having a symmetrical circular row of sawlike teeth on

its lower jaw. Then, using suction, it literally forces these teeth into its prey, scooping out a one- to two-inch disk of flesh or blubber before it can be shaken off. Most Hawaiian porpoises and whales are dotted with scars from this source, especially those that live far offshore and those that feed deep below the surface. The spinners are less afflicted than most, but, still, such scars are common amongst them. I have seen them with fresh wounds, piercing through the blubber and exposing the raw flesh beneath.

The cookie-cutter shark is strange in other ways too. Its body is luminescent, and it is perhaps part of the fauna of fishes and squids that daily migrate from the dark sea below the levels of light penetration to the surface. Jones feels that it may mimic squid, allowing it to get close enough for a dash to the unwary animal's side, a quick attachment, and then flight with its disk of flesh.

Other sharks, larger and more dangerous, obviously take their toll of porpoises in Hawaiian waters. Some recorded scars are ugly lunate rows of tooth marks, so broad the porpoise's whole tail must have been grasped by a giant shark before it somehow shook loose. Fins and flukes, too, are rather often tattered in ways that suggest shark attack. The communal alertness of the porpoise school, we realized, is an essential component of survival in these shark-filled waters, and even that sometimes is not enough.

After seeing the porpoises swim so close to the cliff base, we knew we needed a cliff-top camp. Somewhere along that imposing rim there should be a vantage point where one could observe and photograph, wholly without disturbing the porpoises. So one sunny morning Dave Bryant, Tom's quiet young assistant, and I started up the back slope of the cliff. It proved a long, hot climb through shoulder-high tussock grass growing from a hidden mass of jumbled boulders. The pitch increased until Dave and I were on hands and knees swinging from clump to clump. Then, finally, we reached the crest, and a lovely, savanna-like parkland opened before us. Undulating grassy slopes studded with spreading monkeypod and inia trees provided cool shade for sleepy cattle. Our passage jarred their slumbers, but soon we left them and plunged into a dense hale koa thicket that skirts the cliff edge, making our way by parting the bushes at each step. Finally, the brush thinned at a little promontory on the cliff edge.

A ledge of huge lava blocks hung over the sheer drop. Dave scaled a stone out arcing into the air, and we listened until it whumped into the water below. The whole character of the bay was different when one looked down upon it, rather than across its surface. Close against the cliff shore castellated domes of submerged coral showed clearly, flickering beneath the water: green, yellow, and white, each with its halo of fishes. Dozens of black triggerfish that the Hawaiians call *humu humu ele ele* cruised just beneath the surface, while deeper yellow flashes came from butterfly fishes and tangs. Beyond the shallows the coral became a tracery between the light blue of coral-sand "meadows," and then beyond all deepened to indigo where deep water lay.

"There they are," Dave said quietly. I followed his pointing arm with my eyes and saw a school of porpoises not far from shore. They were brownish torpedoes, rising to the surface in unison and submerging seconds later. A spin briefly left a splotch of white foam on the glossy sea surface. A couple of seconds later we could faintly hear the splash as the animal fell back into the water.

Later, with the gracious help of the local rancher, Sherwood Greenwell, camp was made nearby. We pitched a tent, suspended shade awnings, built ourselves a big stone fireplace for an evening campfire, and began regular observations. With this work and the SSSM observations we could piece together a daily routine for the porpoises. We knew now that they enter certain bays around all of the Hawaiian islands in the morning. They come in from the sea in a broad rank, many leaping and spinning. At this time they are sociable and, in fact, are usually divided into small social groups that will ride the bow of the SSSM and will sometimes peer in through the capsule windows

Kathy, a bottlenose porpoise, closes her eyes as blindfold is adjusted by John Prescott during an experiment in porpoise navigation. One problem was finding a blindfold that would adhere to the slick skin of the animal. *Below,* Blindfolded, Kathy locates and presses the lever, after which she will receive a reward fish.

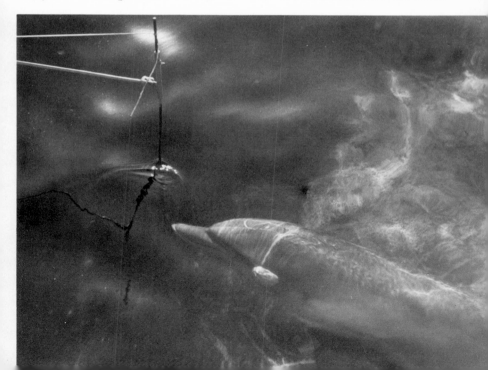

Trainer Dotty Samson works with Pono at Sea Life Park, Hawaii. CAMERA HAWAII. *Below,* Pono in her stretcher before riding to Pokai Bay. "She rolled her goggle eyes up at us in curiosity, but without the slightest show of concern." CAMERA HAWAII

Left, Steno porpoise in hoop training for open-sea diving tests. Bill Evans and Bob Ballard look on. PHOTO BY COLES PHINZEY FOR SPORTS ILLUSTRATED

Pono jumping for joy. *Below,* She presses the diving lever, about seventy-five feet below the surface. CAMERA HAWAII

Looking for Pono. Dotty scans the horizon while Howard Baldwin runs the skiff. "Dotty's taut posture and concentrated gaze told eloquently enough that for her this was not just an experiment gone awry but a wrenching separation from a dear friend." CAMERA HAWAII

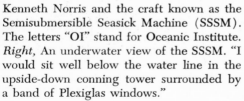

Kenneth Norris and the craft known as the
Semisubmersible Seasick Machine (SSSM).
The letters "OI" stand for Oceanic Institute.
Right, An underwater view of the SSSM. "I
would sit well below the water line in the
upside-down conning tower surrounded by
a band of Plexiglas windows."

A chance to study porpoise behavior in the wild. Here, spinner porpoises as seen from the SSSM.

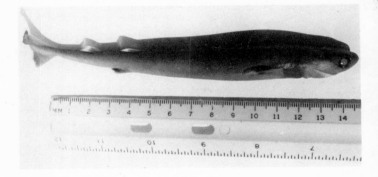

The cookie-cutter shark. Most Hawaiian porpoises and whales are dotted with circular scars resulting from the bite of this insidious little fish.

A spinner porpoise back-slaps, Kealakekua Bay.

Kenneth Norris holding lower jaw of bottlenose porpoise. This discovery on the Baja California peninsula led to a scientific adventure in sound transmission whose outcome is still unknown.

to make their own observations of the strange air-encased creature inside. Their stomachs are full, and soon the water is filled with contrails of fecal material as the night's catch of lantern fishes, squids, and shrimps is metered through the digestive tract from storage stomachs, where it has been packed during the night. Gradually the school slows and the spins become less ebullient. In an hour or so no leaping animal can be seen. A desultory slap of the tail or the head is all we see. Then that too is gone. The porpoises quietly rise to the surface and dive as one. They begin to surface and for so brief a time that it is easy to miss them, even though they swim in calm water directly below us.

A curious thing happened during this subsidence into porpoise rest, or "sleep." They ceased to act like porpoises and began to act like herrings. When the animals entered the bay, they swam in little subgroups, roughly abreast of one another. Each of these subschools dove and swam as if partly independent of the school as a whole. One subgroup or another was usually at the surface. This is what the observer normally expects to see in porpoise schools. But by the time the porpoises slowed into the resting pattern, they came to dive in unison, and subgroups were no longer evident. The school became a tight disk of animals, quite as structureless as a herring school and without any apparent leaders.

This became obvious when Tom brought the SSSM near one such school as it swam quietly close to the cliff base. Even though we bobbed silently in the water with our engine shut down, the porpoises were fully aware of our presence. They always are, by the way, no matter how stealthy one tries to be, even from hundreds of yards away. The school surfaced, and we could see that the disk of animals was dented inward on the side nearest us, as if our presence had forced animals away from us from a distance of thirty yards. The school moved down the sixty-yard corridor between our vessel and the cliff. It stretched out into a dumbbell shape, bulging out on either side of us, as if the cliff and our little craft had combined to squeeze the school almost to the breaking point.

Beyond us a passing motorboat caused the school to reverse its direction abruptly, so that followers instantly became leaders. I feel that this kind of behavior represents what I call "sensory integration"—that is, in the absence of a leader, each school member receives sensory information about the surrounding world and reacts to a greater or lesser degree depending upon how close he is to the source of disturbance. Then, because schoolmates also react to each other, the school as a whole moves in a useful way. Probably such an arrangement requires less individual alertness than for a single porpoise to make decisions independent of the whole school. Thus, I suspect that when the porpoise school subsides into rest, a measure of relief comes to each animal—they needn't be alert in the same way as in a socially structured school. It's not your sleep pattern, or mine, but perhaps it's the best a porpoise can afford in the hostile world of the sea. It's probably why they enter calm coves, such as Kealakekua Bay, where some of the awesome predators of the deep sea are absent, or at least scarce, and where the protective sea bottom is close at hand.

Then, as I described earlier, after three to five hours of rest all the porpoises abruptly become alert again, begin aerial behavior, resume their socially structured school, and begin zigzag swimming. Toward dusk the porpoises begin to edge out to sea, sometimes directly, and sometimes angling slowly away from the coast. As they do so, their school spreads and a new diversity of social activity begins to appear.

At twilight from the bow of a ship traveling with such a school, it is possible to see all kinds of social encounters, whose meanings are mostly hidden from us. Porpoises swim upside down, slapping their flukes on the water surface while emitting streams of sound so loud an observer above-water can hear them as high-pitched air-borne squeaks. One baby seems to be practicing his spinning technique as he vaults from the water repeatedly, coming closer to the ship with each leap. Finally, when he is all but in the bow wave, he "looks up" to find the boat bearing down on him and quickly veers off. Chases and matings are common.

As night comes, the school has spread across a great swath of sea. Its parts can be located only when animals leap or when a few black fins can be seen out on the graying sea. Even though the animals are spread over a mile or more, all know precisely the position of all parts of their school, for often the school changes direction, and the new course will be quickly taken by all the far-flung groups of porpoises. Our ship turns belatedly, like a member of a platoon who didn't hear the command "To the rear, march!" Soon, as darkness closes over us, the only hint of the school comes when a few animals race in to the ship's bow for a brief ride.

By this time the ship is usually two to four miles at sea, over water varying from a hundred to a thousand fathoms or more in depth. A look at the chart will show that whatever the depth, the animals have taken up station over an underwater cliff or slope; a vast dropoff in which the submerged base of the island descends into the true abyss. It is here, we and other cetologists such as Bill Evans think, that deep-sea fishes, shrimps, and squids which form the porpoises' diet rise in greatest abundance toward the surface. Together these deep-sea creatures form what is called the "deep scattering layer," so called because in certain parts of the world the sheer mass of this rising cloud of animals is so dense that fathometer sounds beamed downward against them return echoes that have led mariners to talk of a "false bottom." Each night this deep scattering layer (or DSL) rises from dark waters over most of the oceanic world away from the poles. Its organisms feed on the abundant planktonic food of the surface at night and descend again before daybreak.

By the time darkness comes, our porpoises are swimming over this layer with their food rising toward them. They don't wait, though, but begin to dive far down to meet it. Other scientists have made echo traces that show porpoises descending to such a DSL, and one can clearly see the animals on these records in the midst of the rising mass of scattering layer organisms, as deep as seven hundred feet below the surface.

Subtropical waters such as those of Hawaii are not noted for having dense scattering layers, so we decided to see for ourselves how difficult it would be for a porpoise to find enough food. At dusk the *Westward's* lines were cast loose and she took us a few miles offshore. A big light and reflector were rigged over the water from a spar. Soon fish began to dart in and out of the halo of light. At first surface creatures like flying fish came in, their long wings folded against their sides for speed; small barracudas and needlefish skittered in tight against the surface. Later came the first lantern fish from the depths. These strange light-bearing creatures darted in rapid, erratic paths beneath the light. A swift swoop of a dip net and the three-inch fish lay flopping in the meshes. In the dark, away from the boom light, one could see rows of gleaming bright-blue jeweled buttons running down its belly and scattered over its head. Each tiny light was directed downward as if to signal those beneath. It seemed able to turn the light on and off at will—cold, strange, beautiful light from another world, and a sight to stir the wonder of the naturalist.

We knew that squids formed an important part of the diet of our porpoises, yet at first we saw none under the light. Then we noticed, out at the light perimeter where the disk of light faded into darkness, forty shining amber eyes staring at us— squids at the ocean surface and too timid to enter that glaring disk. Later some came in—darting, milky arrows. A few were caught in spite of their speed, perhaps because the light blinded them to the danger from above. Some of these creatures, too, had bioluminescent lights. As they lay before us with pulsing mantles, spots of light glowed, showing that they too were dwellers of the depths and not surface squid. Some scientists have even dipped up the cookie-cutter shark in these same waters.

At any rate, even though the DSL is a faint trace or none at all on fathometers in Hawaiian waters, we knew it was there, part of the vast worldwide movement taking place every evening and morning around the globe. And from the variety and numbers of organisms we have been able to catch, we surmised that a much more adept porpoise would have little trouble making a living.

Perhaps the most perplexing feature of our porpoise school is its habit of spinning. No one really understands its meaning. Porpoises of the group to which ours belong occur around the world in tropical and subtropical seas, and wherever they occur, they seem to spin like dervishes. So there is almost certainly a genetic aspect to the behavior, a racial memory of the patterns involved.

Actually the Hawaiian porpoises do much more than spin. Tom and I have catalogued eight different kinds of aerial behavior. The simplest is the desultory tail slap, in which an animal lifts its flukes free of the water and smacks them down again, sometimes with a resounding slap that can be heard for dozens of yards. Another common behavior, a bit more energetic, is the head or back slap, in which the animal lunges from the water for three-quarters of its length and then slaps its body back against the water, producing a cascade of spray and a sharp, slapping sound. But these minor displays are not even worth watching when a school member begins to spin. To perform a true competition-grade spin, the porpoise swoops down deep beneath the surface and comes up in a swift arc. At the very last instant, as its body darts free of the water, it tilts its flukes, catching the water and sending its body into a dizzying spin that may cause it to revolve four or five times around the long axis of its body before it crashes back into the sea. Usually, as it lands, its rotating body scoops out a hollow of water which claps together over it as it sinks, jetting a column of white water upward from its entry point like a boy doing a cannonball dive.

But for sheer grace and athletic prowess I prefer the head-over-tail leap. This magnificent leap can often be seen when a school is in the height of excitement. The animal leaps free of the water in a graceful arc, and when seven or eight feet above the water whips its tail over its head, slinging trailing spray for many yards into the air like the sparks from a pinwheel, and enters the water tailfirst. Exhibitionist porpoises sometimes combine the spin and the head-over-tail leap. This is too complicated to be beautiful, but I suppose it must represent a joyful degree of bodily control for an animal.

To suggest, as some of my friends insist, that pure joy motivates these leaps is, I think, begging the question. Even so, the best I can conjure up as a halfhearted explanation is that the intensity of leaping indicates rather precisely a level of "school excitement" or alertness. A resting school leaps not at all. A fast-moving school in deep water will usually leap more than one swimming more slowly in shallow water. The leaps are most common when the schools are spread far across the sea. Their slapping return to the sea may produce underwater sounds that let schoolmates know where others are. They may serve to shake off parasitic fish like remoras and maybe even the cookie-cutter shark. I don't know. All I know is that so far I'm unsatisfied that I understand them. But seen in evolutionary perspective, it seems clearly a pattern that has evolved through time. And such things do not happen just for the joy of it.

From my studies with Alice and Kathy I knew that sounds probably controlled much school behavior. So we rigged hydrophones, tape recorders, amplifiers, and the like and began to listen to what the porpoises in our school had to say.

As an aside, before telling what we heard, I want to explain that in all my work with porpoises I have never seen any evidence that suggests to me that they have a language like ours. I'm not surprised about this, either, since our strange method of acoustic communication is almost grotesquely clumsy and difficult. What other creature, for example, would want to wait around for the message involved in a long sentence; to wait until all the little abstract symbols like prepositions and adverbs and participles were arranged according to an arcane plan before meaning could be extracted? Only, I suggest, an animal deeply involved in cause-and-effect sequences, like those that result from and allow the use of tools. Each time we use a tool, we make a set of predictions to ourselves: "If I turn this screwdriver so far, it will release the window screen, and if I don't step aside now, it will hit me on the head." We are predictive animals par excellence, and nearly everything we do, from our technology to our language, involves looking at time spans longer than the moment just before us.

Porpoises are almost wholly nonmanipulative, as one would expect from an animal whose fingers are encased in a smooth glove that makes their hands into diving planes. Probably, like most other animals, porpoises look largely at the moment, and also like most other animals, it is likely that most of what they think, do, and say is related to relationships and emotions and not to complicated abstractions. Certainly I have seen no evidence to the contrary.

Purely as a prediction, I suggest that when we truly understand the sounds of porpoises and their meanings, we will have found that they have incredibly refined capability at "seeing with sound," to the point that they form sonic images of their environment. Further, it is already clear that they can hear the composition and texture of objects around them. I suspect they look into each other in eerie ways, inspecting the contours of internal air spaces like lungs and upper respiratory tract spaces, and that information about emotional states is to be gathered this way, even though the external surface of the animal is smooth and expression-free, having been dictated largely by the demands of hydrodynamics.

Then, I suspect that their whistle signals will be found to carry a variety of meanings, like the cries of wolves which carry information about the state of the chase—"I'm closing in now"; "The prey is a long way ahead"; and so on.

So it was with these personal prejudices (in my case at least) that we began to listen to the Kealakekua Bay school. One of our hydrophones was affixed to the hull of the SSSM, just in front of the viewing windows. Its cable ran through a stuffing gland in the hull to the tape recorder lying on the little shelf in front of the observer. With Tom topside steering us toward the porpoise school, I spoke into the microphone to identify the sequence for the later time when we would analyze it in the laboratory.

May 2, 1970. Observers are Tom Dohl, Larry Hobbs, and Ken Norris. We are approaching a school of approximately 30 *Stenella longirostris* that entered Kealakekua Bay, Hawaii, at 8:15 A.M. It is now 8:35 A.M. and the animals are still in rank formation headed for Observation Post No. 1, 1,500 yards offshore. Occasional spins and head slaps can be seen. The weather is clear, sunny, and calm. Recordings are being made with an LC32 hydrophone, a 466A Hewlett-Packard Amplifier set at −20 db, and a Uher 4000 Report L tape recorder set at 7½ inches per second. The animals have just come in sight of my capsule at 11 o'clock. They are swimming toward the bow of the SSSM. Recording starts.

One five-porpoise subgroup of the school cut toward us, swinging around a few feet from the windows and taking up station directly ahead of our bow. Their tails beat up and down a foot or so in front of the Plexiglas windows. The sleek porpoises jockeyed for position, poking each other with the tips of their pectoral flippers, or occasionally nudging one another body to body. A stream of bubbles issued from the blowhole of one and trailed back past my capsule. At the same instant a chirping whistle, so high I could scarcely hear it, issued from the tape recorder speaker. I heard no clicking sounds until another group joined the first, and when they came in, heading directly toward the capsule, a barrage of clicks, like rain on a tin roof, hit my capsule. As the animals turned their tails toward me to take up station, the sounds ceased. Their directional beams now shot forward into the water ahead, out of my hearing.

Hours of listening to a resting school revealed no sounds other than desultory clicks when a school headed toward us. But after they aroused themselves, whistles became prominent. Once, when a newly aroused school had begun zigzag swimming out into Kealakekua Bay, we still heard nothing but clicks until another school, alert and leaping, approached them from across the bay. This record is then dotted with a peculiar double-parted whistle that we have yet to hear again. The two groups joined and left the bay, heading for Keawekaheka Point to the north.

Fully alert traveling schools are sometimes very noisy indeed.

We encountered such a school several miles south of Kealakekua Bay, in the deep-water cove called Hookena. We swung the skiff just ahead of the leaping, spinning animals and dropped our portable hydrophone in the water. Moments later we had drifted to a stop, and as the hydrophone hung quietly a few feet below us, cascades of clicks could be heard. Clearly by now the porpoises knew all about us. Still, they came toward us. Some were within a few yards when the clicks subsided and a weird chorus began. Bleating and quacking sounds issued from animals up and down the passing rank, and an undulating chorus of very high-pitched whistles arose, rising and falling in volume as animals closer and farther away spoke their piece. Presumably they were reacting to us, since once they passed abeam the sounds ceased.

Later, by slowing the tape recorder, these sounds could be brought down to levels where humans could hear them easily. The bleats became moos that sounded for all the world like those of a barnyard. The high, squeaky whistles resolved into long, rising, pure-tone whistles coming in sequential chorus. The whistle of one animal seemed to evoke that of a nearby animal, and so on down the rank and back again.

What do the sounds mean? That very difficult question is a long way from solution in our work, or, for that matter, in the work of all others who study porpoises. At last we can begin to relate certain kinds of sounds to certain parts of the daily activity cycle. But I suspect it will be a long time before we can truly unravel the intricacies of porpoise sound communication.

Many other questions remain. We know that in late summer and fall all the porpoises from the lee side of Hawaii seem to gather in a sort of "Porpoise National Convention," usually off Keahole Point. Many young appear about that time, but birth seems clearly not restricted to such a short time but is instead spread over most or all of the year.

Even with the SSSM and our cliff-top observation post, much porpoise social behavior remains a mystery to us. For instance, most of the subgroups we see in active schools have no clear function. Are they family groups, play groups, are they divided by sex or age? As yet we have few answers to these questions, but we must continue to learn, in order to understand wild porpoise life.

What is it that regulates porpoise school numbers? Why don't their schools grow and grow until every scrap of natural resource is used, as humans are busy doing? What racial wisdom, somehow lost by humans as they adopted civilization, keeps them in balance? If we can answer that by watching the Kealakekua porpoises, they will have told us a great deal.

CHAPTER TWELVE

The Jaw-Hearing Porpoise

This is the story of a scientific adventure whose outcome is not yet known. If I tell it correctly, it will carry some of the excitement of such a pursuit as well as some of its frustrations, and it will tell something of the scientific method. It should also show that any scientist's ideas are fair game for all. The real story is much longer and more complex than I can describe here, involving many workers whose names and contributions will not be mentioned. I will, of course, tell it from my own viewpoint, which is composed partly of intuition and partly of fact. There is here, too, the human desire to be right. You may also note that it leads me far away from the field I usually till into what is terra incognita for the field naturalist. I couldn't help that. The mystery simply went in that direction. It begins, like all such stories, with a simple observation, and it does not end at all.

If sometime you see a porpoise up close, for instance when he is being carted from one tank to another at an oceanarium, see if you can locate his external ears. They're there all right,

but you may not be able to find them, since they are tiny pin-
holes at best, located a couple of inches behind and below the
animal's eyes. I've even looked at some porpoises in which the
ears were completely covered with skin. How, one wonders, can
the porpoise hear through a pinhole, especially when we know
his sense of hearing is very important to him and is extremely
acute?

As I began to learn about porpoise hearing during our work
with Kathy, I had thought about these things. I knew that beneath the pinhole of the ear lay cartilages and muscles somewhat similar to those in the human external ear. One theory
held that these were functional and that they served to cast
sound shadows and thus help the animal determine the direction from which a sound came. I knew, from an old parlor trick,
that our own external ears, or "pinnae," worked this way. The
trick is to close your eyes and have a friend shake a bunch of
keys somewhere in front of you. Point your finger at the spot
where the sound seems to originate. Then open your eyes and
see how good your directional sense is. Usually it's pretty good.
Then do it all over again, only this time bend the tops of your
ears over with the fingers of each hand. This time when you
point, you will likely be off by several feet. Your external ears
are involved in isolating the sources of sound. They have other
functions, too, such as collecting and concentrating sound.

I pondered these things when I remembered how blindfolded
Kathy had zeroed in on a tiny piece of fish sinking in her
tank and snapped it up without hesitation. How could she do
such a thing with that smooth head and those tiny pinhole
ears? I remembered that when she located the bit of food, she
came in with her head waggling in a jerky circle at first, as if she
was either listening alternately with her tiny ears or shooting
a sound beam out into the dark and scanning for the sinking
food morsel. Maybe she was doing both. At any rate, no one
knew.

I filed the mystery for future reference and forgot about it.
Then one morning, months later, it began to unravel itself for
me. My wife, Phyllis, and I and some friends were camping far

down the Baja California peninsula, waiting for our bush pilot friend, Francisco Muñoz, to pick us up. We had time to kill, because he wasn't due to land until afternoon. So the group of us wandered off down the lonely strand, looking at the fleets of fiddler crabs and poking at the debris on the beach. Soon I gave a yelp of joy, which my wife has learned to interpret as "Valuable junk ahoy!" and ran up to a bleached porpoise skeleton jutting part way out of the sand.

Phyllis groaned and said, "Now I suppose you're going to scoop that smelly thing up in your shirt. Francisco will turn right around and leave us *all* on the beach." As usual, I wasn't listening at that point but digging furiously with my hands to uncover the prize.

It was a big bottlenose porpoise that had died from some unknown cause, washed ashore, and become partly buried in the sand. Time and beach creatures had picked the skeleton clean, and the sun had turned it white. The skull was perfect; even the tiny cheekbones, which in porpoises are reduced to thin, almost threadlike strands, were intact. I held the head up, like Hamlet, gazing intently at that curious skull. It was like that of no other animal. The long bones of the snout jutted out like a broadened trough-shaped tube. The nose and forehead had been pushed back by millions of years of evolution until the nostrils pierced the skull far back of the snout. This change let the porpoise glide to the surface and breathe all in one smooth arc, without having to raise its head and "break stride" every time it needed air.

All these marvels I pointed out to my companions, who seemed more interested in sea shells. Setting the skull aside on the sand, I continued digging for other parts of the skeleton. Soon I unearthed the lower jaws, their peglike pointed teeth all still in place. I dusted off the sand and held them up. What peculiar jaws they were! Most land animals have stout jaws adjusted to the forces of chewing or tearing, or of pulling up grass or the leaves from trees. One can see strong flanges where jaw muscles attach. Nothing like this seemed to be represented in the porpoise jaw. In fact, it was so thin toward its rear end that I could see sunlight shining through the translucent bone, which at its center was less than a millimeter thick. I learned later that in some species, such as the pygmy sperm whale, this "pan bone," as the old whalers called it, is so thin it often can scarcely be dissected from a dead animal intact.

I knew that other mammal jaws had what is called a mandibular canal running down their length. This canal is usually a tube surrounded by solid bone, and carries blood vessels and nerves to the teeth and tissue of the lower jaw. It seemed lacking in the porpoise jaw, until I realized that instead it had been immensely increased in size until all that was left was that thin, translucent bone. On its outer side lay a flat wafer of bone, while on the inside bone was excavated away altogether until one looked forward to where the canal closed and began to be roofed over with bone. Finally, toward the front tip of the jaw, it tapered down into a perfectly respectable mandibular canal.

Nothing in nature as bizarre as this is created unless the forces of survival hold out value for it. Why, I wondered, did a porpoise find it useful to have a jaw as thin and delicate as finest porcelain, and a nerve and blood vessel canal that consumed the whole rear end of the jaw?

Picking up the skull again, I looked to see if the ear bones were present. They are nearly free of the skull in porpoises, and often fall out and are lost in beach skulls such as this. My prize was so complete, however, that both were there. I'd marveled at them before, but took a moment to look at them again on this animal. They are like ivory; in fact, they are the densest bones of the porpoise body. Each is like a tiny clenched fist, composed of two bones. One, like the ham of your hand, is a dense blob of bone that houses the organ of equilibrium and the peculiar curled organ of hearing, the cochlea, which lies twisted like a tiny sea shell inside it, its ends communicating through minute windows to the cavity of the middle ear. The fingers of the clenched fist are formed by the other bone, called the tympanic bulla. It arches over one side of the blob-shaped bone and encloses the cavity of the middle ear.

I knew that this intricate complex of bones hung suspended inside an air-filled cavity at the side of the skull in the live animal, its connection to the skull being the nerve of hearing and the blood vessels that supplied the tissue of the intricate structures within. I also knew that the tympanic bulla was supported on its front side by a fatty pad thought to hold the whole complex bone firmly in the skull.

Then I fitted the jaw to the skull, taking care to mesh the upper and lower teeth alternately with one another, as they are in the living porpoise. The jaw hinged far back on the skull, just to the side of the little clenched-fist ear bone. I saw that the mysterious mandibular canal pointed right at the ear bone. In fact, the lower jaw ended right over the ear-bone complex.

Could this peculiar canal somehow be the path of sound for a porpoise? Could Kathy, when she swung her head back and forth, have been directing sound to one ear and then the other through these canals in each jaw? The idea was exciting, but by this time my companions were far off down the beach, intent on their own affairs. So, with no students to preach to, I gathered up the bones in my shirt and hurried after them.

Those few moments of wonder on that warm desert beach have led to a whole series of experiments, meetings, scientific papers, and friendly arguments with my colleagues, and the mystery is even now far from solved. It does look to me, however, as if my insight is, in the main, correct, though not everyone in the scientific community agrees with me. Come to think of it, I can't remember a time when they ever all agreed with me. But that is part of the lure of science. The flux of ideas, the engagement of lively intellects, the coming together of people whose viewpoint and expertise differ, and finally the emergence from this bubbling pot of an enduring idea or two—that is science, and if one particularly minds being disagreed with, he should have taken up landscape gardening.

It's useful enough to make theoretical predictions such as these, but the proof of the pudding lies in what the animal actually does. So I began to experiment. My first test left me thoroughly perplexed. Dr. Kenneth Bloome, a treasured friend and associate

on other scientific projects, and I took old, tired Alice out of retirement for the occasion. We first renewed her acquaintance
with the ball bearings, requiring her to choose blindfolded the
larger of a pair and indicating her choice by pressing the appropriate lever. She whistled at us each morning just as she used
to, and she balked just as often as she ever had, but in a few
weeks she was repeating the same basic test she had performed
for so many months.

Our approach was to devise a cap of acoustically reflective
material that Alice would wear over the tip of her lower jaw. We
made it out of diving-suit foam rubber and attached it with
elastic over her snout. It came back along her jaw and covered
about half of the pan-bone area on each side. The idea was to
block incoming echoes of Alice's clicks. If our theory was correct, she should no longer be able to tell us which ball bearing
sphere was largest. In fact, it seemed likely that she would
even be unable to locate the target or the levers at all. If this
happened as planned, we would open small holes through the
rubber in the suspected areas of reception. At some point their
size should be big enough for Alice to begin to find her way
around again.

As so often happens, things didn't work out that way. At first,
just as we had planned, Alice was totally befuddled with the
jaw cover on. She seemed unwilling to move in the tank at all,
and couldn't find the levers. Our confidence in our own wisdom
leaped up. Then Alice brought us crashing back to humility,
which is certainly where we belonged anyway. She began to
emit echolocation sounds with remarkable intensity. When Ken
put his hands below the surface at these times, he reported that
he could actually *feel* the sounds she was emitting on the skin
of his hands. Then fitfully, grotesquely, Alice began to discriminate between a very large and a very small sphere. We had,
we knew, done something to Alice's ability to echolocate, but obviously, by making some mysterious corrections, she had been
able to solve her dilemma without our help. All the sites of
sound entry we suspected might exist were covered. In our ignorance, though, what we didn't do was to cover the rear end

of her jaws or her throat, and, as I will point out later, that was our undoing.

Ken and I set our perplexing results aside to think about them for a while, and Alice went back into retirement.

I continued dissecting porpoises any time I could lay hands on a dead one. Soon I began to doubt my original premise that sounds entered the jaws near their tips, and began to believe it more likely that sound penetrated right through the thin pan bone at the back of the jaw. The thinner it was, the easier it could be penetrated. This, of course, would at least partly explain our perplexing results with Alice; we simply hadn't shut down her hearing entirely with our jaw cover, since the rear ends of her jaws had remained uncovered.

I began to trace where fat was found on the porpoise head, since, as you may recall, water-borne sound has less trouble penetrating and traveling through fat than any other tissue. It could, in effect, form channels for sound, just as our air-filled ear canals do. The more I dissected, the more interesting little tidbits I found, and the more coherent the story seemed. Also, the more complicated it became. This all seemed right and proper to me, since nature almost never builds simple mechanisms. What emerges from the trials of natural selection, instead, are intricate and elegant systems whose refinements you almost never see *in toto* at one glimpse.

If that pan bone was the point at which porpoises received sounds, its thickness relative to the incoming sound would change every time the animal moved its head. That is to say, a sound beam hitting the bone diagonally would penetrate at an angle and would have to go through more bone than a sound beam hitting it directly from the side. With this thought in mind, I began to notice that the pan bones of porpoises were tilted outward in the living animal. In fact, the duties of porpoise jaws seemed twofold; the normal function of catching and holding prey was relegated to the tooth-bearing jaw in front, while hearing was presumably restricted to the rear half of the jaw. In some, like the sperm whales and the river porpoises of South America, the front of the jaw, which bore the teeth, was a simple rod of stout bone, while the pan bone behind flared to each side at about a twenty-degree angle. Such an animal might be able to switch its hearing from one jawbone to the other by simple movements of its head. I found that in some degree or another all porpoises showed this feature. Further, to my delight, I found in a physics book a discussion of experiments by a man who had tested the transmission of sound through ivory. I've never understood why he performed his experiments, but they were wonderfully relevant to the questions I was raising, since a porpoise jawbone is remarkably like ivory.

The experiments indicated that sounds of the kinds porpoises use would penetrate easily with almost no loss in intensity when hitting the pan bone at right angles (90 degrees), but if the bone was tipped with regard to the incoming sound beam, less and less would penetrate until very precisely at 8.8 degrees the sound should cut off altogether. If the porpoise jawbone acted acoustically like ivory, porpoises could indeed swing their heads across a group of echoes or other sounds and turn one jaw on and the other off.

A physicist friend, Dr. Scott Johnson, took this information for me and ran a series of tests on his computer. The resultant piles of computer paper showed that not only might the animal turn one jaw on and the other off by swinging its head, but such swings would sort out the returning echo with regard to frequencies (pitch), since each frequency had different capabilities for penetrating bone. Thus, one might envision that a porpoise hearing through its jaws would also hear a changing series of pitches as it swept across an echo field. It would thus be provided with a remarkably sensitive way of learning about the composition of sounds.

The story I found by tracing fat deposits was even more fascinating. One species, the pygmy sperm whale, had a perfect pipe of oil starting just beneath its skin that led directly from the sloping jaw and throat to the bulla of the ear. In fact, over the almost paper-thin pan bone of this species lay a cylindrical area filled with waxy spermaceti oil, limited only by the skin and blubber. This same liquid material was contained inside the jaw and tapered back in a true channel to the ear.

In porpoises the oil was supplanted by fat. Just beneath the skin of the rear jaw where the pan bone lay buried, one could see an oval area of pellucid fat, with muscles invading the tissues on all sides. This oily fat extended clear down to the bone and, once again, filled the interior of the jaw and extended back to the ear-bone complex. Thus, my predicted channel was there and seems to be present in all toothed whales and porpoises. But it extended farther forward than I expected, invading the throats of some species and even extending up into the base of the tongue.

Thus, I was almost, but not quite, prepared to accept the findings of some neurophysiologist colleagues who had succeeded in placing tiny electrodes in the hearing centers of the porpoise brain. These electrodes picked up a minute electrical discharge every time the sense of hearing of the animal was excited in some way. Further, if the hearing apparatus of the porpoise detected a loud sound, a large electrical discharge would be recorded, while a small one produced a small discharge.

Using this system, the scientists could map the sensitivity of the animal, by moving a sound source over its body. Porpoises heard six times as well when sounds were played to their lower jaws as when played to their tiny pinhole ears. The throat and tongue were highly sensitive, and, in fact, with the jaws, were the spots most sensitive to sound on the animal's body. Imagine —an animal that seems to hear with its jaws and throat! This made excellent sense when one considered the distribution of fat in the porpoise head. Kathy, when she swung her head around and around, was listening not just with her jaws but also with her whole lower head. The neurophysiologists found that the sides of the porpoise head remained as separate receivers, though, and sounds played to different sides of an animal's throat appeared in different sides of its brain.

All this was exciting to me, in view of my predictions about jaw hearing and the fat guidance of sound, but I was quite unprepared for the scientists to report that their porpoises heard almost as well through their *foreheads* as through their throats and jaws! Sounds played there were 5.5 times as effective as those played over the pinhole external ears. How a porpoise might hear with its forehead escapes me to this day. No acoustic nerve penetrates that area, and there seems to be no route for sounds hitting there to get directly to the ear.

Also, nothing I have said will explain how sounds might get from the porpoise jaw to the organ of hearing, the cochlea, that tiny coiled organ encased inside the dense ear bone. In human hearing, sound travels to the inner ear through a chain of three tiny bones, the malleus, incus, and stapes, the outermost of which is attached to the eardrum. When the drum is set in motion by air-borne sound, the malleus moves too, communicating its vibrations down the bony chain to the cochlea. That incredible little device translates these movements into nerve impulses which are a faithful description of the sound just received. These then go to the brain for further processing and interpretation.

The middle ear of the porpoise is different. Its eardrum, a slackened cone of tissue, seems degenerate to me. I suspect that when the early porpoise ancestor first entered the water, the eardrum became useless (in exactly the same way that our ears are virtually useless under water), and a new mode of sound transmission developed. I suspect that sound came in through the blubber and thence to the conchlike bulla, to whose outer surface the jaw fat attaches. Whereas in a normal land-dwelling animal sound comes in through the tympanic membrane to the tiny middle-ear bones, this seems to have changed in the porpoise. The outermost of these bones, the malleus, is attached to the porpoise bulla. I suspect sound comes in through the jaw fat, to the bulla, thence through this tiny bony strut to the inner ear and brain.

All of this is supposition, supported here and there with just enough fact to allow various scientists to explain what they see in different ways. This is always the case when you find yourself at the fuzzy forefront of science. Here, equipped with such

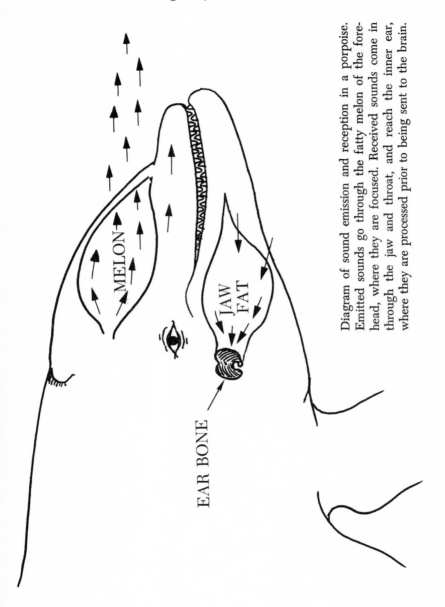

MELON

JAW FAT

EAR BONE

Diagram of sound emission and reception in a porpoise. Emitted sounds go through the fatty melon of the forehead, where they are focused. Received sounds come in through the jaw and throat, and reach the inner ear, where they are processed prior to being sent to the brain.

facts as one knows, one moves by intuition and wonderment. A person without real curiosity has no hope of functioning very well, it seems to me. One tries to perceive a mode of functioning in the shapeless and complex mass of blubber, muscle, and bone. The trick is to know what facts are relevant, and often to dig them out from disciplines far removed from your own, and to imagine how all these disparate pieces fit together. It's not an orderly process for me, involving as it does many incorrect scenarios, a disorderly store of information, and a deep, and I hope reasonably accurate, feeling for how nature builds things and how animals work. I treasure my ability to throw ideas away quite as much as the ability to pursue and develop them.

Thus "pet theories" come to be, and thus scientists argue interminably with one another over various interpretations of the phenomena they see. This need for argument is integral to science, and even though science is human endeavor, there is no need for the arguments to become personal. But, of course, they often do. It's easy enough to jab at your fellow scientists for their apparent myopia about some idea or other, and I suppose it keeps them on their toes. It certainly works the other way, too. The higher the pitch of the argument on both sides, the more craft and effort the participants are apt to apply to the discussion. This often causes scientists to look deeply into the phenomena they study, and more critical science is apt to result. The trick is to argue about phenomena and not personalities.

The science of porpoise hearing is lively at the moment because three separate theories remain unresolved. My little store of facts and intuition leads me in one direction, and other observations and experiments have led other workers in other directions. It's instructive in understanding how science works to mention one of these intellectual exchanges. One group of workers, amongst them treasured colleagues of mine, also found the jaw area to be the most sensitive hearing locus. I could, of course, accept this without argument. These scientists penetrated the porpoise ear by surgery and found that cutting the tiny chain of bony ossicles did not cause a great reduction in the porpoise's hearing sensitivity. Therefore, they concluded that these tiny bones are of little importance to the hearing of porpoises. If the porpoise hears, as I surmise he must, by sound transmitted through this chain, this result is perplexing.

So I dug into their experiment in detail. I concluded that their surgical procedures do not allow them to say that the ear ossicles are of little importance in porpoise hearing. To get to the ossicles, they had to cut open the bulla. To my way of thinking, the moment they cut the bulla, they severely reduced the hearing of the animal, before they ever severed the bony ossicular chain. The additional cutting of this chain, or so my hunch tells me, would have made little difference and tells us little.

My theory seems to require that sound go from the jaw fat body and through the bulla to the middle-ear bones. How, I wondered, could it do this? Once again delving into the literature of physics, I came up with some papers by a scientist who had studied how water-borne clicking sounds like those used by porpoises behave when they hit spheres of various kinds. Now, to be sure, the bulla is not a sphere, but it *is* a thin, curved surface like the wall of a hollow sphere, and the sounds coming to it from the fat body of the jaw should be like those coming through water. The analogy is not perfect, but it may be useful. The physicist showed that sounds hitting a thin-walled sphere produced a "flexural wave" in the wall of the sphere. If the bulla is like a metal sphere, then a porpoise click echo coming down the fatty jaw channel should produce such a flexure in the bulla; it should travel around the wall of the bulla, be picked up by the thin, bony stylus of the first ear ossicle, and be transmitted thence to the inner ear and brain.

The workers who cut the ossicular chain must have found it hard to explain how their animal could hear well at all. Their tests didn't support those who feel the pinhole ear is the site of hearing, or the work of those who, like me, suggest a route through the bulla and ossicles. They fell back on the conclusion that the animal hears by "bone conduction," which presumably includes flexural transmission around the bulla, since there is no other bony route to the cochlea, but bypassing the chain of ossicles. I presume they mean that the bulla flexes and passes its vibrations on to the heavy ear bone to which it is attached. This bone, containing the cochlea, is then stimulated.

Two things make me feel this is incorrect. First, when the entire bone that houses the cochlea vibrates, the result is hearing, but it is a general sort of hearing that tells the animal little about pitch. Presumably the cochlea cannot discriminate well when sounds come in to it from all directions. It has to receive them from one end and to process them in an orderly manner to discriminate pitch. Second, I cannot imagine that nature would build an intricately structured chain of bones, modifying them in very specific ways that would seem optimum for the transmission of high-frequency sounds (such as porpoises use), and then abandon the effort.

Who's right? Well, I see no reason to abandon porpoise hearing through jaw, throat, bulla, and ossicles for the moment, and I think time and more experiments will bear me out. I could be wrong, too. Perhaps my own experiments will disprove my theory. That's a comfortable thought, since I could then proclaim in a clearly audible voice how I myself had advanced the field and proved my old notions wrong. But then, maybe the guys who cut the bulla are right.

Looking back on other sagas of investigation like this, I see that nature has nearly always fooled the scientist. At first he looks at what he considers to be a broad and simple truth. Then, with more work, complexity appears and his chief wonder, in retrospect, is how he could have perceived any pattern at all. Always, it seems, animal structure and function are more subtly balanced to serve the many needs of the animal than even the most sophisticated scientists at first can imagine. Very likely that is what we will find when all the dust settles.

CHAPTER THIRTEEN

Cachalote

Berit Bloome pressed the soft ear cups against her head and listened. The cord from her earphones led to a tape recorder resting on the deck. From it a cable looped over the scarred gunwale into the sea. She was silent a moment while the little felucca rocked quietly in the mirrorlike water. She looked upward in concentration, and said, "I hear knocks."

Later when we listened to the tape, they sounded like someone tapping on an empty keg with a fist. Ken Bloome lifted the earphones from her head and listened. He too reported knocking sounds. "Do you gals see anything anywhere near?" he asked.

The two women, who were hunkered down alongside the weathered cabin bulkhead, shaded their eyes and scanned the flat sea. It was empty except for the line of faint, far-off hills of Mejillones, ten miles to the southeast. Leanne Hinton, the second woman, switched on the tape recorder, watching its reels come up to speed. She adjusted its volume delicately until the VU meter wavered at minus 20 decibels. Each knock caused the needle to jump a little, but not enough to reach midline on the gauge. This setting, she knew, would ensure a clear recording. Sharp sounds like these are apt to bang into the electronic innards of a tape recorder and "overload" it unless the settings are made carefully. Then she too listened in puzzlement to the barrage of banging sounds that coursed through the sea below.

Leanne beckoned to Enrique, the felucca's skipper. Enrique, a graceful man tanned like dark leather by the northern Chilean sun, was our teacher. He seemed to know all the secrets of everything that lived in the Chilean sea. He swung up from the open stern cockpit and came forward to listen. When the earphones were in place, instant recognition spread across his face. "Cachalote," he said firmly.

"Cachalote" meant sperm whale, and one wonders how he knew what they sounded like under water. Sperm whales never seem to cease making these bangs, and perhaps he may have heard them through the hull of his ancient little craft sometime at night as she slept offshore in the great Humboldt Current. Who knows? Anyhow, Enrique left no doubt that there were sperm whales about, even though no one could see them.

The tape brought back to me by Berit, Ken, and Leanne tells the rest of the story more eloquently than words can. For minutes the knocks continued, coming in long trains, a few each second. Then a burst, much louder than the rest, began to rap faster and faster, ten, twenty, thirty bangs per second, merging into a crescendo whine that rose and ended in a desultory scattering of bangs. Almost at once it began again, this time louder still. Leanne hurried to the recorder and twisted the record-level knob almost as far down as it would go. Finally there came a long cascade of even louder knocks that rose to a loud whine because the individual sounds came so fast. The whine ended in a crash, the sound of rushing water, a roar of the felucca's engine starting, a clash of gears, and then the overwhelming noise of hasty acceleration.

Ken told me they had seen nothing until the huge bulk of a sperm whale rose beneath the gently rocking felucca. The whale had headed straight for the hydrophone directly below the ship, spraying it inquisitively with sound. It actually hit the instrument with its snout before rising to the surface, thus accounting for the final crescendo of knocks, the initial crash, and the water noise. Then the whale surfaced, blew, and rolled onto its side, only a few yards from the frail craft. That instant of cetacean curiosity was quite enough for Raul in the engine well. He immediately started the engine, and Enrique, concurring, swung the felucca away from the whale as fast as he could go. It was clear from the tape that they "got the hell out of there."

The whale was a little one, as sperm whales go, probably not yet into its maturity and still full of "puppy" curiosity. Ken and the women said it was very close to thirty feet long, and I believe them, because when the animal rolled onto its side, it was almost exactly as long as the felucca, whose length was thirty feet.

The recorder tape of this event my crew brought back meant much more to me than they could have guessed. It was unique in that for once we knew exactly which sperm whale was making the sounds we recorded, and we knew rather precisely how long its body was. Most tapes of sperm whale sounds consist of ten or twenty animals all banging at once, and there is no way to tell which whales are responsible for any of the sounds. I needed to know, and the tape would let me test one of my more bizarre and seemingly untestable ideas.

The idea, succinctly put, was this. I thought I could perceive from the almost unbelievably peculiar anatomy of the sperm whale head that sperm whales produce sounds with a pair of huge lips located inside the soft tissue of the forehead (the lips were picturesquely called *museau du singe,* or monkey's muzzle, by French anatomists of the last century), and then rocket them back and forth between a pair of air sacs also located inside the forehead, to produce the loud banging sounds we heard. For a whale or porpoise swimming in water, you will recall, such air spaces as the sacs make nearly perfect sound mirrors.

The key to the validity of my idea lay in the structure of the sperm whale click. It is not just the simple bangs or knocks we hear but is actually a reverberant series of much smaller and briefer signals produced so quickly that, to our ears, a single noise is all that is evident. When a single bang was taped and slowed down to a fiftieth of normal speed, one could hear that it was actually composed of an initial loud click followed by six or seven clicks of diminishing intensity:

click- click-click-click-click- click-click-

It went, all complete in about 25/1000 of a second. If this peculiar composite noise was produced by reverberation within the whale forehead, I thought, the time between the diminishing clicks should relate to the distance between the sound mirrors. These mirrors, I assumed, were the pair of huge air sacs, also in the forehead. The biggest sac was plastered against the dish-shaped front face of the sperm whale's skull, and was, in a big sperm, big enough to hold two men sitting upright side by side. The other mirror was clear out near the tip of the snout, as much as twenty feet away, buried a few inches beneath the surface of the whale's bluff bow. Between these supposed mirrors lay one of the strangest organs in the animal kingdom—a huge, curving cylinder called the spermaceti organ, filled with hundreds of gallons of a strange waxy oil, which is liquid in a living sperm whale. I felt that this organ might be the reverberation chamber, and the oil the medium for sound transmission.

If I had a record of a single sperm whale's sounds, I could listen to some of them and determine exactly how much time there was between each pair of click sounds in a single bang. This time should represent the time it takes a sound to travel down the spermaceti organ from the huge lips, bounce off the great rear sac "mirror" plastered against the face of the skull, and return to the front mirror. Repeated reflections would produce the entire sound, and a leakage at each reflection of part of the sound out into the sea would result in their diminuendo. Thus, with certain additional information, I should be able to convert the time between reverberations into a measure of the animal's total length.

The additional information I needed was as follows. First I

had to know how fast sound traveled in spermaceti oil. So I sent a sample to an acoustician friend, Dr. Jerry Diercks, in Texas and he performed the needed measurement. He told me that, surprisingly enough, sound traveled quite a lot faster in this peculiar oil than it did in sea water. Next, if the size of the whale had anything to do with these time relations within its sounds, a single whale should always produce the same kind of bang. It should always have its click-click-clicks equal distances apart in time.

By measuring many signals, I had become convinced that this was true. Even within the cacophony coming from a school, one can detect the trains of sounds made by a single animal. Each of these, when its tape was slowed down, showed its bangs to be composed of reverberations evenly spaced apart in time. Furthermore, each whale, though consistent with regard to its own sounds, was different from most of the others. This was just what one would expect from a school of animals composed of many sizes.

All this was to the good, but two major questions and some minor ones remained. Before I could place any reliance at all on the idea, I had to know how far apart the air-sac mirrors were in whales of various sizes. Then I could convert Dr. Diercks' sound velocity measurement into travel distance and then to whale size. Only then could I see if it matched the approximate length of the Chilean whale that had so frightened my fishermen and friends.

Next, it simply wouldn't do for the sounds to continue to reverberate between the two proposed mirrors in the whale's forehead. The whole packet of reverberations had to get out into the sea somehow. The scientific literature I had searched did not clear up this question for me, so there was no recourse but to find a sperm whale and to dissect it. I thought that my friend Bernie Lenheim, a biologist with the government Fisheries Service, could probably help. Bernie's job was to check the whales that came in sporadically to the only American whaling station operating at that time, the station at Richmond, California, in San Francisco Bay.

When I called Bernie he assured me that some sperms had been caught that week. He'd call, he said, when the catcher boat radioed in the news of a sperm whale catch. Since most captures were made about a hundred miles at sea, we would have time to gather our gear together, hop on a plane from Los Angeles, and be at the whaling-station dock when the ship came in, towing its whales alongside.

Early one evening about two weeks later, Bernie called me to say that four sperms were coming in and the catcher ship would dock about midnight. I hastily gathered my team together. In preparation for the effort, all the necessary gear had been assembled in my garage. We carefully loaded the trunk and back seat of my car with oscilloscopes, sound generators, dissecting tools, notebooks, sample jars, and other items we felt might be needed and headed for the airport. Once there, I apportioned the equipment to each person as hand luggage, since we could not entrust much of it to the delicate ministrations of the baggage personnel. A few anxious moments passed when the largest part of it refused to be "placed beneath the seat in front of us," as is required by FAA regulations. A sympathetic and curious stewardess solved our problem by letting us put most of it in her coat closet, in return for a detailed explanation of what we were hoping to do.

At San Francisco we started off in a rented station wagon in the black night to search for the Richmond Whaling Station. The station, I knew, was somewhere up in the tough waterfront of Richmond, along the shore of northern San Francisco Bay. In my Navy days in World War II, this area had a justifiably evil reputation. If one was looking for trouble, it was a sure place to find it, as we all knew from the battered crewmates who returned to our ship. On the night of the whales it proved calm enough, though; we found a dilapidated waterfront lined with ramshackle rusting metal buildings, doors slack on broken hinges, dust-encrusted windows, mostly shattered, facing on rutted dirt streets that wandered uncertainly along the bluffs. Our lights flashed up and down across these old, settling hulks as we picked our way amongst the ruts and railroad tracks. Down at the end of one such track was a gaunt building whose sign dimly proclaimed, "Del Monte Fishing Company." A single dirty bulb depended from a metal yardarm over the dirt street. From inside, through the grease-covered windows, came a hum of activity. A dump truck, comfortable in its rusting old age, stood slumped under a chute that pierced the building wall. From the chute came a mass of formless whale parts and oily fragments of blubber, sluiced into the recesses of the truck by a man standing in hip boots deep in the gurry. That truckload of assorted whale parts, it turned out, was almost the last of the four sperm whales we had hoped to examine. They were already on their way to the rendering plant.

What an end, I thought, to a magnificent and mysterious animal. Then I thought, Now what do we do?

Inside we entered a vast cement-floored warehouse with a broad cement slipway running up into it from the murky bay below. Blood and oil lay in slippery pools across the deck. A weblike mass of cables and hooks lay snarled amongst the blood, where they had been left once the "blanket pieces," or sheets of blubber, had been stripped from the whales. To our right an awful giant of a machine gobbled up the last remaining pieces of the four animals. A huge steel shaft, as thick as a man's waist, rotated, bringing ponderous hooked steel arms one after another down upon the last six-inch-thick sheets of blubber, forcing them into the maw of a grinder that then spat them out the chute into the waiting truck. The blubber sheets, some fifteen feet long, writhed and recoiled with each blow, and crawled jerkily forward into a hole in the deck like huge living things in their death throes.

The whales had come in early, and the flensers were finishing them off, paying no attention to the forthcoming arrival of the scientists. That, we found, was the way they treated all visitors. This was the only operating whaling station in the United States; many scientists had visited there, and not a few had proved a nuisance in the dangerous operation. The gaunt old Norwegian flenser who ran the crew had nothing but contempt for such interruptions. When he answered us at all it was curtly, with the implied message that it would be to his liking if we got the hell out of the way of his men and stayed well clear of cables and bone saws.

"Well," I asked my crew, "what now?" Should we get some sleep, curse the catcher-ship skipper for reporting in his position incorrectly, and go home and wait another two weeks?

It wasn't until the operation was complete that we learned four more whales were due in the next day. If we waited, we might work with the last animal after the others had been cleared away. The flensers would cut the huge head free, slide it to the side, and let us putter around with it once the other work had been done.

We trudged back out into the night, packed our gear in the car, and sought out a place to sleep. At 2 A.M. we found an ancient pistachio-colored motel whose plaster fell free of the lathing in many places, featuring enough aged, sway-backed beds for us all.

Next day we did indeed get our whale. It was a little one as sperm whales go, just over the thirty-five-foot lower legal limit. I walked beside it as it was winched up the slip. What a strange animal! About 35 percent of its length was a great, bulbous head. The rugose body tapered to a narrow tail and then spread to giant flukes. The head didn't look like the pictures I had seen. The bow was bluff, to be sure, as one sees in old whalers' paintings, but from the front the upper part of the head was rounded, almost cylindrical, like the end of a boiler, and then just below it was narrowed and indented, and a foot or so above the upper jaw it finally bulged again. The lower jaw was all but invisible under this peculiar snout, a long, thin rod of bone lined with teeth.

I later learned that the upper cylindrical bulge was the front end of the spermaceti organ, the indentation beneath it lay just over the strange buried lips (the *museau du singe*), and the lower swelling was the front of what the whalers called the "junk." They gave it this derisive name because it was made of fat not nearly so valuable as the spermaceti oil above.

Far up on the front tip of the snout was the peculiar S-shaped blowhole. The left nostril, of which it was the termination, pointed forward, instead of upward as in other whales, causing the whale to spout at an angle when it rose to breathe. From a distance one can usually tell a sperm whale from any other species by this feature of its spout.

The whale's lower jaw dragged open as the animal came to a halt on the flensing deck. It looked like a long, cylindrical branch that forked abruptly outward near its rear end. Stout peg-like teeth, yellowed and glistening, lined its border in two close-set rows, and one could see where they rested in indentations of the toothless upper jaw when the animal's mouth was closed.

Just below and behind the angles of the mouth were the two closed eyes, covered with heavily folded lids. Obviously, in life the whale couldn't see forward past its great nose, which swelled above and ahead of those now sightless eyes, but it could look down on either side of its mouth. That's presumably where its food was being caught, so sight might help in the last stages of capturing a big squid, but it would be blocked out during much of the course of hunting. That job, I supposed, was left to the whale's biosonar or echolocation system—whose banging sounds my team heard off Chile.

I pondered those eyes. They were so far out on prominences that I wouldn't be surprised if the animal could simply roll them back and see dead astern, even though it couldn't see very well where it was going.

The whaling-station crew made quick work of their part of the whale. They slashed the whale's blubber coat in a circumferential cut back of the head. A flap was cut, a slit made in its corner, the cable slipped through and secured by a heavy wooden toggle. The old Norwegian flenser raised his hand to the winch operator, who took a strain on the cable. It snapped taut and pulled at the blubber. The flenser sliced with quick strokes between blubber and muscle. A great blanket piece ripped free of the animal with a noise like crumpling paper, to be slid quickly into the grinder. The head was cut free and the carcass disposed of while we got to work on our bloody prize.

Instead of the great hockey-stick-sized knives used by the

flensers, we set to work with tiny scalpels. To help understand what we found, it would be best to refer from time to time to the diagram of the structures, since it was a bizarre creature, unlike any other in nature, that we explored.

My first cut was in the indentation below the bulbous cy-lindrical forehead, above the upper jaw. I cut crossways across the face of the snout along the line of the groove. The tissue was tough and fibrous, but only about two inches in I felt my knife push through into a cavity. It was the distal sac, the front of the two sound mirrors I felt the animal possessed. Here should be the secret of how the animal's sounds were able to emerge into the water as a packet of brief, almost explosive sounds, and here we should find the lips I thought were sound producers.

We cut a large flap in the sac wall and pulled it upward. There lay exposed a black semicircular pair of rounded, arcing lips. They were nearly as broad as the snout and perhaps two and a half feet wide. We tried to open them but found them pressed tightly closed. I forced a hand inside them and felt them grip me very tightly. Two of us finally pulled them open. Above and below, around the perimeter of each lip, was a grooved band of hard, translucent tissue, almost like horn, that looked as if it had been machined on a lathe. The two bands met each other tightly in the closed lips. We surmised that the ridges of one lip fitted in the grooves of the other when the *museau* was closed, forming a sort of mortised border.

Behind the lips lay the walls of the broad, flat, horizontal right nasal passage. Each wall was striated with hundreds of curving black lines, each ending against the rear wall of the lip borders. Later we found these were actually tiny pigmented grooves, and came to suspect that they collected and distributed air to the back of the lips when the animal swam in the deep sea. The evenly distributed air might force the lips open and let them clap back together to produce a bang. When these strange whales dive a mile and a half down, such air as they contain is com-pressed almost into a fluid and comprises less than 1/200 the volume it had at the surface. A thin air film is all the whale has to work with at such depths in producing its sounds, and perhaps these tiny grooves help to guide it, I thought.

I looked for the sound window that would let the rocketing, reverberating sounds out of the spermaceti organ. They had to cross the air-filled distal sac somehow. In moments I thought I had found it. Across the entire front of the air sac, just under the surface of the snout, lay a triangular ridge of stout tissue, standing out white against the otherwise black sac wall. This, I could see, would fit precisely between the line of the lips behind, and when the animal swam below the surface, would be pressed between them very tightly. Perhaps sounds emerged from the upper lip of the *museau* and directly into this tightly pressed ridge and thence into the water ahead. Above and below the smooth ridge, the sac wall was wrinkled and folded like stout cardboard and would keep the sac walls from pressing tightly against one another. Air contained in the sac would stay between the tissue folds, and thus continue to act as a mirror to sound above and below what I perceived as the animal's sound window.

I began to trace the spermaceti organ. We peeled the blubber from the head and came at once to what whalers had called the "case." It was the container which held the prized spermaceti oil. In the days of hand whaling the sperm whale head had been too heavy to hoist aboard with hand-operated block and tackle. So it was simply secured upright in the water alongside the ship and a whaler was lowered over the side onto it. He opened it from the upper end as if slicing a watermelon, and then lowered a bucket repeatedly to "bail the case" of its prized oil. Old sea stories have it that this job was sometimes dangerous because of the swarms of sharks that tore at the whale, or because occasionally whalers slipped and fell into the cavernous case to drown in the oil.

Once I had stripped away the blubber, I could see the entire case stretching ahead yards from the ridge of the skull clear to the monkey's muzzle. It was a cylindrical barrier of hundreds of parallel ligamentous cables, most as thick as your thumb, all

glistening and white. I could scarcely force a scalpel blade between them. When I succeeded at last, it was as if I had cut
into one of those puncture-proof inner tubes; a clear, waxy
spermaceti began to ooze forth in a welling pool. Once we had
opened the great oil-filled chamber, we found it almost completely hollow, only crisscrossed by weblike connective tissue
bearing tiny blood vessels for its nurture. Such strange oil! It
spilled in a cascade on the flensing deck and in the cool air
congealed into a soft white wax. Our little animal held perhaps
sixty gallons of the fluid oil in its nose.

The spermaceti organ ended, I found, in the upper lip of the
museau du singe, as a broad, shallow wedge. The organ widened
behind until it was oval-shaped, and at its rear end it was
bounded by the great air sac spread across the skull forehead.
That structure, I felt, would hold some surprises for us. I predicted that in it we should find the secret of how a whale could
make its sounds at any depth of water and in any body position
and yet have its rear air mirror remain intact. There should
be a way of trapping air over the face of the sac even if the
animal turned upside down, as we knew them to do. I reasoned
that the whale's echonavigation could not function if the air
collected up in one corner of the sac during a dive. The whale
could not be expected to produce its reverberating sounds in
the deep sea if its mirrors were not complete.

I cut the rear of the spermaceti organ free. It looked for
all the world like the face of a bass drum, but, unlike a drum,
its surface was soft and I could dent it easily with my thumb.
This wall formed the front of the great frontal sac, which ad-
hered tightly to the bony forehead of the skull. All across the
skull face it was covered with a pavement of spherical knobs,
each an inch or more in diameter. Later, when we were able
to examine these more carefully in the laboratory, we found that
each was a tough, hollow, fibrous sphere, filled with fluid. In
between each lay a channel that would be air-filled in life.
Every so often a thin membrane blocked these tortuous channels, and is, we think, the way the sperm whale keeps its mirror
intact in the deep sea. The film of air trapped between the

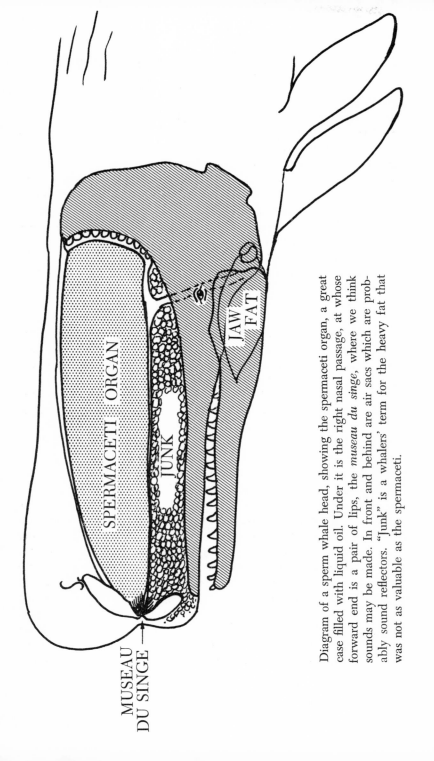

Diagram of a sperm whale head, showing the spermaceti organ, a great case filled with liquid oil. Under it is the right nasal passage, at whose forward end is a pair of lips, the *museau du singe*, where we think sounds may be made. In front and behind are air sacs which are probably sound reflectors. "Junk" is a whalers' term for the heavy fat that was not as valuable as the spermaceti.

knobs (the soft rear wall of the spermaceti organ must press tightly against them in life) could only move a short distance in any direction before encountering one of these membranes. A filigree of air between the knobs would remain in a whale's sac during a deep dive and would continue to reflect sound even under the enormous pressures of the deep sea.

The dissection had taken several hours. About midnight I called a halt, literally climbing out of my dissection, covered with blood and spermaceti. Dave Bottles, one of my companions, thrust a cold beer into my greasy hand. I sat exhausted on the occipital condyles of the whale sipping my beer, satisfied that we had learned a great deal.

Now, inferences like these, made from anatomy without actual tests of true function in life, are speculations. They are apt to be castles in the air without foundation in reality. So, while I thought I could see how this incredible system might work, I did not know that my speculations were right. In fact, I am not now satisfied that I know with certainty, though some additional evidence has accumulated to support the ideas I have given here.

Our measurements of the spermaceti organ in relation to body length were compared with other measurements of this sort published by Japanese whale biologists. Combining our data, we were able to calculate how long the animal should have been from the structure of its sounds. Our figures showed that it should have been thirty feet long—just what Ken and the others had told me! My theory leapt up another notch in my estimation.

Next I went to my colleague, Dr. George Harvey, an ingenious instrument designer and biologist. "George, can you build me a sperm whale?" I asked, half facetiously.

George, who takes such challenges seriously, without cracking a smile asked me to explain myself.

"Well," I told him, "do you think you could take the dimensions and other design criteria we think we see in the sound system of the sperm whale and build a mechanical model to see if it can be made to produce sperm whale clicks?"

George, who was present at the dissection, asked me a few

questions to fill in his knowledge: How long was the spermaceti organ in different-sized whales? How wide across? Did it narrow or curve? Did I think the air sacs covered all of both ends? How big was the sound generator?

I discussed these things with him, and he hummed to himself, turned, and left the lab. Next day he returned and announced that his plastic sperm whale was making good clicks, and would I come and see.

I was flabbergasted, since I had thought such a model would take weeks to make. In George's lab, surrounded by the banks of electronic gear and cables of his trade, there stood a piece of plastic pipe, about three feet long. George flipped a switch on a gray-colored instrument and asked me to look at his oscilloscope screen. I did so while he tinkered beside me.

Instantly traces of clicks appeared on the screen, and I could see at once that they looked for all the world like those of the sperm whale. Each was a diminishing packet of bursts.

George's "whale" consisted of a tiny speaker, some earphones, a sound generator, the piece of plastic pipe, and two boards. George had carefully measured the pipe, which was his spermaceti organ, to compensate for the fact that his whale "talked in air," where sound went one-fifth as fast as it does in water. The boards were his sound mirrors. Though they were not as efficient as the air sacs would be, they produced a good echo. The top board was slid a bit to the side, partly off the end of the pipe, simulating the sound window I insisted must exist at the front of the spermaceti organ. The rear board covered the entire pipe, just as the giant knobby frontal sac did in the living whale.

A series of single clicks came in electronically to the speaker and rocketed back and forth between the boards, some energy escaping out of the incomplete mirror at the top with each traverse. These escaped reverberations bore a close resemblance to sperm whale bangs. Each single click made by the generator produced a packet of clicks, starting with an intense signal and diminishing in strength until, after six or seven reverberations, it disappeared.

This "whale" was a bit unstable, and its clicks were apt to change with slight readjustments of the parts, but later George refined the apparatus and could always produce good sperm whale signals with his contraption. George's whale made me feel a little bit better about the theory.

While we were busy trying to simulate whale clicks recorded in the ocean, I was wondering why the sperm whale should make such peculiar sounds in the first place. All other toothed whales that had been studied produced simple clicks, or, at the most complicated, pairs of clicks. What was different about the way a sperm whale lived that would require these particular bursts of sound? The only possibility that came to mind was that sperm whales feed in the deep sea, sometimes several thousand feet down, and eat mostly very large, swift prey—very large squids, some of which may be ten or even twenty feet in length. Probably the range at which the sperm whale locates its food is very long—a mile or more.

It occurred to me that if the sperm whale did what Alice, the bottlenose porpoise, did, I might have a partial explanation. That is, Alice sent out a click and waited for its echo before sending out another. Because most of her echonavigation was close in, a matter of dozens of yards or less, she could emit large numbers of sounds in a short period of time and still retain this relationship. We came to suspect, as you may recall, that in this way she was able to compare the outgoing signal with its echo and thus gain a whole galaxy of information about a target.

Now, a sperm whale trying to do this with a squid a mile away could emit just about one click per second. I doubted if this would be enough to tell the sperm whale much about the size, composition, speed, and bearing of a prey animal. *But,* if the whale used packets of clicks instead, perhaps the internal relationships of the echo would tell the whale enough to be useful even with sounds emitted at this slow rate. The more I thought about this and discussed it with colleagues, the more I became convinced that this might be correct. For example, if the sound packet of a sperm whale hit a small squid, each of the little clicks that make it up might come back as a discrete echo, simply because each little click would have time to travel on before the next arrived a thousandth of a second later. Thus the animal would hear a clean echo much like its outgoing sound. On the other hand, if the squid was a big one, each little click would hit the squid at many places and return multiple echoes. The result should be a "mushy" echo, in which the little clicks merged into one long sound.

Another possible function was demonstrated to me by a physicist friend, Dr. Vern Knudsen. Cautious scientist that he is, he refused to answer me directly when I asked him how the sperm whale's sound might work. He beckoned me to follow him to his laboratory. Once there, he led me into a strange room called an anechoic chamber—that is, a room designed so that no sound could produce an echo. We entered through a wall and walked to the exact center of the room on a scaffolding of stainless-steel wires. All the walls were covered with long wedges of glass wool, their points facing us. Any sounds we made would be trapped between these wedges of wool and no echo would come back.

Dr. Knudsen produced a starter's pistol from his pocket and fired it into the air. *Pop,* it went, like a cap gun. Next he led me into an echo chamber, a tall, walled room lined with hard plaster. Once again the gun was produced and fired. The noise was long and painfully intense. The doctor explained that in the first room the sound had passed my ears once, while in the latter room it had gone by many times as it was reflected from one wall to another. My ears had failed to distinguish these individual echoes but instead had summated them into the painfully intense sound.

Without further explanation the doctor left me to ponder and draw my own conclusions. I wondered if the packet of clicks produced by the sperm whale might do the same thing in its ears; that is, would a faint echo from a very distant target be summated by the whale, allowing it to hear tiny sounds that would otherwise be lost in the background noise of the deep sea? In fact, such repeated clicks do provide a major way for animals to detect their own echoes in otherwise noisy and confusing environments. The click trains are predictable because the animal has heard them when they were emitted, but extraneous noise is apt to be random.

It's exciting to predict something in science, like predicting and finding the knobs on the big sac, which we think may hold the air film, but it's also time for caution, since, however much I want this strange system to work the way I think it might, no one will know until it is tested on a living whale.

We must find a way to get up close to a living sperm whale and to listen in to his sounds. If, say, we can press a microphone against the front of his snout, over the *museau du singe,* we should be able to hear the whole packet of sounds. But if we shift our microphone up or down, we should be over the sound mirror, and the sounds should diminish or cease. This kind of test will make us more confident that there is indeed a sound window over the lips. Other tests of this sort should allow us to prove our ideas, to modify them (which is the most likely event, I feel), or to cast them off altogether.

Now, how do we catch a living sperm whale? And what do we face when we try to press a microphone against its head?

CHAPTER FOURTEEN

Porpoises, Whales, and Men

I

Beyond sight of land the angular little craft rolls easily in the glassy morning swell. A small, leathery man encased in an ancient quilted jacket that hangs below his knees leans forward from the flying bridge, his dark eyes all but closed against the sea glare. A mile ahead forty falcate fins quietly cut the surface, marking it with slight, spreading Vs as they dive. Fifty feet down, playing shafts of blue light shine upon the slim little whales. Their snouts are reminiscent of those of sharks—underslung and filled with large, conical teeth. A brushing of white lines their lips like the mask of a clown. In the dim, wavering light, threadlike lines of almost luminous white shine from their sleek bellies. All else is black.

The nine-foot animals, a pod of pygmy killer whales, bunch tighter together, spraying beams of sound into the impenetrable blue curtain that circles them. No echo returns, but every little whale can hear the distant soft, thumping voice of the ship be-

hind them. Together they turn thirty degrees to the left. Then,
faintly, they begin to hear an insistent higher-pitched thrum off
ahead of them. They know from long experience that has become pure "feel" that the new ship is at least two miles away,
so they continue toward it, rising to the surface in scattered
groups of twos, threes, fives.

Glistening heads roll into the air, the water slipping from
them. Staccato puffs of wispy vapor hang in the cool air as the
whales slide below again. Long, slow sweeps of their slim tails
stroke the invisible water with the grace of a hula dancer's hands.
Once the descending glide levels, they turn together again so
that the strongest ship voice is behind them on the right, and
the faint one dead astern.

Soon the merest hint of a new thrumming comes into audible
focus nearly ahead; a faint noise evident only as repeated em-
phasis in the ever-present hissing of the sea that one can hear
beneath the water when he closes his eyes. The little whales
bunch closer and imperceptibly tense the great propulsive muscles in their flanks.

Dawn has turned to noon. The sun overhead has burned the
haze away, revealing not four but fifteen battered, sea-beaten
sampans, deployed in a broad arc over the roughening sea. Land
lies ahead—a jagged, grayish outline of folded hills and coves.

The little whales plunge along together now, tight upon one
another in the only security they know—that of proximity of
whale to whale. Froth churns as their phalanx hits the sea, the
animals lunging into the swells. The arc of boats has tightened
until each is 150 yards from the next, their bow wash mingling
behind as a common wake. The wrinkled little man deploys the
boats behind the frightened whales with all the delicacy of an
orchestra conductor. A feint from the whales is followed by an
almost reflex movement of the boats, causing the animals to turn
inward toward the center of the boat arc. These maneuvers head
the whales toward a hidden indentation in the coast, where all
hands know the animals can be cornered and blocked from escape with a short piece of net.

Close to the shore the most delicate part of the chase begins. The oceanic whales, unaccustomed to the sight of the bottom rising beneath them, might bolt seaward in fear. They have to be kept from swimming under the closing semicircle of ships. The equilibrium of fear has to be greatest behind.

Over the sides of the respective ships go the noisemakers—devices that will turn the whole semicircle of boats into a curve of menace. Big bamboo poles poked vertically into the water are a favorite, with a hand clapped over the open end producing a resonating underwater thump. Newer but equally effective are automobile axles. A sharp blow on the upper end produces a ringing clang under water. A boy's cherry bomb sets off a reverberating bubble of gas and a cascade of noise. Thus, ringed from behind, the safety of the blue depths gone as shoals rise from below, the school plunges on wildly, subject to the whim of the implacable, sharp-eyed man who now senses success. He steers them, in their thoughtless, mindless fear, into the gap in the hills, within which lies a calm bay and a clean sweep of beach upon which he will soon strand them, every resource of their familiar world gone. Thus they die en masse, victims of their own instincts and the almost infinite cunning of their pursuers.

This chase is *oikomi* to the Japanese, who every year harvest in this way several species of porpoise and small whales for the markets of certain parts of Japan. It is, with variations, the design of the pilot whale, or "pothead," catch of Trinity Bay, Newfoundland, or of the Faeroe Islands, and of the communal canoe porpoise fishing of the Malaita Islanders, who save only the porpoise's teeth from the catch to pay the bride price. Nowhere in the world is the impact of such fishing very great, for the human advantage over the animal is not overwhelming and many escape. Then, too, the circumstances that require many vessels and an appropriate shore are not common, so I suppose such fishing does not pose a deep threat to marine mammal populations.

II

The loquacious beluga, the white whale or sea canary, descends far into the Gulf of St. Lawrence when those waters are free of ice, sometimes as far as Quebec. In this area the gulf narrows and tides become extreme. The tugs of the moon and sun set the long wedge of water rocking in its basin. A man on shore who can look only at a segment of this dynamic system sees nothing but the great tides, the swift currents rushing over stones, creeping sheets of water inundating broad mud flats to the rocky headlands above.

The beluga may know more. At least he is an expert in dealing with these tides in their totality. He feels them go slack and begin to retreat, and he knows that he must head for deep water away from the shallows where his food congregates.

Along the shore of Île aux Coudres such a beluga cruises quietly along the shore in the falling tide. As he slides along over the mud, ahead of him he hears a vibratory sound so low it is difficult to localize. The lower the pitch of a sound, the more it seems to come from everywhere. From this sound and echoes of his own signals he knows only that it lies ahead. He swings to the side, churning across the flat, his flukes sending boils of silt into the moving water. The sound appears ahead again, capriciously, as if it had skipped a hundred feet over the water. It is, he knows, caused by water racing past saplings, for he has heard it in nearby river mouths where the water is partly fresh and trees grow to the water's edge. It speaks of shallows and of danger in the falling tide.

As he turns, there seem to be many sound sources in each sector, and every way he turns he sees no hole. He must move fast now as the tide is rapidly receding. The water is shoaling beneath him as he turns completely around and wallows in the swirling water, his back part way above the surface. The sounds still come, though weaker now, but weaker only because the tidal waters have left only a yard or so of each sapling beneath the surface to vibrate its tune.

The whale circles in confusion and turns back upslope, the way he came. With a violent rush, the animal races up the flat and jams fast in the receding wedge of water against mud at the water's edge. He makes a frantic turn, flailing the mud with his flukes, and then lies stranded in a little muddy pool of his own making, opaque brown water lapping over his eyes so that he can see nothing. His whistles and clicks travel uselessly around his body in this tiny pocket of water.

Light-footed crabs appear tentatively at the mouths of nearby burrows in the surrounding mud and sidle out on the sharp tips of their delicately placed claws—alert, spiderlike. Suddenly twenty of them nearest the beleaguered whale flow seaward and pop down their water-filled burrows. The cause of their fright quickly becomes evident. Slogging down the beach, his rubber hip boots sucking in the mud at each step, comes a grizzled wool-clad fisherman, his breath trailing clouds of vapor which quickly disappear in the morning air. A rope and a knife swing from his belt. One can see ahead of him the curving wall of poplar saplings driven in the mud to form a flask-shaped enclosure, its mouth now opening high above the receding tide. The saplings are twelve feet apart, and one cannot see how they could hold any animal, but they do.

Not many belugas are taken by this old method. Most are run down on the flats by fast skiff, harpooned around river mouths, netted, or taken by Eskimos in winter as they rise to breathe at holes they keep open in the ice. Some are even harpooned by "hunters," who pay for the dubious privilege of lancing an animal from the bow of a skiff.

In spite of these depredations, the beluga remains the most numerous modest-sized cetacean in Arctic waters. Its numbers are still high enough for some game managers to consider them a menace to small salmon making their first run to sea. These men try to control their numbers by hunting, and they are now learning to drive them from river mouths by playing the peculiar resonating calls of the killer whale. Such barriers of sound have succeeded in turning back beluga schools. However, one wonders if this simplistic tinkering with natural balances is truly likely to return more salmon to the fisherman. Perhaps, but it seems likely that other controls on the salmon at sea may make it a futile gesture. At any rate, the beluga yet holds its own, though the match is an unequal one, and only the rigors of Arctic weather, in which many fishing methods cannot be used, swing the balance back toward equilibrium.

III

The harried school is skittish. Overhead a light plane circles, adjusting the loops of its arcing course to hang over the leaping animals below. A hundred porpoises plunge in ragged formation, breaking into three smaller schools as pongos are launched from a distant mother ship. The pongos, fast skiffs driven by powerful engines, skim toward the animals, circling around them and driving them together. The skipper on the mother ship brings his big white craft near, heeling her over as he turns hard after the plunging animals.

"Damn 'em. They're getting tougher to wrap every season!" he grumbles.

And well might the porpoises be frightened. From bitter, terrifying experience, they knew the climactic moments of this frenzied race. Soon the captain will bark an order and the flaked net will slip into the water, its lead line sinking rapidly 420 feet down. The ship will cut around in front of the huddled school. In minutes the racing ship will draw a circle of net 2,500 feet around, which will close like an old-fashioned purse beneath them. Then they will mill helplessly in this gauzy teacupful of sea, with no route of escape open to them except to leap the bobbing cork line, which no experience has taught them to do. If the tuna fishermen have been lucky, the school of tuna that swam beneath the porpoises will be trapped too. The fish will mill in the net in a dense, flashing horde, deep beneath the surface. The skipper's practiced eye tells him at a glance the extent of his catch, using signs too subtle for the untrained observer.

Then the net will begin to shrink as the fishermen "dry it up." As the net walls close, some members of the porpoise school bolt in terror, with nowhere to go but down. Born and nurtured in the open sea, these porpoises have known no barrier except when a seiner has caught them before. A few times during the lifetime of these animals they have moved close to Alijos Rocks, forbidding oceanic pinnacles of rock jutting from the open sea. The ocean ground swell heaves up against these crags almost constantly, retreating in cascades and foaming rivers of sea water. The porpoises have heard the heaving sea complain against the rocks, and have seen the water beneath them turn to light blue as the bottom rose from the darkness of the deep sea. These signs were enough, even though the porpoises were a quarter mile from shore. They turned away as something akin to a ripple of fear passed through the leaderless school, causing them to shift course back into the relative safety of the deep sea.

Now, four hundred miles at sea, by contrast, the giant capture ship hangs in the surface, a few dozen yards away, pulsating with painfully loud engine noise, the shouts of men, the clatter of plastic corks, and the cascading of net as it pays onto the deck from the hydraulic block affixed to the boom head dozens of feet above. The fifty sleek, slim-nosed "spotter" porpoises huddle against the far cork line, sweeping the water with staccato trains of clicks whose echoes tell them of no escape.

The net narrows and a causeway appears to some of them as the captain tries to release them with a maneuver called "backing down." The captain has brought the full power of the mother ship to bear against the net as he backs away in an arc from its side. This pulls out an elongated lobe of net, one end attached to the boat and the other streaming away behind.

In this corridor the porpoises huddle at •the far end, as far away as possible from the ship. The tuna school paces back and forth, up and down the corridor, looking for an escape route. The captain must now move with great finesse, pulling hard when the tuna are away from the net barrier, pulling the corks and net under the hapless porpoises, but when the fish come near again slacking off so the corks will pop to the surface and prevent their escape.

Men from the attending pongos lift some porpoises across the corks, but most that are not released by backing down simply bolt and dive mindlessly downward, to be brought up short by the taut nylon mesh. Some jerk free to rise again and breathe explosive breaths. Others, not as lucky, come up in a bulging belly of net that blocks them from the surface. They ram their slim beaks through the mesh, tangling flippers and flukes, and are drawn drowned on deck by the block. Some who have escaped race in disorientation into the melee of patrolling sharks outside the net and are killed amid greenish clouds of blood. How many die there no one knows.

The decimated school, shattered by its experience, regroups in twos and threes as the ship moves away. The fear dissipates slowly, since the social structure of the school has been broken. Sleep and play patterns are only haltingly reestablished, because habitual partners are missing. To be sure, there is normal attrition in such a school and death is no stranger, but a netting such as this constitutes a disaster.

The tuna fishermen, caught between the economics of their business, in which a fast trip is a rich one, their feeling for the porpoises, and pressure from the bank that holds a mortgage on their boat, strike an unsatisfactory compromise. They try to release as many porpoises as they can, but often a few are lost, and on occasional sets when something goes wrong, a thousand or more may die at a time. They are discarded over the side, because space in the hold is too valuable to be occupied by low-priced porpoise flesh. Tuna are worth many times more. The fishermen, tough-minded marine businessmen, many of whom have everything they own invested in the huge, intricate boats and nets, have protected their own in any way they could, first by secrecy and, when that failed, by making their own modifications in nets and procedures designed to allow porpoises to escape. Their efforts have helped, but do not solve the problem.

Statistics are hard to come by, but some say as many as a thousand porpoises drown during the capture of a boatload of

tuna. In all, it may mean the death of 250,000 to 400,000 porpoises per year in the eastern tropical Pacific tuna grounds alone.
And now porpoise-based tuna fishing has spread to other parts of
the tropical world, and no one knows the extent of the worldwide kill.

If the pressures of the seiner fleet, which is growing, continue
to increase upon these schools, their populations face collapse.
The trends are hard to read because reliable information is so
scarce, but it seems unlikely that the porpoise populations can
stand much if any more. Even if the remaining animals are left
alone to recoup their numbers, it may take many years to accom-
plish. It has happened before. In the Black Sea a common dol-
phin population was fished to the brink of extinction. Russian net
fishermen all but wiped out the animals before their government
afforded protection. Today, decades later, the school is only just
beginning to show signs of satisfactory growth.

Other men are trying to stem the tide of disaster for the porpoise-based tuna industry. Government scientists are attempting
to build special nets from which porpoises, but not tuna, can
escape, and there is some hope they will succeed. Unless these
efforts succeed, the tuna fishermen will lose too, since their
markers will be gone. Tuna catching without porpoises to pin-
point the fish is only about one-fifth as efficient as with them.

The demise of the porpoises may affect the tuna industry in
another way. No one knows for sure why the tuna follow the
porpoises, but it may be that porpoises, with their amazing
echolocation capability, may be able to locate food better than
tuna. This may be a parallel case to the porpoise schools which
become social parasites to pilot whale schools. Without such a
food guide, tuna populations might decline or change their behavior in a way to make them more difficult to catch. No one
knows. In any event, the present methods, if unmodified, spell
nothing but disaster for the tuna industry as well as the porpoises. The problem seems to be spreading around the globe,
and growing in severity as new nations join the fleet.

These three vignettes run the gamut from beluga trappers
who seem to leave the basic animal population intact to tuna-

porpoise seiners who bid fair to shatter the animal populations upon which their industry is based. Many other examples could be cited. The decline of worldwide great whale populations under the relentless and disastrously efficient methods of modern whaling is well known. Less well known is the fact that overfishing of great whales in the Antarctic has left the great shoals of krill, on which they depend, to other predators—especially the crabeater seal and the penguins—and the seal, which may now be the world's most abundant pinniped, is being tested for exploitation.

However, the ramifications of the tuna seiners' use of porpoises as markers remains among the most ominous of problems. Too little information exists to be sure what level of kill those porpoise schools can endure, but it seems doubtful to me that it is as high as the present catch. We simply do not know enough to make a rational estimate, and the secretiveness of tuna fishermen compounds the problem.

The tuna-porpoise story is an especially disturbing one to me for two reasons. First, we know so little of the biology of oceanic porpoises that we cannot say what the impact upon their populations will be. We don't know how many porpoises are involved, and we don't know their normal replacement rate. We don't know whether porpoises within the tuna-fishing area are sedentary and hence subject to great fishing pressure, or whether they move long distances and thus move in and out of danger. The affected population size may be very much greater than the number of porpoises found at one time in the tuna area. Our ignorance of these and other vital facts is deep.

The second reason I am concerned about the tuna-porpoise story is that it has revealed a potent new fishing method to the world, and an unexploited source of animal protein. Porpoises literally cannot, for long, escape purse seiners with large nets and high-speed boats. Unlike the fish that associate with them, they must return to the surface to breathe, usually at least every four minutes or so, and when pursued, much more often. The fisherman, with his fast skiffs, has every advantage—greater speed, greater endurance, a predictable prey that cannot disappear beneath the surface to escape. Whole schools are wrapped in minutes, and when they die, an entire porpoise lineage may die with them, for such schools may have long continuity through time. The fisherman has only to wait, keep a sharp lookout, and move in wherever the animals surface.

If seining *for* porpoises instead of *with the aid of* porpoises starts, we will at once find ourselves facing a deeply serious worldwide problem. A new and uncontrolled fishing industry will be at hand, and any regulations that are proposed will be based upon the flimsiest of biological data. Experience shows that no industry is willing to regulate itself on the basis of guesses but instead will refuse all regulation until the scientists can make a strong enough case to muster public opinion. And seining *for* porpoises is not at all unthinkable, in view of the growing world shortage of protein. Porpoises may also provide other products that may be of commercial value. For instance, the finest of machine and watch oil has been made from the melon and jaw fat of porpoises.

The advent of the seagoing processing ship, many of which are at sea now under the flags of such countries as Japan and Russia, adds another ominous dimension. Some of these ships can take anything available over a wide range of market values. Sharks, tuna, sauries, or porpoises can be processed by them, leaving the catcher boats to spend their time fishing. Thus relieved of the necessity to judge what goes into the hold by its price, the fishermen might be expected to pursue the easy-to-catch porpoises. They can also be expected to resist any attempts to modify their nets to allow porpoise release. I do not know whether this happens now, but I would not be surprised if it did.

Man's wholesale destruction of nature is evident to all rational people. Our race has elbowed its way into every nook and cranny of the world and no creature is free from our influence. Is decimation in store for the porpoises of the sea, as has repeatedly been the case for the large whales and the seals? Is it moral to hunt these marvelous animals? If we can reconcile ourselves to such hunting, how is it wise to proceed? These and other questions arouse controversy whenever stories of porpoise hunting are told. There is such empathy between porpoises and people that emotions nearly always run high and the issues tend to become hazy. As one who has caught, studied, and become deeply attached to a considerable number of porpoises, I have naturally pondered these matters. But even with the facts at hand, I feel less sure about solutions.

The answers, such as they are, seem tangled with our concept of ourselves and how we fit into our world. Our myopia has led us to believe we can guide our own destiny on this planet while all other creatures must respond to the dictates of natural law. We face the same problems wherever we try to "manage nature," but they are especially difficult in the open sea, which nobody owns and which no nation can manage by itself.

Should we hunt porpoises at all? This question, often enough heard in our country, even within the halls of our national congress, is quite irrelevant in most other nations. Wherever life is hard, the protectionist-conservation ethic appears more and more effete. The prevailing view is that the world is here to be used, or at best managed, for human purposes. The problems of survival, wealth, or position override other considerations. Whatever personal feelings I may have, I find it hard to defend a position which says that no porpoise should be killed for commerce when our entire meat industry is built on practices that are equally cruel. The young Four-H boy selling his prize steer faces a similar emotional dilemma. Only when he is able to depersonalize the slaughter and take tenuous refuge in the fact that it is routine everywhere can he function without emotional upheaval. The same refuge from reality is sought by every farmer, by every bomber crew, and certainly by those who hunt whales. I don't condone the morality involved, but simply point out that it represents a human frailty, and a pervasive one.

The ethics of exploitation cannot, I fear, be expected to change in the world at large. Only a few rich nations seem able to afford the concept of "leaving the seas to the whales." One wonders how our own ethics will stand up if our economy changes

in the face of the population and resource crunch which is beginning to emerge.

Even if our national posture continues to be the seeking of a
worldwide moratorium on killing, I think we must prepare for
international management. The call for a moratorium is useful
on the world scene, even though, in my view, it is unlikely to
be achieved on a worldwide basis. But it is useful because it
raises people's passions and awareness of problems, and activates
national and international forces which would never be involved
in a calmer, more scientific debate. Nevertheless, beyond the
call for a moratorium on killing, we must learn to know our
animals so that the inevitable killing can be judged by its impact
on the animal populations involved. There is desperate need for
this in some sectors, especially with regard to open-seas seining, where in a few years we may see the worldwide destruction of porpoise populations, a gruesome rerun of the same scenario that has reduced species after species of marine mammals
to near extinction.

So I say support those who fight for a ban on the killing of
marine mammals, but, equally important, support those who demand more knowledge of their basic biology as the essential first
step in the fight for their nondestructive exploitation. With such
tools available, perhaps rational solutions can be found. The history of previous attempts gives reason for guarded optimism.

For example, with the help of aroused public sentiment, the
much maligned International Whaling Commission has recently
begun to succeed in its long and frustrating efforts to bring whaling nations to their senses regarding how many whales may be
taken without causing the extinction of the basic source. In
nearly every case the larger whales are no longer being fished
so hard that their numbers are declining toward zero. The most
seriously endangered species, like the blue whale, the right whale,
and the humpback whale, are now totally protected. However,
none of this was achieved until the biologists were able to provide the basic data showing approximately what numbers did
exist and approximately how hard they could be fished. Nobody

listened until the facts were in, based on the best possible evidence. Now the job of the commission is to persuade the whaling nations, principally Japan and Russia, to cut their quotas still further, allowing a little surplus reproduction which will eventually build the whale stocks up toward their former abundance. Here one must convince businessmen, who typically base their planning on short-term gains of at most five to ten years, that it is to their ultimate advantage to embark on a program that may take thirty or even fifty years to complete. It will take a long time for the whales to reconstitute their stocks, their destruction has been so great.

The history of the International Whaling Commission is illustrative of the problems of all international high-seas resource management. Although its scientific counsel was the best available, and was deeply concerned about the unbridled exploitation by whalers, member nations refused to listen as long as the scientists continued their usual habits of differing about detail and methods. Even after the scientists presented a united front, the fishing nations balked at the necessary controls. The problem, as the biologist Garrett Hardin points out, was the "problem of the commons," or the problem faced by farmers who grazed their stock on a commons which nobody owned. The seas belong to no nation, and hence every nation feels it can exploit them as it sees fit. Competition rises between nations at the expense of the beleaguered resource involved. Only when public opinion became aroused did change occur, for there were no binding laws or stringent punishments.

The lessons are clear. First, we must learn the basic facts in each case, and, second, world opinion must be aroused. Either alone, it seems to me, is unlikely to meet with success.

A third problem, which is really a corollary to the problem of the commons, is that of the proliferation of fishing nations. Once a new resource is located, everybody wants in on the act, and the basic problem of control becomes increasingly difficult. It is heartening, in this regard, to see the principle of "limited entry" increasingly being considered in high-seas ecological management. That is, since the Bering Sea, or the California Current, or the Mediterranean Sea is bounded by a limited number of nations, that segment of world population should devise rules for its ecological health and other nations must work within those rules.

Human beings are bewildering animals. One of our outstanding differences from the rest of the animal kingdom is our ability to predict far ahead from what we have learned of the past. To be sure, many animals do this to some extent, but prediction in the non-human world is based largely upon innate patterns, and little of it, where learning is involved, seems to span many years. Yet, remarkable as we are at looking ahead, it is our limitation in this respect that may be the fatal flaw in our ability to manage our own affairs within the closed system that is our world.

For, haltingly, we have begun to realize that we must manage our affairs, including all resources—not just those of the sea —or we shall feel the full bite of natural selection at its harshest. We have become heavily dependent on, in fact addicted to, enormous sources of power and food, and now we must consider not only where that food is going to come from but the consequences, in thermodynamic terms, of the injection into the world system of so much of what would otherwise be stored energy. We must learn to do these things while at the same time we learn to manage our own numbers; these numbers unquestionably must, in time, be drastically reduced.

Basically, we must learn to control our attempt to run nature for our own ends. This is an incredibly complicated business whose ramifications and rules cannot be understood or even contemplated in short frames of time. When the world is viewed in five- to ten-year pieces, as the whaling companies tend to do, causes and effects appear simple. If a longer view is taken, we will always find that nothing is linear. There are no such things as simple causes and effects. Instead everything is related to everything else.

To take a hypothetical case, if we now take a long view of the disastrous reduction of the great whales in the period between 1930 and 1970, we might find that the balance of life in the sea has shifted, and that, try as we might, no management will completely restore it to its former condition. Whale destruction has promoted the increase of plankton-eating birds and seals, and food limits might be reached before the whales' former abundance could be reestablished.

I don't know what will happen, and I can't predict, because the world is composed of such unimaginably complicated interlocking systems so full of feedback loops that what will actually happen as a result of human tampering is likely to be counterintuitive. In fact, it may be that most results of such tampering will be different from anything we expected. It is our dilemma that within this complexity we must learn to manage our affairs.

How? How can you manage something you can't predict? It seems to me we have tried in three ways. In the first, whereby we tamper in a major way with natural systems for our own ends, the results are usually horrendous and unexpected. Any time we build an Aswan Dam, or introduce smog into a populous area, or become drug addicts on chemical pesticides, we can be sure the ecological consequences will be large, diverse, and disastrous. Many will be counterintuitive.

The other two methods of human resource management, it seems to me, have some chance of success. One involves developing systems which we militantly keep as simple as possible, guarding them from the natural world. An example is a corn field. We have learned to plant hybrid corn that is resistant to known diseases. Periodically, a new disease sweeps like the plague across field after field. This represents the real world battering at the system we have created. It is the real world demanding variability in our corn, which we have systematically bred out of it for the sake of predictable quality and uniformity. When this happens, the plant geneticists desperately go back to wild stocks of corn, which they know to contain great potential for variability, and they begin to build another hybrid corn stock that is resistant to the new disease. The corn exists only because we protect it—not only from disease but also from weeds. In nature these weeds would be its natural competitors, and because the weeds have great reserves of variability in their genes, they would have the *flexibility* to withstand the passing flow of disease, climatic change, periods of drought, and so forth. Our corn could never survive. This human method works to our advantage, but it requires constant intervention to keep these human creations going, be they domestic chickens or hybrid corn.

The last method we humans have used is to tamper gingerly with natural systems, relying upon their own internal integrity over a space of time to reveal the consequences to us. This, I think, is the lesson of sophisticated resource management. Most natural populations, including those of porpoises and whales, maintain a surplus of individuals over and above those needed to maintain the population. There is, in other words, some flexibility in a population in terms of optimum numbers, and some surplus over what is actually needed to maintain the organism's place within the ecological system to which it belongs. Taking this surplus for human needs is the least disruptive level of utilization. Usually some changes in the parts of the system most utilized by the resource organisms can be expected, but they can be expected to be slight, and, if detrimental, should be rather quickly reversible.

What is not known is the exact function of the buffer of surplus numbers which we take away. Does a species maintain such a surplus as a means of coping with noncyclical change in the environment—say, a long-term nonrepetitive change in climate due to variation in the sun's energy? Even if this is true, the results of operating in this way—of using the natural system empirically instead of trying to anticipate—is bound to be easier and is perhaps the only possible way for the human manager to function successfully. He does not need a depth of ecological wisdom, only alertness to change and the chance to reverse himself. He needs only to tinker carefully and to watch for results as they appear. Then he needs to be able to change the rules. This is the most difficult problem, since society quickly incorporates resources into its fabric and change becomes difficult.

So, in human relations with porpoises, let us first recognize that they are part of enormously complicated systems in the sea, whose intricacy we can scarcely hope to understand fully. Next, let us gain enough wisdom about their basic biology for us to lay guidelines that will let us tamper with them in such a way that their integrity, both as species and as parts of the living web of the sea, remains intact and responsive to the flux and flow of the world. Finally, let us look with wonder at all the capabilities of these superbly adapted marine mammals, for themselves and not for any relation they may have to human affairs.